# TINSEL, TREES
## AND
# TREACHERY

A SMILEY AND MCBLYTHE MYSTERY

Published by Jubilee Publishing, LLC
Ebook ISBN: 978-1-958252-43-7
Paperback ISBN: 978-1-958252-44-4

Cover design: Streetlight Graphics
Editor: Teresa Lynn, Tranquility Press

# TINSEL, TREES
## AND
# TREACHERY
A Smiley and McBlythe Mystery

# BRUCE
# HAMMACK

# 1

Heather wasn't expecting a rebuke from Steve so soon after he arrived that November morning. He leaned forward with hands on her desk and spoke louder than necessary. "You weren't listening. It would help if you took those earbuds out and put away the spreadsheets." He let out a huff of exasperation and asked, "Are you unplugged and ready to hear what I have to say?"

Heather released a moan of regret and mumbled, "You caught me again. How can a man who can't see be so aware of what's going on around him?"

"My dog tells me what you're doing. It helps that he's a giant schnauzer, thinks he's human, and is smarter than both of us put together."

"Hilarious," said Heather without a hint of mirth in her voice. "Let's start over, and you tell me who's coming and why."

"It's a woman I went to high school with and her husband. Her maiden name was Lola Caine, but everyone called her Sugar."

A snort came from Heather. "Was there anyone in your high school who was called by their given name?"

"A few. Her sister's nickname was even better. Her given name was Lauren but everyone called her Candy."

This time a snort of disbelief came from Heather's nose. "Sugar Caine and Candy Caine. They both sound very sweet."

Ignoring her sarcasm, Steve said, "Candy was, and I have no reason to believe she's changed."

"What about Lola, AKA Sugar?"

"Sugar was quiet and reserved, the proverbial wallflower. By the way, they spelled their last name C-A-I-N-E, not C-A-N-E. Sugar now goes by her married name, Andrews. She and her husband, Randy, should be here in about five minutes."

Heather spoke as she collected papers and put them into file folders. "That takes care of the who, but not why Sugar needs to consult a couple of private detectives."

Steve returned to his desk, which sat some distance from Heather's in her oversized corporate office. "Sugar believes her sister is in danger. I assured her we'd hear her out and not make fun of her for being frightened. Do you think you can do that?"

Heather spoke with confidence. "I'll make a pinkie-promise to be on my best behavior and to listen carefully."

Steve's dog, Le Roi, sat up in his bed. Heather's German shepherd, Princess, did the same. Steve said, "They're early. Are you ready to see them?"

"There's no time like the present."

Heather stepped toward the door as Steve rose from his chair and spoke to Le Roi in French, the dog's preferred language, "*Les amis.*" The one-hundred-pound mass of muscle sat at Steve's side with ears up and eyes fixed on the door, ready to welcome his new friends.

Heather's personal assistant, Pam, opened the office door and allowed the couple to pass into the office. "Don't worry," said the PA to the visitors. "Both dogs have been through extensive training. They won't harm you unless you attack Ms. McBlythe or Mr. Smiley."

Heather extended her right hand to the man. "It's so nice to meet both of you. I'm Heather McBlythe." The man shook her hand without looking at her, as he scanned the office with wide eyes. It was obvious he wasn't used to the corporate world. The woman stood with head down, looking as if she'd bolt if someone shouted, "Boo!"

"Steve tells me your name is Lola, but you prefer to be called Sugar. Is that correct?"

The woman raised her eyes to meet Heather's then lowered them again. "Most people call me Sugar, but I'll answer to either name."

Heather made a three-second inventory and committed Sugar's hair-to-shoes appearance to memory. Gray strands highlighted her dark-brown collar-length hair. She'd done a relatively good job of putting body into it with a curling iron. She wore what looked like drugstore reading glasses as if they were a tiara. Probably an oversight. Her dark slacks, pewter-colored blouse, royal blue windbreaker, and plain brown shoes were clean, well-worn, and inexpensive. The purse she carried was utilitarian, the cheap material beginning to crack on the handles. Her wedding band was just that, a simple gold circle, less in width than bulky knitting yarn. Makeup was unusually heavy, especially around her eyes, as if she wasn't used to wearing makeup, or perhaps, she was hiding signs of abuse.

Heather looked for something to compliment her on. "That's a lovely pin you're wearing, and such an appropriate sentiment. *Give thanks.*"

Sugar touched the pin and brought her gaze away from the floor. "Only three days until the second-best holiday of the year. If it weren't for celebrating our Lord's birthday, it would be number one in my book."

The husband interrupted. "Sugar, everyone knows about Thanksgiving and Christmas. Look at this office. Any fool can see that Ms. McBlythe and Mr. Smiley are busy people. They don't have time to listen to your superstitious nonsense about your sister being in danger. We should leave."

3

Steve approached with Le Roi at his side. "Leave? You just got here."

While Steve took charge of the conversation, Heather gave Randy a visual once-over so she could give Steve a description of Sugar's husband. He looked remarkably unremarkable, an easily overlooked and quickly forgotten man. Like his wife, he was average height and weight with no visible scars or tattoos.

She focused on his clothes. He wore a dark blue off-the-rack sports coat, gray slacks, baby blue shirt with stains, and rubber-soled black shoes that should have gone to shoe heaven hundreds of miles ago.

She tuned back into the conversation as Steve said, "You've caught us at the best possible time. Heather has nothing important on her schedule this morning, and we're leaving for the day at noon."

It was only half a lie. She had plenty to do as she was under doctor's orders to limit her time at the office to thirty hours a week. She sometimes stretched her day's work to seven or eight hours, but gone were the sixteen, seventeen, and eighteen hours of toil. It was a pleasant surprise when she discovered that her careful selection of department heads meant her company and its subsidiaries functioned well without her. In fact, her absence allowed new ideas to come from many of her employees, especially the team who did research and acquisitions.

Steve gently directed Randy and Sugar to seats near the head of the massive conference table. He and Heather sat on the opposite side of the table with their backs to a wall, their dogs lying beside them. Steve sat with palms flat on the table. "Now then, who wants to tell us why you think Candy is in danger?"

"Not me," said Randy. "I believe imaginations and folklore have gotten the best of both sisters."

"The letters aren't our imaginations," countered Sugar in a timid voice.

Steve interrupted. "I've always found that the best place to start a story is at the beginning. Who wants to go first?"

Randy leaned back in the leather chair and crossed his arms. "Sugar, you go ahead. This wasn't my idea."

Sugar examined her work-worn hands, an obvious sign of timidity, and perhaps something more serious. She seemed to wrestle with herself before looking up and blurting out a question. "Have you ever heard of Krampus?"

Randy shot her a daggered glare. "There you go again. I knew it was a mistake for us to come here. You're embarrassing yourself."

Heather came to Sugar's rescue. "I know what a Krampus is. I had a nasty encounter with one at a Christmas market in Germany when I was on a winter break from Princeton. It beat me with a whip, placed a hood over my head, and roughed me up enough to leave bruises that lasted weeks. I finally kicked it between its cloven hooves."

Steve issued a one-word appeal for an explanation. "Huh?"

Heather expanded her story. "At Christmas, Saint Nicholas gets credit for giving presents to boys and girls as a reward for good behavior throughout the year. Krampus predates Saint Nicholas and is the antithesis of Father Christmas, or the American version, Santa Claus. To be accosted by Krampus signifies you haven't been good and you're getting what you deserve. They're fierce-looking creatures with devil horns, a forked tongue, cloven hooves on their hind legs, and claws for hands."

Sugar found her voice. "*Krampus* is German for claw. My maternal grandmother was from Bavaria, up in the Alps. While our mother emphasized Santa Claus, my Oma warned us what Krampus would do to us if we misbehaved. My sister scoffed at the idea of a hairy beast punishing us, but I believed Oma." She took a breath and qualified her last thought. "Don't get me wrong. I now know Krampus doesn't exist, but people wearing costumes and doing bad things are real."

Randy challenged her. "Candy lives in Branson. The last time I checked a map, it's in the Ozark Mountains of Missouri, not the Alps. I still say we're wasting their time."

Sugar didn't respond to the stinging remark, so Steve took over. "You said something about threatening letters. Tell us about them."

"The letters are real," said Sugar. "They came on plain paper with a Branson, Missouri postmark on the envelope."

Heather asked, "Can you describe the stationery?"

"It has the image of a Krampus centered at the top."

"Anything else?"

Sugar reached for her purse and pulled out a single envelope. She handed it to Heather and said, "Candy was going to throw this one away like she did the other letters she received. I talked her into sending it to me so I could show it to Steve."

She slapped her hand over her mouth and dragged it down past her chin. "I'm so sorry, Steve. I didn't mean to say anything about you being blind."

Randy broke in with a snapping rebuke. "First you waste their time, and then you make fun of Steve. We should leave."

Steve waved off Sugar's choice of words. "There's nothing to apologize for. You wanting to *show* the letter and envelope to me is a compliment. It tells me you trust me to find someone to analyze it and give you advice on what to do about it. Heather, Le Roi, my dog, and many others are my eyes, and my other senses are better now than they were when I had my sight. Hand me the letter and the envelope."

Steve placed the letter on the table but focused on the envelope by touch alone. "Inexpensive stock paper with moisten-and-seal glue on the envelope. The person, most likely a male, used a standard ballpoint pen to write your sister's name and address."

"How do you know that?" asked Sugar.

"The roller-ball of a ballpoint pen does exactly what the name implies; it rolls and mashes the fibers in the paper. Fountain pens and quills leave tiny tears in the fibers."

Randy challenged him. "Are you sure it's a man's handwriting?"

"Great question, and the answer is no, I can't be definite

6

about that. The depth of the indentations generally point to a man's heavy hand, but it could also be someone in a hurry, angry, or both." Steve removed the letter from the envelope, ran his fingers over it and smelled it. "It's the same quality paper as the envelope. No trace of aftershave, cologne, or perfume."

Heather took over. "I'll give Steve a little help with the image on the letter. A rubber stamp created the Krampus image. A right-handed person printed the letter and signature."

Steve slid the envelope to Heather. "A good handwriting analyst might match the writing to the sender if they had a large enough sample of other writings. Without knowing the identity of the sender, the letter and envelope aren't much help."

Randy looked at his wife. "I told you the same thing. They need something to compare it to. This letter by itself means nothing."

"I wouldn't go that far," said Steve. "Sugar read the letter to me over the phone. Someone is threatening her sister. It could be just a sick joke, and no matter what the letter says, there may never be any consequences. Or the sender could be deadly serious."

"I don't think it's a joke. There have been other letters."

"Oh? Have they all demanded money?" asked Steve.

Obviously holding back tears, Sugar replied, "The first one sounded like a weird prank. There were just a couple of lines that said something like bad things happened to greedy people. Candy wrote it off to a weird fan. Then the next one demanded a thousand dollars or there would be a price to pay. That part was generic sounding. Candy ignored it again, then ended up with four slashed tires. In this one they demand five-thousand dollars. Candy still said to ignore it, but I'm scared for her."

Steve said, "I understand, but even if she pays the demand, it won't end there. There will almost assuredly be a larger demand next time."

Randy leaned forward and shifted his gaze between Steve and

Heather. "So you two believe there's cause to worry about Candy?"

Heather used her training as an attorney to sidestep the question. "It's always a good idea to be prepared for trouble, especially when there've been multiple letters warning of physical harm."

Steve followed this with, "Heather's one hundred percent correct. That's why I'm going to call Candy to tell her how she can protect herself. I've become an expert on the subject in recent months. It's a long story, but a guy assaulted me and later set fire to the condo I owned."

Heather added, "The fire spread to my condo, which was next door to Steve's, but unfortunately, I wasn't home to help him. Following the fire, Steve and I built homes next door to one another in a gated community on Lake Conroe. That was just part of our security solution."

Randy tilted his head and asked, "What was the most effective thing you did to protect yourself?"

Steve raised his voice and said, *"En guarde."* Le Roi sprang to his feet, locked his eyes on Randy, and emitted a loud growl with teeth bared. Princess did the same.

Randy fell back in his chair as Steve smiled and said, "They're called man's best friend for a reason."

"Sorry," said Heather, then she gave commands in French and English for the dogs to lie down.

With Le Roi still on high alert, Steve asked, "By the way, what kind of work do you both do?"

Sugar went first. "I work at a dollar store and do alterations on wedding dresses as a second job. I've always enjoyed working with fabric, but there aren't as many seamstress jobs anymore."

Randy cut her off. "I'm in regional sales." He pushed up from his chair. "If that's all, your dogs are giving me the creeps. I'll be out in the hallway."

Steve ended the meeting by saying to Sugar, "I'm taking the threats to Candy seriously. So far there have been three threats, with the second one resulting in property damage. If this continues, someone will get hurt. If Candy will do what I tell her, she'll minimize the chances of something bad happening to her."

Sugar's phone came to life with a text alert. She slipped it out of her pocket and gasped. "It's from Candy. Her car caught fire in the theater parking lot two nights ago."

Steve clenched his jaw. "Whoever Krampus is, they mean business. I'd better call Candy."

# 2

After closing the door behind Sugar, Heather returned to her desk and resumed studying spreadsheets.

She worked for ten minutes before realizing Steve still sat in his chair at the long table. "Why are you still sitting there? I thought you were returning to your office to call Candy and write the next great American novel."

"I'm taking a break from writing while my editor critiques the short story I sent her."

"A break? I guess the next thing you're going to say is advice to Candy won't be enough and we're going to investigate the letters from Krampus. Besides my terrible memories of that costumed buffoon, may I remind you that we're private detectives who specialize in homicides. We have no reason to start an investigation. No one has been assaulted, let alone killed. Can't you tell Candy to call the local police?"

Steve changed the subject. "That Krampus thing intrigues me. Tell me more about it."

"As I said, I ran into one at a Christmas market in Germany. I can still feel him dragging that claw across the back of my legs. It tore my leggings and left deep scratches. He must have been drinking gluhwein, or as we'd say in English, glow wine."

Steve scrunched up his nose. "No wonder he was mean. Hot wine with spices doesn't appeal to me."

"Gluhwein is the European version of antifreeze for humans. When it's snowing at a Christmas market in Munich or Salzburg, it's pretty good. It warms you up from the inside out. It also makes Krampus lose his inhibitions."

Steve's brow wrinkled, a sign he was thinking. "Krampus is a novel way to introduce a frightening character into American Christmas traditions. The closest things we have to something scary at Christmas are lumps of coal in a stocking, Ebeneezer Scrooge, and a Grinch who burglarized every home in Whoville. A hairy Krampus who assaults and punishes children is enough to give anyone nightmares."

A shiver started at Heather's shoulders and worked its way down. "I hope I never run into one again."

"No wonder you gave him a swift kick between the hooves."

Heather cringed again at the memory and said, "I hope he's still singing tenor." She shook herself back into the safety of her office and narrowed her gaze. "You were quiet for too long. What are you cooking up in that shrewd mind of yours?"

"I'm dredging my brain for memories of Candy, thinking about what I'll say to her."

"Was she pretty?"

"She was the total package: pretty, smart, talented, and ambitious." Steve held out his left hand in front of him at something invisible less than five feet off the floor. "And about this tall with no curves."

Heather chuckled. "Perhaps she had a late growth spurt."

"She needed to."

Heather changed the subject. "I didn't know you had a new editor."

Steve moved on before she could ask for details. "I'm between projects, and Sugar's story intrigues me. I want to spend the Thanksgiving break learning more about Candy, Krampus, and Branson, Missouri. There's a reason she's receiving threat-ening letters and I'd like to know what it is."

"Is she wealthy or currently getting a divorce?"

Steve lifted his shoulders and let them fall. "I'll find out when I talk to her. The main thing I remember about Candy was her singing voice. She made people sit up and take notice when she stepped up to a microphone. She earned a scholarship to Belmont University in Nashville."

"Belmont?" said Heather with surprise in her voice. "That university is an incubator for professional musicians and enter-tainers. Their famous alumni list reads like a who's-who of coun-try-western and gospel stars."

"It's no wonder she lives in Branson," said Steve. "I've never been there, but I've heard about it all my life. It's known for good, clean entertainment, the type children, parents, and grandparents can enjoy together."

Heather's mind for business engaged. "Now that you mention it, I've heard people talk about the shows and attrac-tions in Branson and how much they enjoy them. I wonder what kind of business opportunities might be there."

Steve wagged his head. "You can't help but think of ways to make the next hundred million, can you?"

She countered with, "It's a dominant gene my father passed down to me. New projects to us are like drugs to a junkie or free booze to an alcoholic."

"And just as dangerous to you," said Steve. "I want another pinkie-promise that you'll not spend over one hour a day on any new project."

"One hour? That's not nearly enough time to get a new project off the ground. I'll need three hours a day added to what I'm currently working."

"Two hours," said Steve with extra firmness. "Or do you want to spend Christmas in a hospital bed?"

"Oh, no," she said quickly. "I had enough of that last year

when I almost worked myself to death. Two hours to my current schedule is acceptable."

"Good," said Steve. "I'll tell Rasheed that we won't need him to drive us home until two o'clock today. That will give you time to brainstorm and get with the head of your acquisitions department. It shouldn't hurt you to pick up the pace of your work but do so slowly and be prepared to slack off if it's too much for you. Who knows? We may not go to Branson. If Candy takes good security precautions, Krampus may get tired of trying and fade into the night."

Heather returned to Steve's earlier remark. "You said you have a new editor. I hope this one works out better than the last two."

"So far, so good," said Steve.

Heather picked up her phone.

"Who are you calling?" asked Steve.

"Acquisitions. All new projects begin with thorough research."

Steve issued a last condition to Heather. "Don't you dare make the people in that department work over the Thanksgiving holiday. A few days' delay won't make any difference, even if they find a new project for you to play with."

Heather's first inclination was to stick her tongue out, but what good would that do? Instead, she punched a series of numbers into her phone and heard, "Research and acquisitions."

After the normal salutations, she directed the department head to put Branson, Missouri on his list of places and things to investigate. His response took Heather by surprise. She turned on the phone's speaker so Steve could hear.

"Did you know Branson once had more theater seats than Broadway in New York City? Somewhere between five and six million visitors came to Branson last year."

"You sound like an expert," said Heather.

"I'm a third-generation tourist. My kids are fourth-generation. There are so many things to do in the Branson area."

"Make the report detailed," said Heather. "Tell me what they have, and kick around what they want or need, even if they don't know it yet. Don't be afraid to be creative."

"When do you want the report?"

"I want it yesterday, but Steve just reminded me that patience is a virtue I need more of."

Steve broke in. "More means there's some patience in her now. We all know that's not true."

Heather spoke over the chuckles coming through her phone. "Start working on it after Thanksgiving. Don't make it a top priority, but I'd like to have it sooner rather than later."

"This will be fun. The team will enjoy the challenge."

The call ended, and Steve spoke to Le Roi. "Let's go to our office and let the financial horticulturist plant another money tree. I need to call a woman named Candy."

"After the call," said Heather, "get to work on that next story. It won't hurt you to put in a few more hours of work."

"That's what my editor says."

---

STEVE AND LE ROI ALMOST MADE IT TO THEIR OFFICE without stopping. Rasheed, a former philosophy professor, met them in the hallway with a warm greeting. "My two best friends, I trust you are both having a joyful and profitable day. To that end, I have written a new proverb. Would you like to hear it?"

"Will it bring me joy and wealth?" asked Steve.

"You lack neither, my friend."

"You're right, but why does man always want more? Why aren't we satisfied with what we have?"

"You ask a profound question. I believe the answer lies in the holiday's name we are soon to celebrate."

Steve nodded. "Thanksgiving."

"Precisely," said Rasheed. "Joy follows giving thanks as sure as day follows night. That is the basis of the proverb I wrote."

"You also wished me a profitable day. Will more money increase my joy?"

"I said nothing about money, only profit, which is defined in a thousand ways. Money comes and goes, but true wealth is found in relationships and giving. You have a generous heart. That makes your soul very wealthy."

Steve asked, "Did you forget to bring money for lunch again?"

"Not only are you generous and full of joy, you possess the ability to spot a beggar a mile away."

"Lunch is on me," said Steve. "Your proverbs are usually worth a sandwich, chips, and a drink. But save it for lunch, I need to make a phone call."

Steve couldn't help but smile at Rasheed's antics, which were small miracles in themselves. The Middle Eastern philosophy professor had spent a couple of years in prison following a regime change in the land of his birth. Radical leaders had no use for independent thinkers or those who taught anything but their rigid doctrine. Rasheed fled his native land at his first opportunity, which was thanks to a clerical mistake. A few months ago, Heather's father had hired him to drive her and Steve wherever they needed to go.

Le Roi led the way into Steve's minimalist office and settled in. Steve realized too late that he'd failed to close the door, so he spoke to his dog. *"Fermez la porte, s'il vous plaît."*

Le Roi made the six-step walk to the door and pushed it shut with more force than necessary.

Steve took out his cell phone and told it to call Candy Caine. It rang six times before a woman's voice came on in a recorded message. "This is Candy. I'm watching a workout video and burning fat. Can't come to the phone right now. If I'm still alive at the end of my workout, what's left of me will call you back. Don't forget to leave your name. Bye, now."

He followed her instructions then placed his phone on his

desk. "Candy certainly sounded joyful. She and Rasheed would get along fine."

Steve turned his computer on, but that's as far as he got before his phone rang and announced Candy's name. He answered with a quick, "Hello, is this Candy?"

"In the flesh, which there's still too much of. Sugar told me she and what's his name were coming to see you."

Steve chuckled. "You never thought much of Randy, did you?"

"I guess he isn't the worst man I ever met, but Sugar deserves better." She took a breath and lowered her voice. "How are you, Steve? It tore me up something terrible when I heard about you and Maggie being attacked."

Steve swallowed. "Time dulls the hurt, and I have much to be thankful for. Thanks for the audiobooks you sent me. I was so messed up I didn't listen to them until a year had passed. How about you?"

"Probably the same as with you. I lost my husband, Jim, three years ago to leukemia. At least I've finally stopped reaching for him when I wake up in the middle of the night."

Steve continued, "I had to sell my house and move from Houston. Our home held too many memories for me to stay there."

"Sugar tells me you're a private detective now. That sounds exciting."

"My business partner and I work a few cases a year. Like me, she's a former cop. Heather was a detective in Boston, Mass."

"She's a lot more than a former cop. Randy did research on her before your meeting. Sugar said he couldn't stop talking about Heather McBlythe and how many companies she owns." Candy sputtered out a laugh. "He thinks the dividing line between rich and poor is whether you receive an overdraft notice by the end of the month. He and Sugar qualify as habitually poor."

Steve asked, "Is Randy a rainbow chaser?"

"Unfortunately, he hasn't changed since high school. Still taking shortcuts, looking for his big break."

Steve wanted to get down to business, so he changed the subject. "Heather and I examined and discussed the threatening letter you received. Sugar said you received others but threw them away."

"Two others. The first came in late summer. I don't know if Sugar told you that I have my own musical show in Branson. I receive a fair amount of fan mail, so I didn't think much of the first letter. There's no shortage of crackpots in the world, and entertainers attract their fair share of them. Even though it demanded money, I ignored the second one, too. I thought it was somebody trying to make some easy money with a baseless threat. Then, my tires were cut. Do you think the person who wrote the letter did that?"

"It's possible."

"The last letter made me angry. That's the one Sugar brought you. Do you believe I should be concerned?"

Steve leaned back in his chair. "Did you report the slashed tires to the police?"

"An officer came out and took notes. He looked tired and bored, so I wrote it off to kids with nothing better to do. I think he did, too."

Steve moved on. "Have you noticed anyone following you, or waiting outside the theater after a performance?"

"Have you ever been to Branson, Steve? Traffic is bumper-to-bumper nine months of the year. Someone is always following me in a car or truck from late spring until the shows close after the Christmas performances. I stay inside and sign autographs for as long as it takes. I make a point not to go to the parking lot alone, especially after what happened last summer."

"What happened last summer?"

"The police say it was a robbery gone wrong. It happened long after I'd left our theater that night. The woman who took care of our wardrobe stayed late to make repairs and adjustments to costumes. She was the last to leave. There was no sign of a struggle, and the official cause of death was a heart attack."

"Was anything missing?"

"Only her purse. The detective said if it had been found with her, they wouldn't have suspected foul play. Just because her purse was gone doesn't necessarily mean she was attacked. He said it was possible someone not connected with the death could have driven through the parking lot, saw the woman on the ground, and taken the purse."

"Was an arrest ever made?" asked Steve.

Candy's response came with an undertone of disgust. "No arrests, nor do I expect any. The theater put up more lights in the back parking lot, and the cast and crew now use the buddy system to go to their cars. Branson is a very safe place to live and work, but that doesn't make it immune from all the problems other cities have, especially drug abuse."

"That checks one box. You've already taken some of the precautions I was going to recommend. Have you noticed anyone hanging around your home?"

"I don't want to sound pretentious, but my home sits on a tall hill, behind an eight-foot wrought-iron fence and gate. I think it would take a professional to get onto the grounds. It's more house than I need, but I love it."

"Excellent," said Steve. "Do you have a dog?"

"No pets because I travel at least two months out of the year. Should I consider getting a dog?"

"That's a decision you'll have to make. It's a huge commitment, especially for the type of dog I'd recommend."

"And what type is that?"

"A big one who will accompany you everywhere in public, protect you with its life, and respond immediately to all commands. You'd have to go through specialized training with it."

"That's a problem. I'm booked through the Christmas season

here in Branson and I go on tour in January. Any other recommendations?"

"Does your home have a security system?"

"Jim insisted on it. It's top-notch."

"How many years have you had it?"

"Twelve. That's when Jim designed and built our home."

"Have an expert check it out and make recommendations for an upgrade. The technology has advanced tremendously in the last few years."

"Anything else?"

"I keep going back to recommending you get a dog. Even if it isn't a trained police dog, find one with the temperament to guard your home and bark like crazy when people come to your door."

"Thanks for the advice." She paused, then lightened the conversation. "I want a commitment that you'll come to Branson. You'd love the Christmas show we're putting on. If you can't come this year, come next. I have plenty of bedrooms for you and whomever you want to bring. Jim loved people and we had plenty of guests. All that changed when Jim died."

"I know what you mean about things changing. Maggie and I had planned to come to Branson for our next wedding anniversary. Life happened instead."

Silence reigned before Candy broke the awkward moment. "I'd love to see you again, Steve. You're welcome anytime."

"Thanks, Candy. Call me if you get another letter or if there's any more property damage."

The call ended as waves of nostalgia and curiosity swept over him. Did Candy really mean she'd like him to visit her, or was her invitation a hollow example of southern hospitality? Time would tell.

# 3

Thanksgiving Day arrived, and Heather welcomed it by sticking to her normal routine of stretching exercises every other day. After thirty minutes of yoga, she rolled up her mat from the living room floor, poured herself a cup of coffee, grabbed a blanket, and went to her patio overlooking Lake Conroe. She loved her new home, which sat at the apex of a peninsula jutting into the lake.

Normally, she would spend fifteen minutes in the pre-dawn quiet, listening to nature as it awakened the sun. What had once been a mad dash to get to her office seven days a week impressed her as foolishness. She now practiced a minimum of fifteen minutes of silent meditation before preparing for the pressures of owning multiple companies and a bulging portfolio of investments. A mental breakdown and subsequent hospitalization had forced her to take drastic action. She'd gone from a sleep-starved, frenetic routine to a full stop in the mental ward of a hospital. Since then the gradual return to her work life and society had worked its magic. She was well on her way to living a balanced life.

Since today was a holiday, there was no need to limit her time on the porch to fifteen minutes. She heaved a sigh and gave thanks for a myriad of things that flowed in and out of her thoughts, including her father and late mother. Both parents came from Boston's top tier of generational wealth. Their marriage started as a merger between two wealthy families and morphed into something much more human, even though they shunned open displays of affection. A sudden heart attack took her mother but helped transform the grieving widower from Father to Daddy.

Her thoughts moved to the man in her life, attorney Jack Blackwood, and his daughter. Heather would have already married Jack but for the unexpected arrival of Briann into their lives. She was a blessing from Jack's brief fling with a fellow attorney from Louisiana a decade and a half ago. The mother, a fiercely independent woman, refused to acknowledge Jack as the father and never told him he had a daughter. A letter following the woman's death informed him of his status as a father.

The teen had no family that was willing or able to raise her. To his credit, Jack, the bachelor, embraced his paternal responsibilities, and with the help of his mother, welcomed Briann with open arms. She'd adjusted better than expected and was thriving in school and helping in Jack's law practice.

As for Heather's delayed nuptials, at first, she used work to console herself. Over time, she and Jack had embraced their status as the adult version of going steady. Perhaps they would tie the proverbial knot someday, but not until Briann took wings and flew from Jack's nest. The girl's desire to become an attorney, like her mother, meant many years would pass before Heather and Jack had the marriage conversation again.

The early morning unfolded as various names and faces floated through her mind. Princess jerked her head to the right, ears erect, while her tail ticked back and forth.

Heather spoke to her guardian. "Do you hear Le Roi and Steve? It's past their normal time to join us for coffee."

Princess's tail swung again as Steve and the giant schnauzer made their way across the connecting backyards. Heather waited until Steve was within ten feet of the patio before she asked, "Did you two sleep in?"

"I did," said Steve. "Le Roi comes and goes all night, just like Princess does. Pet doors are great inventions. Where's Max? If he were here, he'd be weaving in and out of my legs."

Heather took a quick peek at the pet door to make sure the portly Maine coon cat wasn't joining them. "He helped keep me warm out here before losing patience. I'm sure breakfast was on his mind, and now he's probably putting a dent in my pillow."

The sound of an outboard motor caught Heather's attention. "There are very few people on the water today. That's only the third boat I've seen since first light."

Steve said, "Thanksgiving Day is perfect for sleeping in. Even the fish don't wake up early. No fish, no fisherman."

Heather looked up as high gray clouds scuttled southward. She spoke while considering the chance of receiving stray sprinkles of rain. "Were you studying Branson last night?"

"Uh-huh," said Steve through a yawn. "Let me get a cup of coffee, and I'll amaze you with my vast knowledge of the Ozarks."

"That sounds too much like detective work. I've been giving thanks for everything and everyone I can think of. Get your coffee, think about what you're thankful for, then come back and tell me."

Steve stopped in his tracks. "What have you done with the hard-charging businesswoman who had to have six projects going at once to be happy?"

"She called in too thankful to work today, but promised to be back tomorrow."

Steve soon returned and sat in the patio chair next to her padded chaise lounge. He remained silent until a helicopter flew over the lake. "That must be a person hoping to copy you and build an empire like you did."

"I wish them luck," said Heather. "I almost choked trying to chew and swallow a project as big as this one."

Steve felt for and located the small table beside his chair. "What do you think about everyone going to Branson for a week?"

Heather cleared her throat. "That was a quick transition. Who are you including in everyone?"

"The usual suspects. You, me, Jack, Briann, Jack's mother, Rasheed, Junani to keep Rasheed out of trouble, Bella, and Adam. Your dad might want to come, too. Rasheed and I could drive up soon after Thanksgiving and you and the rest could fly up a week or two later."

"Bella's mom and dad won't be back until a few days before Christmas. They seem to enjoy owning a winter home in Puerto Rico and a summer one here next door to Bella and Adam. When did you want to go to Branson?"

"That depends on Krampus. Rasheed and I will go early to see if the threat is legitimate. You and members of your team can join us a few days later to look into business opportunities."

Heather challenged him. "Working on a case without a victim isn't what we agreed to."

"Fine," said Steve. "If there's still no victim and no case by the time you get there, we'll let it drop."

Heather knew there was more to Steve's plan than he was telling her. "Your voice has a Svengali tone to it. What kind of web are you weaving for me to fall into?"

Steve placed his hands over his heart. "Your words of distrust have pierced me like the slings and arrows of outrageous fortune."

"Svengali and Shakespeare? Now I'm sure you're plotting something special. Why do you really want to go to Branson?"

Steve huffed. "All right, I'll confess. Speaking with Sugar and Candy took me back in time. Although Maggie didn't go to high school with me, she did meet some of my friends when we attended a high school reunion, including the Caine sisters. All three women are lumped together in my memories. Hearing Candy talk about Branson reminded me that Maggie and I were supposed to go there to celebrate our next wedding anniversary. I'm calling this trip unfinished business."

"Oh," said Heather. She hadn't expected Steve to bare his soul. She searched for a way to respond and said, "Is this a door you have to go back through before you can move forward?"

"My former therapist would probably say it was."

Heather paused, considering the layers of meaning in Steve's words. "If this is something you need to do, I'll support you. But let's keep our priorities straight and make sure everyone's safety comes first."

"You stated it more clearly than I could. Candy and I have similar stories. She's a widow and I'm a widower. We both work because we want to, not because we must. Someone's threatening her. I didn't protect Maggie. Perhaps I can keep Candy from harm."

Steve took a full breath. "Finally, I don't make a habit of overemphasizing coincidences, but you and I are both interested in Branson, although for completely different reasons. I believe you, me, Rasheed, and our four-legged friends should scout out the land before we take a week off to rest and enjoy some time off."

He'd convinced her, but she had questions about logistics. "When do you want to go?"

"Soon for Rasheed, Le Roi, and me."

"What's the rush?"

"In the Central and Eastern Alps, people usually celebrate Saint Nicholas Day on December sixth. Krampus punishes children who misbehaved the night before. If something is going to happen to Candy, it will be on the night of December fifth or before dawn on the sixth. Therefore, arriving early would give us time to make our presence known."

A sense of wanting to protect Steve swept over Heather. "I'm coming with you."

"I won't tell you no, but Le Roi and Rasheed are all the body-guards Candy will need. Missouri is a constitutional carry state, and Rasheed has gone through firearms training. He's finally overcome his fear of pistols. Don't forget, your main reason for going to Branson is to find a business to invest in, not get tangled up in what I'm doing before we know if we have a case."

Heather ignored Steve's halfhearted attempt to dissuade her from going. "I'll have Pam arrange lodging for us."

"I've already taken care of that," said Steve. "It's a full day's drive to Branson. Rasheed, Le Roi, and I will leave very early on December third. You can fly up on the fourth with your head of acquisitions and as many of his staff as you want to accompany him. Pam will only need to arrange lodging for your pilots and acquisitions team."

"Why not have Pam arrange lodging for the three of us and the dogs?"

"We're staying with Candy. She has plenty of room and is looking forward to meeting you."

Heather wagged her head. "Once again, you're three steps ahead of me. When will Jack and the others join us?"

"I don't want to wear out our welcome with Candy. We'll play it by ear, but I don't want us to stay with her for over a week."

"You'd better write a letter to Krampus and tell him we expect full cooperation in identifying him by December sixth."

Steve asked, "What makes you think I haven't already sent him an email? He's a modern Krampus who uses electronic as well as regular mail."

Heather ignored his attempt at humor. "Where will we go after we leave Candy's home?"

Steve rubbed his chin. "My crystal ball can't look that far into the future. I thought we'd ask Candy for her recommendation of where that many people could stay."

Heather rose from her lounge chair. "You've done enough with planning the protection portion of this Christmas adven-ture. I'll plan the second half."

Steve agreed, and they went inside for a light breakfast. A button-popping feast would come mid-afternoon, the perfect time to discuss going to Branson to catch the sights and sounds of the Christmas season in the Ozarks.

# 4

Heather scurried to open the front door for the first guests to arrive for the Thanksgiving feast. Adam carried a massive roasting pan covered with aluminum foil. Bella, his blonde wife, who looked like a Scandinavian goddess, followed him in carrying a pan not much smaller than Adam's. "Cornbread dressing," said Bella.

"They smell amazing," said Heather. "The oven's warm and empty, and there's spiced cider to sip on."

She took the time to examine the Ken and Barbie couple as they slid their offerings into the oven. As usual, Heather found nothing to criticize. Bella wore her silver-blond hair in a tight braid that reached to the waist of her skinny jeans. The loose-fitting cowl neck knit top made her look like the fashion model she was. Adam also wore designer jeans, but with a skin-hugging black turtleneck that showed off his athletic torso and arms.

The trio's conversation began with Heather speaking to the back of Bella's head as she closed the oven door. "It's a shame your parents aren't able to join us this year."

"The repairs to their home outside of San Juan are taking longer than expected. That late-season hurricane resulted in supply chain issues for roofing materials. They're scheduled to install the new metal roof in two weeks. I told Dad I'd give him a pass on Thanksgiving, but they had to be here for Christmas. No excuses."

"Help yourself to a hot drink and let's go into the living room."

"Yummy," said Bella as she dipped a ladle into the steaming liquid that spread the aromas of apples, cloves, and cinnamon throughout the home.

Bella handed Adam a mug shaped like a plump turkey and asked, "Where's Steve?"

"He and Le Roi should be here soon. He took his golf cart to the fitness center for a workout before gorging himself."

Adam joined the conversation. "I should have gone with him. His self-driving golf cart is amazing. I'm glad I invested in the company that developed the satellite technology that's so precise the visually impaired can experience a new level of independence."

Heather spoke in a matter-of-fact tone. "Did I tell you I obtained the franchise for retail sales of the leading brand of self-driving golf carts for all the southern states? Sales in golfcart communities are taking off like wildfire. Steve is the company's best passive salesperson. When people see him step out of his cart carrying his white cane, they have to know where they can get a cart like his. Most are interested in something that allows them to have a few cocktails then let the machine carry them home safely."

The conversation paused when the doorbell chimed again. Heather and Princess went to welcome the next guests, who turned out to be Rasheed and his love interest, Junani Hasan, an attorney in Heather's legal department.

Junani carried a large platter covered with sheets of clear plastic-wrap. Heather took a quick look and said, "Please tell me those are stuffed grape leaves."

"I call them by their Turkish name, *dolma,* but they're also called *sarma,* or *warak enab.* There are many recipes, but I fill the grape leaves with rice, ground lamb, parsley, mint and pine nuts."

Rasheed added, "Lucky is the man whose future wife knows her way around a kitchen. His stomach will seldom growl."

Junani rolled her large, brown eyes. "Your latest attempt at writing a proverb has fallen as flat as unleavened bread."

"Get in from the cold, and let me take your platter to the kitchen," said Heather. "Help yourself to the hot cider on the stove. Bella and Adam are in the living room."

Heather was following Junani to the living room when the doorbell sounded again. The smiling face of Jack's daughter, Briann, greeted her, but her gaze quickly shifted to Princess, who received a hug that set her tail to wagging.

"She'd love it if you took her to the backyard. Her tennis ball is on the table. A game of fetch would earn you a lifelong friend."

"Come with me, Princess," said Briann as she shot through the house.

Jack hollered from the driveway. "Come give me and Mom a hand."

Heather pulled the door to but didn't fully close it. She then scuffed her house shoes up the sidewalk and onto the driveway. Cora met her carrying two pies. Heather gave her an awkward hug as she said, "There's a red velvet cake in the back seat that Briann was supposed to bring inside. She was so excited about playing with Princess and Le Roi that she forgot her responsibility. Jack will bring the other two pies."

"My taste buds are already celebrating. Thank you so much. You've earned a mug of pre-dinner hot cider. It's on the stove."

Cora made her way inside while Heather approached Jack. He all but swallowed her in his arms and delivered a kiss that left her wanting another. He whispered, "Can we stay out here a few more hours?"

"I love the idea, but your timing is off. We'll have a riot if the meal isn't on the table soon."

"Who are we missing?"

"Steve is the only one. He went to the gym for a long workout. I think he's justifying the overeating he's looked forward to all week."

The front door opened, and Steve appeared on the front porch. "My green bean casserole is getting cold, and the natives are getting restless."

He disappeared back into her home, and Heather said, "He and Le Roi must have come across the backyard. Hand me the cake and grab your pies."

Everyone had yielded to Jack's mother as matriarch over the kitchen by the time she and Jack delivered desserts to a narrow table that stood against a wall in the dining room. Heather walked into the kitchen and found Rasheed carving the turkey, while Junani ferried hot and cold dishes to the table. Heather's contribution was three varieties of salad from the gourmet natural foods store that stood near the entrance of her housing development. Learning to cook more than breakfast and throw together a healthy salad was on her 'someday' list. Until then, she was content taking advantage of the myriad of healthy commercial alternatives.

After everyone was seated, Heather asked Jack to offer thanks. The sincere prayer from his heart lasted longer than she expected. "Amen" marked the end of the prayer and the beginning of a cacophony of voices in separate conversations. Rasheed heaped slabs of turkey onto empty plates. Junani added dressing and gravy. All other dishes passed clockwise, as people took or rejected sides.

Steve shocked her as he held up a palm when asked if he wanted seconds. Instead, he said, "I walked two miles on the treadmill today so I could have half-portions of all the desserts Cora baked."

Eventually, dessert plates were being pushed away around the table. Steve scraped the chocolate icing off his plate and settled back in his chair with a contented sigh and a cup of coffee in his right hand.

"If I can have your attention," said Steve, as he waited for conversations to end. "Thank you for your culinary skills; I believe everyone agrees that this was a meal to remember. Heather and I want you to know what we have planned for the near future and how it will affect everyone at this table."

Steve waited a few seconds before saying, "Rasheed, Le Roi, and I will drive to Branson, Missouri next week to investigate a possible extortion case."

Heather took over. "I'm also leaving for Branson with members of my acquisitions team the day after Steve leaves. It's possible I'll assist Steve in his investigation, but I'm hoping to explore business possibilities."

Steve chimed in. "Everyone at this table holds a special place in my heart, and in Heather's as well. We want to make this Christmas special for all. We're hoping you'll join us in Branson for a week."

Excited conversations sprung up around the table.

Heather explained, "I'm still working out the details of when I'll send my plane to pick you up, where we'll stay, and many other decisions. I can promise you we'll come back home a week before Christmas Day. Pam will be in touch with each of you and address questions you may have."

Jack's smile exposed a row of perfectly aligned teeth. "A Christmas trip to Branson. What a great idea."

Cora clapped her hands. "There's nothing like Christmas in Branson. The shows are incredible and Silver Dollar City is ablaze in lights. This will be so much better than going by bus with a bunch of blue-hairs."

Jack raised his hand. "Briann and I may be late getting there. Her school is touchy about students starting their winter break early."

Steve spoke up. "I'm sure a brilliant and resourceful defense attorney like you can find a loophole in the rules. Besides, nothing important happens in the last days before the break."

Jack rubbed his chin. "Why do I feel like I'm on the verge of becoming an accessory to a crime?"

Heather piled on. "Lawyers seldom get in trouble for creative interpretations of laws, rules, and regulations. We all have complete confidence that you'll find a creative workaround."

"Yeah, Dad," said Briann. "Do some of that fancy lawyer stuff and get me out of that jail they call school."

"If you need help," said Rasheed, "I could make a list of excuses my college students used to justify their absences." He tilted his head. "Then again, the threat of missile attacks probably wouldn't work with Briann's principal."

On that note, Jack rose from his chair, rubbing his stomach. "If you want me to entertain any more suggestions, you'll find me on the couch watching football."

# 5

Rasheed's knock on the front door came precisely at 4:30 a.m. Steve had been up for a full hour, nursing his first cup of coffee. Bella and Heather had helped him pack the preceding evening. With the two of them telling him what he should and shouldn't take, he felt like a child going off to a winter version of summer camp. The two women also took control of packing a large ice chest with frozen steaks for Le Roi, the only thing the ultra-discerning dog would eat.

"Good morning, my friends," said Rasheed as he greeted man and beast. "We should have mostly pleasant weather for our journey. I have charted a route that will bypass Dallas, even though that is said to be the quickest route. My experience as an Uber driver in Houston taught me to be wary of time estimates in big cities."

Steve said, "The maps program said it's about six-hundred miles. With stops for meals and bathroom breaks, we're looking at ten to eleven hours on the road."

"That was my estimate, too," said Rasheed. "We should arrive at your friend's home before dark."

"Not if we stand here talking."

The sound of Steve's suitcase rolling toward his front door

was his cue to grab his computer bag, a jacket, and his travel cup. "Did you bring snacks and bottles of water?"

"Junani packed a cooler with bottles of water and an assortment of homemade delicacies. I fear they're all from her healthy living cookbook."

"That's too bad," said Steve. "I have a hankering for waffles and sausage this morning. I thought we'd stop in a couple of hours and have breakfast at a place with plenty of pickup trucks in the parking lot."

Rasheed fired back, "It is said that if you travel two counties or more from your front door, your secrets get lost trying to find their way home."

"Did you make that up?"

"Yes, my words are a complete fabrication, but that won't stop me from soaking my waffle in syrup." Rasheed added, "I appreciate Junani trying to keep me healthy, but my desire for western foods often wrestles with her cooking. It is a weakness I have yet to overcome."

The sound of Rasheed loading the suitcase in the back seat and placing Le Roi into the back cargo area of the Mercedes SUV reached Steve's ears. He climbed into the passenger seat and put on his seatbelt after closing his door. Rasheed soon joined him, the click of his safety belt breaking the silence.

Steve picked up the conversation where they had left off. "When it comes to diet and exercise, I'm a casualty in the battle of the bulge. Being blind doesn't help. My senses of smell and taste are so much keener than when I could see. Exercise is a constant battle between my desire to do what I know is best for me and wondering why I bother. Holidays and vacations are extra hard to maintain discipline."

Rasheed backed out of the driveway. "If we keep talking about food, it may take us an extra day to get to our destination."

"You're right," said Steve. "You drive and I'll try to sleep."

"I won't wake you until I find the restaurant or diner you described."

Steve asked, "What route did you choose?"

"The most scenic I could find without sacrificing too much time. It's divided between interstate highways and roads that connect rural towns. We'll go from Conroe to Huntsville, through Davy Crockett National Forest, and on to Nacogdoches. It's a college town, so there should be multiple places that will satisfy our desire for waffles. After we eat, we'll go northeast to Texarkana through dense forests."

Steve added, "Most people don't realize how big the lumber industry is in East Texas. You'll get your fill of looking at future telephone poles on this trip. Where do we go after Texarkana?"

"It's interstate all the way to Little Rock, Arkansas. From there, we'll switch from I-30 to I-40 and go north until we reach Conway, Arkansas. We'll then take Highway 65 all the way into Branson. It's a four-lane road, but goes through many small towns."

Steve nodded his approval. "You've done well in choosing our route. I'm looking forward to you describing the landscape after breakfast. I already know what's between here and Nacogdoches."

The drone of tires on the highway worked its magic, and Steve soon drifted into that state of being between asleep and awake. He stayed in that timeless place until his phone rang.

Groggy, he fished his phone from the front pocket of his jacket. He'd missed the caller's name, so he issued a simple, gravelly, "Hello."

"I'm sorry, Steve, I thought you'd be awake by now."

He recognized the voice and cleared his throat. "Candy? What's wrong?"

"I hope nothing, but I received another threatening letter."

Steve located the button that brought his seat to an upright position. "Did you open it?"

"No. Once I saw it looked like the others, I put it on the kitchen countertop. I'm treating it like it's a poisonous snake."

"Good. Use gloves and put it into a plastic bag."

"Will a sandwich bag do?"

"As long as you don't bend or crease the envelope. Be sure you seal the bag. I may be able to detect a smell on the envelope or letter." A thought occurred to Steve. "If I can't, Le Roi can. I should have had him smell the last letter. I'll call Heather and get her to have Princess take a good sniff of it. She'll join us in a day or two."

A few seconds of silence aroused Steve's suspicion. "What else is wrong?"

Candy released a soft moan. "It's nothing but a touch of paranoia. The Christmas show I'm in is an experiment. An actor dressed as Saint Nicholas starts the show and begins with an explanation of when and where the idea of gifts at Christmas originated. St. Nick is suddenly interrupted by Krampus in full costume, who tells the boys and girls there is no hope for presents if they misbehave. He then takes a present from a child actor and runs offstage, leaving the child crying."

"That doesn't seem very family-friendly," whispered Rasheed.

Candy either didn't hear Rasheed's comment or ignored it, as she kept talking. "St. Nick always has the last word and tells the audience not to worry, that the spirit of Christmas is stronger than any troll who comes against it. Saint Nicholas then introduces the first act, which is one of my songs.

"As the show progresses, St. Nick talks about hope, joy, peace, and love. He's interrupted by other characters, each based on a scary legend. Trolls, witches, a scarecrow, a really nasty man, and even a cat from hell make an appearance."

Rasheed blurted out, "It is good versus evil. That theme never grows old and sounds very educational."

"It is," said Candy. "I never knew there were so many traditions around Christmas dealing with punishment for unacceptable behavior."

Steve answered an unasked question. "That's Rasheed. He's Heather's driver and works for her in other capacities. I borrowed him to drive me."

"Hello, Rasheed," said Candy. "I'm looking forward to meeting you."

"Many blessings to you. To paraphrase the poet, 'There are many miles to go before we sleep.' However, your talk of trolls and witches may make sleep difficult tonight."

"I must admit," said Candy. "Watching the show yesterday wasn't a good idea. The image of Krampus and the others is firmly stuck in my mind now that I've received another letter."

Steve knew Rasheed's gift of gab would hijack the conversation unless he cut in. "Candy, I'd like a full list of the evil characters in the show. Send it to me as soon as you can. If possible, get me the names of the actors who play each character. I'll also need the names of everyone who has access to the costumes."

"Ah," said Candy. "You suspect someone will borrow the Krampus costume and try to scare me, or worse."

"The thought crossed my mind, but I don't want you to worry about the threats. I'm going to call Heather and set up a three-way conversation. You should receive a call within the next fifteen minutes."

"Thanks, Steve. Knowing you're on the way and taking the threats seriously is very comforting. You always were a guy who could get things done." With a smile in her voice, she said, "Don't tell anyone, but I had a big crush on you when we were in school."

Not sure how to respond, Steve stumbled over his reply. "I... uh. I thought you didn't know my name."

Candy chuckled. "You don't need to worry. I got over the crush by the time I went to college. Music was my life until I met Jim. I made room for him and still miss him like crazy. I won't be resurrecting my crush. You'll be safe staying in my home."

Moving on to safer ground, he said, "It's not *my* safety I'm concerned about. Expect a call soon."

The phone clicked off, and Steve spoke Heather's name into the phone's microphone. She answered on the second ring. "How far have you gone?"

"Beats me," said Steve. "I spent about twenty minutes talking to Rasheed, an unknown length of time in dreamland, and the last seven to ten minutes speaking with Candy. She received another letter. When we're through talking, I want you to get us on a three-way call with Candy. I want you on the phone when she opens it."

Heather spoke with a pretend-serious tone in her voice. "I hope Krampus is a little more forthcoming with his instructions this time."

Steve said, "My research indicates a Krampus is neither male nor female."

"The one I kicked was definitely male."

"Are you in a spot where you can take notes?"

"I'm close to the office. Give me five minutes and I'll be at my desk."

"Also," said Steve. "I want you to give Princess a good sniff of the letter Sugar brought to us. I'm a little late, but I realized it should have the scent of whoever sent it."

"How stupid of me not to think of that," said Heather.

"Me too," said Steve. "I'm putting Le Roi's nose to work as soon as we get to Candy's home. Both dogs should react if they get a whiff later of whoever is playing Krampus."

Steve took a quick breath. "That reminds me. The show Candy performs in depicts scary Christmas legends. Trolls, witches, and other nasty characters to scare children into being good little boys and girls. Krampus is one of about six. I've asked Candy for a list of the evil Christmas characters. Put Bella to work researching their origins and practices."

"She'll enjoy that assignment."

Heather paused, then said, "Candy's theater wardrobe should be our first place to look. We'll take photos."

"Great idea," said Steve. "We may need cameras to put on Candy's property."

Several seconds of silence followed before Heather said, "Are you sure you don't need me and Princess to fly up today? I could be on the ground before you pass Branson's city limit sign and bring a stash of cameras with me."

Steve weighed the pros and cons of her suggestion. "Let's stick with our plan until we find out what the letter says. We still don't know whether this is a legitimate threat or a sick joke."

Following the call, Steve leaned toward Rasheed. "Where are we?"

"Thirty miles from Nacogdoches. I've found three restaurants that offer a full breakfast menu, including waffles."

"Go to the one closest to the college campus. The portions are usually bigger and the prices lower. The student's conversations are often insightful, or at least entertaining."

"It will bring back many fond memories of my years in academia," said Rasheed. "The atmosphere should stimulate me to write another proverb or two."

More miles clicked by before Steve's phone rang again. He traded salutations with Heather and Candy. With the groundwork for the conversation already established, Steve gave instructions to Candy. "I want you to put on gloves and get the sharpest knife you own and place it beside the plastic bag containing the envelope. Let me know when you're ready to proceed."

A few seconds passed, and she said, "I'm ready."

"Take photos of the letter in the bag before you begin."

"Front, back or both?"

"Both," said Steve. "After you've opened the bag, place the envelope on the bag and take additional photos of front and back."

"Alright, I did that. It's in the same type of envelope as before with the same stamp on it. What's next?"

"Gently slide the tip of the blade between the gummed seal and top of the envelope."

"Done," said Candy.

"With a single motion, push the knife along the entire length of the envelope."

"It's open."

"Excellent. Carefully remove the letter and read it to us." Steve silently counted to three before he heard Candy say,

*"You'll pay dearly for your sin of greed if you don't repent. Place ten thousand dollars cash in an envelope and be ready to follow instructions. Krampus is watching. If you don't believe me, ask Jim's picture on your nightstand."*

Heather spoke before Steve could. "Candy, expect another house guest tonight. I already told my pilots to be on standby for a quick departure to Branson."

Steve didn't argue with her.

# 6

Steve remained silent until Rasheed announced their pending arrival to Nacogdoches. "Good," said Steve. "Is there a place to pull over so Le Roi can run and sniff some trees?"

The car slowed and turned right as Rasheed said, "I don't see any fire hydrants, but there's no shortage of trees that pierce the heavens. Le Roi will soon enjoy the Shangri-La of potty stops with no homes in sight."

"Take him into the woods and allow him to run for a few minutes." Steve stepped out of the car and took in the earthy smells of pine needles and sandy soil. His thoughts, however, were hundreds of miles to the north. The investigation had shifted from what the police would consider a prank to something more serious. Even though the threat of violence was vague, it carried with it an exact amount of money, which was increasing with each letter. In the grand scheme of things, ten thousand dollars was a paltry sum for extortion. Yet, the demand came with an implication of harm if not paid. Of primary importance, someone had knowledge of Candy's bedroom and the photo of her late husband. This pushed the threat level up considerably.

He took a step and felt a pinecone under his shoe. A kick sent it away as he considered Heather's reaction to the threat. She didn't hesitate to change her plans and join him in Branson. Her priorities had done a fast one-hundred-eighty-degree turn when she insisted on joining him. This case was also a departure from their normal way of conducting investigations. They'd agreed to work murders, not extortions. He appreciated her willingness to make an exception and her desire to protect Candy from what he believed to be the shakedown of his old friend from high school.

Le Roi sneezed as he and Rasheed returned to the car. "Was it a successful trip?" asked Steve.

"A rousing success," said Rasheed. "Le Roi proved himself to be an excellent tree marker."

Steve took in a last smell of pine needles and said, "Waffles and sausage await us in Nacogdoches."

"And perhaps a stimulating conversation with a philosophy student. I'm interested to see if he or she can give the pros and cons of the Socratic method of teaching. I'm prepared to defend either side of the debate."

Steve shook his head. "I'll give you fifteen minutes after we finish our meals to find a victim and cudgel them with your oratory skills. Our goal today is Branson by dark."

"Fifteen minutes isn't much time, but it should be enough."

The smell of sausage and bacon overpowered all others in the restaurant. Steve asked the server to have the cook cut his waffle and meat into bite-size pieces. She responded by saying, "You got it, hun. That's some dog you got there. I bet he'd like a waffle, too."

"He wouldn't eat it. His name, Le Roi, is French for The King. He believes it's his title, not his name. Raw steak is all he'll eat."

"That beats anything I ever heard. Getting steak every day goes to show it's good to be the king."

"He lives by those words."

"I'll tell the cook to make sure he cooks your waffle just right and cuts it up for you. I'll butter it and put as much syrup on it as you want."

Steve thanked her then Rasheed excused himself after he placed his order. He returned a few minutes later, but he wasn't alone.

"Steve, this is Abdul-Ali. I hope you don't mind, but he and I will speak in our native language. He's adequate in speaking English, but not fully fluent. He still thinks in the language of his birth, not English. This is causing him to fall behind in his studies."

"Knock yourself out. My focus will be on my food."

The server returned. "There's two plates for each of you. The one on your left is your waffles, and on the right is sausage and scrambled eggs. Tell me how much syrup you want on the waffle."

Steve unrolled his napkin and stuffed the point of it under the top button of his shirt. "Pretend the waffle is in a dry swimming pool. Pour syrup until it's touching the waffle's waist."

"That's what I needed to know."

The singsong of the mid-eastern conversation gave a surprisingly pleasant serenade to the meal. Steve polished off the last bite and leaned back, full and satisfied.

A few minutes later, the chair occupied by Abdul-Ali scraped as it moved away from the table. "I regret I did not talk to you, Mr. Smiley. Rasheed sings love songs praising you."

Rasheed issued a gentle correction. "A better way of saying that is, 'Rasheed sings your praises.' It is another of those pesky idiomatic expressions."

Steve asked, "Did you and Rasheed discuss philosophy?"

"A modest amount. Mostly, he encouraged me to fully immerse myself in the culture and language of this country. I am to write questions and call him twice a week. He will no longer speak to me using anything but Texas English."

"You have to admit," said Rasheed, "it differs from other dialects found in this country."

"And howdy," said Steve.

Rasheed clarified the phrase for Abdul-Ali. "That's Texan for, 'It certainly does.'"

Steve pushed away from the table. "We're burning daylight. It's time to mosey down the trail."

Rasheed interpreted. "Steve is teasing both of us with two expressions. Write them down and try to discover what both mean. It will be a good learning exercise for you."

"Can I record them on my phone?"

"Even better," said Rasheed.

Steve repeated the sayings for Abdul-Ali, took hold of Le Roi's harness, and allowed his dog to lead him from the restaurant. Once settled in the car, the trio continued their journey.

"We've cleared the city limits. It was a most enjoyable stop. The professors and students are most fortunate to have such a lovely and peaceful place to work and study," said Rasheed.

Steve muttered a quick "Uh-huh," then asked, "I thought you wanted to have a philosophical debate."

"It was more important that I encourage Abdul-Ali. Nothing good awaits him if he goes home without an excellent education. He must change and overcome."

"That's the story of your life and mine, but what's so special about Abdul-Ali that you committed to mentor him two days a week?"

Rasheed chuckled. "You tempt me to engage in a discussion about the value of a lone man and all of mankind. I sense you do this on purpose."

"I didn't want you to feel you'd missed out on anything."

"You are a shrewd adversary," said Rasheed. "State your position and I'll counter it."

"No dice," said Steve. "You state your position by coming up with an original proverb and I'll counter it with one of my own. The time will fly, and we'll be in Arkansas in time for lunch."

The plan worked. In a verbal thrust-and-parry, the two men engaged in a peaceful verbal battle, and the miles clicked by. Both agreed the contest was a draw as they enjoyed a late lunch at a diner in an easily forgotten hamlet on the far side of Little Rock. The hamburgers and fries were adequate, and the bathroom smelled clean.

Steve wasn't particularly tired, but the high-carbohydrate lunch took its toll. He awakened from a nap when Rasheed started an audiobook by the late author Rex Stout. Steve always liked private detective Nero Wolfe and his dutiful, dapper underling, Archie Goodwin. The story lasted through Harrison, Arkansas, where they stopped on the outskirts when Le Roi insisted on another stretch of his legs.

"How much farther?" asked Steve when everyone was back in the car.

"Thirty miles to the Branson Airport."

"Heather may be there waiting for us," said Steve. "I'll call her."

Steve's phone announced a call before he could tell it to call Heather. After trading greetings, she said, "This airport looks amazing from the air. The pilots told me the builders took three mountains, cut off the tops, filled in the land between them, and made a runway that's over seven thousand feet long. There's no taxiway. Planes turn around on the runway for takeoffs and landings."

"That's quite a construction project," said Steve. "We're less than thirty miles from the airport. I'll call Candy and tell her we should be at her home in about an hour."

"Ask her if she'd rather meet us someplace for supper. I hate to barge in and expect her to cook for us."

"Good idea. Where are your pilots staying?"

"The Hilton Promenade at the Branson Landing. They'll return to Conroe tomorrow morning and wait there until my acquisitions team finishes its research and is ready to explore possibilities."

Steve exchanged one phone call for another. Candy answered in a voice that communicated hospitality. "I can't tell you how much I appreciate you coming. You shouldn't have any trouble finding your way to my home. It's only a hop, skip, and a jump from the airport."

"Yes, we have the address. By the way, Heather and her dog will be with us. We're taking the last letter seriously. Have you received any more threats?"

"I hate to admit it, but fear got the best of me today, and I didn't go to the mailbox. I know it's silly to stay behind locked doors, but that last letter has me hearing every creak of this house and imagining all kinds of silly things. Loud music helps, but there's nothing like having someone here."

"You won't be alone for long. I hope you're ready for the invasion of two men, one woman, and two large dogs."

"I always wanted a full house. Since things didn't work out that way, I'm always happy to have guests. Get here as soon as you can."

"Heather wants us to go out to eat after we unload our luggage."

"That's what I was going to suggest, and you've come to the right city for choices of places to eat. I'll narrow down the choices to three."

"Perfect," said Steve. "We'll be at your front gate in about an hour. We don't have to discuss this tonight, but I want you to make a list of people who either have some sort of grudge against you, have threatened you, or believe you owe them something."

"That may be a hard list to compile. I make it a habit of not getting close to many people."

"The entertainment industry is one of the most competitive businesses in the world. You have money as well as fame. That makes you a likely target. Ask yourself this question: *Who do I know that's shown interest in what I am or what I have?*"

"I have a hard time thinking like that," said Candy.

"Heather and I will help you as much as we can, but you'll need to do your part by answering the two questions I posed to you." He changed his voice to a less serious tone. "Don't over-think it. Your subconscious will do much of the work for you. Names will pop up when you least expect them. When they do, don't hesitate... write them down. Carry a notepad and pen with you."

"It will seem like I'm accusing innocent people."

"An observation, a suspicion, or a gut feeling isn't an accusation. That's where Heather and I come in. We take the names of people, gather facts about them, and follow the breadcrumbs until we find the guilty person. Along the way, we eliminate suspects."

"You make it sound so easy."

Steve released the tension with a deep laugh. "What we do *is* easy compared to what you do. Singing before thousands is hard."

"You're making me feel better. I can't wait to see you again and meet Heather, Rasheed, and the two dogs."

"We'll be there soon," said Steve to close out the call.

Rasheed gave his summary of the conversation. "Candy is a most gracious woman, but full of fear."

Steve folded his hands in his lap. "I wonder what she looks like after all these years."

"Her media photos show her as a petite, handsome woman. Her eyes sparkle with joy."

"That's how I remember her."

# 7

Heather rolled two large suitcases along with a smaller one to the curb, then zipped her light jacket up as far as it would go. She wished she'd taken the time to remove the alpaca scarf from her luggage. It crossed her mind to go back into the terminal and get out of the wind, but her SUV appeared before she could make the move.

Princess sniffed the air as she sat with ears erect, her tail sweeping the concrete walk. "That's right, girl. It's Le Roi, Steve, and Rasheed. They drove while we flew."

Rasheed rushed to load her luggage and Princess. The two dogs touched noses, which was the most affection they ever displayed. Steve also stepped out of the car and asked, "Good flight?"

"A little bumpy on the landing, but that's not surprising considering we landed on a plateau in high winds." She shivered. "It's at least fifty degrees colder than it was back home."

"Only forty," said Steve. "I checked every time we stopped."

"It will take me a day or two to acclimate."

"Something heavier than your windbreaker will also help," said Steve.

"I won't give you the satisfaction of telling me how you knew

I'm only wearing a windbreaker. You heard the material flapping in the wind."

"Wrong," said Steve. "The sound only confirmed what I knew to be true. It was over eighty degrees when you left Texas. You didn't know you'd be flying here until you were at work and I called you. That means Pam went to your home and packed for you. She filled your suitcases with winter clothes, including a jacket and a heavy coat. You used your time to work, but you got cold and put on the windbreaker you keep in the plane."

"Very good, Sherlock. How many bags did I bring?"

"Three are on rollers, but only two went into the back of the car with Le Roi and Princess. Hand me your carry-on, and it can ride with me in the back seat."

Heather came back with, "If I were warmer, I'd tell you to get in the front and I'd take care of my carry-on."

"You'll be warm soon enough," said Steve. "I turned the seat heater to high when we neared the terminal."

Heather settled into the front seat and released a moan of pleasurable relief. "This seat is delicious. Remind me to wear something more substantial than a thin dress if there's any chance of flying north in winter."

She then turned to Rasheed. "I should have offered to drive. I bet you're tired."

"I feel surprisingly good. The scenery and conversation kept me stimulated. I even met a young man from my native land... a college student, no less."

Steve broke into the conversation. "I spoke with Candy. She's expecting us, and we need to check her mailbox on the way in."

Heather thought for a moment and asked, "Was she afraid to check it?"

"Yeah."

"That's good. It means she's taking precautions. I'll make sure it's not rigged to explode. I can show her what to look for tomorrow."

"I desire to learn that skill, too," said Rasheed. "I'm sure Archie Goodwin knew what to look for."

Steve spoke to Heather from the back seat. "You missed listening to a Detective Nero Wolfe book."

"It sounds like you boys had fun without me."

"It was enlightening and surprisingly refreshing," said Rasheed.

"Good," said Steve. "You and Junani will enjoy the trip home together. It will be an excellent test to see if you're truly compatible."

Rasheed shot a glance at Heather. "I wasn't aware you planned on Junani and me traveling that far alone together."

Heather played along with Steve's plan. "Does a full day's trip alone with Junani frighten you?"

Rasheed swallowed. "Frightened is not the best word. How can I explain what is on my mind?" He thought for a moment and said, "Happy is the man who takes long walks and short drives with his overly cautious beloved."

Steve let out a guffaw from the back seat. "That's the best proverb you've come up with in months. Make sure you put it in your book."

Heather chuckled. "I agree. With the right marketing, your book of proverbs may become a bestseller."

"You pull my leg again," said Rasheed.

"Not at all. People are always looking for presents to buy around Christmas, birthdays, and for other special events. With a little work, you could have enough proverbs ready for publication next fall, just in time for Christmas."

"Listen to her," said Steve. "Heather knows what she's talking about when it comes to making money." Steve took a breath. "In the meantime, pay attention to your driving. The computer just told you it had to recalibrate. That means you missed a turn."

"I apologize for my incompetence. Visions of dollar bills from book sales were dancing in my head."

The miles passed as they traversed up and down a two-lane

road. The computer gave a final announcement: *Your destination is on the left.*

Heather pointed and said, "Pull up to the mailbox and I'll show you what to look for."

Rasheed put the car in park and joined her. She used her cell phone's light to examine the box and explained to him how the mailbox, with its simple metal door hinged at the bottom, could be rigged to kill or severely injure someone. "If you see any wires or magnets, back away and call the police."

"I see nothing," said Rasheed.

"I don't either. Stand behind the car and I'll open it."

"No," said Rasheed. "My duty is to protect you. You go behind the car."

"All right. Use the light on your phone, stand to the side of the mailbox, and open it only enough for you to get a peek inside. Take your time and follow the same procedure until the door is completely open. Make sure there's nothing but mail inside, remove it, and close the door."

Rasheed did as instructed and brought her a handful of circulars. She examined them then climbed back into the car. "We're good. No letter today." she said.

"The gate code is 8549. Candy's waiting for us."

The black iron gate, festooned along the top with Christmas greenery and a large green wreath hanging in the center, swung open after Rasheed punched in the numbers. The car climbed upward until the driveway made a sharp turn to the left. Before them stood an impressive two-story red brick home with white columns perched on top of a hill that gave a stunning view of the lights of Branson. Large, potted topiary trees, sparkling with white lights, stood as sentinels on either side of the front door.

Rasheed scurried to unload the dogs while Steve waited outside the car for Le Roi to brush against his leg. He took hold of the handle attached to the dog's vest as Candy spoke from the front porch. "Hello. Welcome to Branson." The woman wore designer jeans, a thick sweater with a high neck, and a puffy vest.

She seemed to float down the front porch steps with her tiny house shoes barely contacting the ground. She walked in a straight line to Steve and took his left hand in hers. "Hello, stranger. We have a lot of catching up to do. I hope you're ready to talk... and listen."

She then brought his hand up to her face. "I know your hands are now your eyes. Tell me if I look different."

Steve dropped the harness and used both hands. He gently ran his hand over her hair. "That's different. You wore your hair long in high school."

"It's the mature woman look with only a touch of color and highlights."

Steve felt her forehead and worked his way down to her chin. "No wrinkles unless you smile. I remember hazel eyes."

"Yep. There are still two of 'em, but I use readers now for anything with fine print."

"Excellent bone structure, and you still have a flawless complexion. No scars that I can feel." His hands move farther down. "Do you still have dimples?"

She let out a dainty laugh. "Only when I smile, which I'm doing now."

Steve kept going. "You and my late wife have something in common. Your lips are almost identical in shape."

"I bet you kept hers firm with frequent kissing."

Steve played along. "I never could abide flabby lips." He smiled and asked, "Mind if I work my way down just a little farther?"

"Help yourself."

Heather bit her bottom lip. She'd never seen this side of Steve before and was having a hard time coming to grips with it.

He ran his hands down her neck, and out over her shoulders where he stopped and gave them a firm squeeze. "No double chin; I doubt you've gained a single pound. Of course, I'd have to hug you or dance with you to make sure of that."

"Then you'd better open your arms, 'cause I'm coming in."

Heather looked at Rasheed, who stood with his mouth hinged open, his eyes looking like two full moons.

The clench ended, and Steve spoke as if nothing unusual had taken place. "Candy, it's cold out here, so I'll make introductions quickly. This is Heather McBlythe. She's my business partner and next-door neighbor, among many other things. The gentleman next to her is Rasheed, our driver and resident philosopher. The dogs are Le Roi and Princess. They're both trained police and service dogs." He then whispered, "They think they're aristocratic humans."

Candy placed one foot behind the other, kept her hands to her side, bent her knees, lowered her gaze, and said, "Your majesties, welcome to your servant's humble abode."

Heather chuckled and said, "You've made friends for life."

Candy stood at her full height, which Heather guessed to be five one, and said, "What are we doing standing out in this refrigerator? Let's get inside and warm ourselves by the fire."

"Good idea," said Heather through chattering teeth. "I hope you don't think I'm rude, but I need to put on some layers."

Their petite hostess shut the front door behind them and said, "I'll show you to your rooms. Each one has its own bathroom. That was one of many things Jim and I agreed on and an advantage of being married to a contractor."

In her room, Heather ditched the flimsy dress, put on fleece-lined tights, slacks, a cashmere sweater, a vest and ankle-high boots, then grabbed her coat, the alpaca scarf and a knit cap. She reached for the door handle and whispered to Princess, "We're not in Texas. If you get cold, let me know and we'll go shopping for you."

Once downstairs, she found Steve and Candy in the kitchen. He must have heard the footfalls of her boots on the travertine floor. "There you are. Did you find enough clothes to put on?"

"I'm double-layered from the ground up. I see you're making supper for the royalty."

Candy looked on. "I've never seen two such beautiful, well-behaved dogs. They could teach manners to humans."

Steve said, "They'll do most anything if we give the command in French and German, but they're most valuable as guard dogs. Le Roi crushed a man's arm who made the mistake of pointing a pistol at us."

Heather nodded. "It was a loud crunch."

"I had my doubts, but these two have made a believer out of me. There's a well-trained dog in my future."

"Good," said Steve. "I have one picked out for you. She's in Houston finishing her training."

This was news to Heather and made her wonder if she was witnessing a budding relationship or if Steve was just being his normal self and doing something nice for an old schoolmate.

Steve changed the subject. "We checked your mailbox. There wasn't another letter."

"What do we do about the last letter?"

"Ask Heather. It's her turn to come up with something."

Heather wasn't surprised by Steve's challenge. In fact, she'd used her time on the flight to put together a loose plan. "We'll leave the light on in the entryway and make sure a copy of the letter is in plain sight. I'll also need an envelope to stuff cut up sheets of paper in." She looked at Candy. "If you don't have a copy machine, I brought my portable one."

"It's in the home office," said Candy. "Are you thinking someone might try to break in while we're gone?"

Steve took over, nodding. "We're setting a trap. The thick envelope of paper strips might be enough to trick Mr. Krampus into breaking into your home. By leaving Princess here with orders to guard your home, he'll get the surprise of his life."

Heather said, "It's her turn to attack a bad guy." She bent down and stroked the dog's head. "We don't want Le Roi to have all the fun, do we girl?"

"All right, let's put our plan in motion. Lead us to the office and we'll get things set up."

Ten minutes later, everything was in place, including a bulging manila envelope that, from a distance, should fool the Krampus.

"Now we're ready. Grab your coats," said Steve.

"Wait," said Candy. "We're missing Rasheed."

"He's not coming."

Steve gave more details. "I filled him in while you two were preparing the 'money' bait. If someone tries to break in, he'll need to save them from serious harm then call the police. Besides, he ate a huge late lunch and wants to call his beloved tonight."

Heather nodded in agreement. "If love were a disease, he'd have a terminal diagnosis."

# 8

Heather stood on the front porch and beheld thousands of man-made points of light below her. "Can you see all of Branson from here?"

"Mostly," said Candy as she hooked her arm in Steve's and walked him down the steps. "We're in Hollister, the little sister of Branson. It runs south and east of Branson." She pointed to the left. "The black void is Table Rock Lake. You'll have a good view of it and the dam tomorrow morning. The lake has over eight hundred miles of shoreline in southeastern Missouri and northwestern Arkansas."

"What's below the dam?" asked Steve.

"Water discharged from Table Rock Lake forms Lake Taney-como, which separates Branson and Hollister. It's a narrow lake that follows the route of the White River. The water is cold, and the trout fishing is very good." Her breath formed white clouds in the air. "We're going to Branson Landing tonight, which runs along Lake Taneycomo."

Heather exclaimed, "My pilots are staying there at the Hilton."

Candy asked, "Which one? At the landing or the one across the street attached to the convention center?"

"At the landing," said Steve, before adding, "Can we continue this conversation in the car with the heater on?"

"You need to toughen up, Steve," teased Candy as she opened his door. "You're in the Ozark Mountains, not in the Piney Woods of East Texas."

Heather loaded Le Roi into the back of the SUV and made her way to the driver's door. For a moment she wondered if Candy would climb into the back seat and sit by Steve. If so, she'd feel like a mother taking a fourteen-year-old son and his girl on a date.

Candy deposited Steve in the back seat, then sat up front. Heather masked her suspicions about Candy possibly husband shopping by saying, "It's been a while since I drove my car."

"Why's that?" asked Candy. "It's a gorgeous car with all the bells and whistles. Do you prefer something sportier?"

"Not really. In fact, I have another car identical to this one. My father insists we employ Rasheed as our driver."

Steve spoke from the back seat. "By *we*, Heather means me and her. We're next-door neighbors who share her cat, her driver, and every few months we'll work a case that tests our detective skills."

Heather quickly added, "I'm in an exclusive relationship with an exceedingly handsome defense attorney who drives an old pickup truck with an unreliable air conditioner. We take the other Mercedes when we go out."

Steve asked, "What about you, Candy? Who drives when the men come courting?"

The laugh sounded as if it came from a small silver bell. "You're the detective, Steve. Tell me who you think drives."

Heather looked in the rearview mirror but couldn't see details of his expression in the dark. He waited several seconds before saying, "Candy, I think you and I have something special in common. We both had the type of marriage that many hope for, but precious few experience. For the time being, I think you're satisfied living with your memories, just like I am."

A sniffle came from Candy. "You hit the nail on the head. I've had plenty of offers, but I drive alone when I need to go anywhere."

Heather drove to the gate, which yawned open without her needing to punch in the code. Peace of mind settled on her like a warm blanket. Steve might allow himself to give and receive the occasional banter of middle-age flirting, but his heart still belonged to Maggie.

The car moved through the gate, then she brought it to a stop. "The view from here isn't as good as the one from your front porch, but it's still magnificent. What am I looking at?"

"We've already talked about the two lakes. They built Highway 76 along a ridgeline. It's known as The Strip and is the location of many of the attractions that bring people to Branson. There aren't as many theaters as there once were, but there's still plenty. Live entertainment is the heart and soul of Branson, but excellent restaurants, unique attractions, hotels, and shops line The Strip for miles."

Steve asked, "Is that where you perform?"

"That's right, and mine is what's called a tribute show. I had one big breakout song, but I can impersonate some of the truly great female singers. Give me a wig with long black hair, and I turn into Loretta Lynn. Put me in a teased-out blond wig and plenty of padding, and I'm Dolly Parton. My favorite singer to cover is Patsy Cline. It took me years of practice to come close to copying her voice. I'm still not there, but I'm close enough that most people can't tell."

"I can't wait to see you perform," said Heather. She pointed again. "Is that a Ferris wheel in the distance?"

"It came from the Navy Pier in Chicago. It looks small from here, but it's huge. We'll ride down The Strip after we've eaten and walked through Branson Landing."

An undulating dark two-lane road took them toward their destination. It wasn't long before streetlights shone down on four lanes of traffic. Candy acted as a tour guide. "To your left is College of the Ozarks. It's known as *Hard Work U.* Every student is required to work somewhere on campus fifteen hours a week and two, forty-hour weeks per year. This guarantees they will graduate debt-free."

"How can the college afford to do that?" asked Heather.

"It's a small Christian university that lives within its budget and has a dedicated faculty and staff who don't receive exorbitant salaries. The students work to produce many products for sale to the public. They also run their own hotel that has one of the premier restaurants in the area. In addition, the college produces much of their own food and have faithful donors and alums who support them."

Heather asked, "How are they ranked academically?"

"Consistently in the top ninety-five percent of other regional colleges of their size."

Heather thought about how much her diploma from Princeton and her law degree had cost and shook her head. How many students would all that money support here?

On they drove and went through what looked like a hamlet with an old-world European vibe. Candy explained. "This is downtown Hollister in the old part of town."

They kept driving, came to a roundabout, and exited onto a bridge that was about a hundred yards long. "We're crossing over Lake Taneycomo," said Candy. "Follow the road and park somewhere in the lot on the right. We may be able to get close to the Bass Pro store, which is the flagship store and first one we come to. If not, a brisk walk will do us good. I recommend hats and gloves."

Heather watched as Candy once again laced her arm in Steve's as they approached the rustic facade of the Bass Pro Shop. Instead of thinking the singer had matrimonial designs on Steve, she now saw them as two old chums, enjoying each other's company. Skirting two ten foot silver reindeer sporting green wreaths sparkling with blue and white lights and ornaments, they veered to the right and walked on a wide sidewalk between two rows of top-of-the-line fishing boats for sale.

Candy spoke to Steve over the Christmas carols playing through poorly concealed speakers. "Branson Landing is a menagerie of shops and restaurants, along with several attractions. It runs parallel to the lake."

Steve said, "I hear people going into and coming out of shops on both sides of me."

"That's the sound of tourists' shopping." She tucked her scarf into the neck of her coat. "Your dog is attracting all kinds of attention."

"He always does." Steve lifted his chin. "I smell fudge, popcorn, steaks, seafood, and lots of other yummy things."

"The buildings on each side act like a wind tunnel, carrying the aromas from one end of the Landing to the other."

Candy turned to Heather. "What do you think about this place?"

"It's amazing. The people are a wonderful mix of young, old, and everything in between. The Christmas decorations, music, and window displays couldn't be more appealing. It's the American version of a European Christmas market, except you can go inside the shops and get warm."

Steve said, "Spoken like a true entrepreneur."

They kept walking until they reached a large area that reminded Heather of a plaza. An enormous Christmas tree stood to her left, decked in blue lights and oversized ornaments. A fountain stood on her right, as did something else closer to the water, but she couldn't tell what it was.

Candy took over. "If you go up the hill to the left, you'll cross the street and go into the old part of Branson. Keep going straight and you'll cross over Highway 65, the road to Springfield and all points north. After passing over 65, you'll start your journey along The Strip."

Heather nodded and cast her gaze back to the right. Christmas trees lit with blue and white lights illuminated steps marching down toward the boardwalk bordering the lake. "Is that an amphitheater?"

"It is, and once an hour, from noon until 10 p.m. you can see a water and fire show at no charge. They choreograph music to fountains of water and fire shooting upward. It's similar to what the Bellagio Hotel and Casino does in Las Vegas but in miniature."

Steve asked, "When is the next show?"

Candy looked at her phone. "It should start about the time we finish eating."

"Now you're speaking my love language," said Steve.

"Your choices are fish, steak, or Southern comfort food."

"Steak," said Steve without hesitation.

"Steak it is," said Candy as she turned to Heather. "Don't worry, the place we're going to has a full menu if you're not a beef eater."

Steve asked, "Is it quiet enough that we can talk?"

"It has white tablecloths, real napkins, and soft music."

"Perfect. We need to talk about your show, who's threatening you, and why."

The north parking lot was in sight when Candy pointed to her right, for the trio, plus Le Roi, to veer in that direction. They passed through double doors made of dark wood and mullioned panes of glass. The woman responsible for seating guests recognized Candy and greeted her with a hug. She then did a double take when she saw Steve's dog. "Uh... we don't normally allow dogs, but I see he's a service dog. Please tell me he's well trained."

Steve answered before Candy or Heather could. "It's not the dog you need to worry about. I'm prone to bite when I'm hungry, and my shots aren't up to date."

The hostess played along. "We'd better get you seated in a hurry. How about a nice quiet booth in the no-biting section?"

"Perfect," said all three at the same time. A server gathered leather-bound menus and walked them to a booth with a view of the river and the homes perched atop the steep cliff on the other side.

Steve raised his chin as they walked to their seats. "I love a place that cooks steak over coals. Talented chefs can really show their skill when they use hickory, oak, mesquite, or pecan."

Candy slid into the booth, and Steve followed her in. This left Heather with a view of them both and Le Roi, who sat next to Steve.

The server placed three menus on the table. Heather reached for Steve's and handed it back to the young woman. "He already knows what he wants."

The server mouthed, "I'm sorry."

Heather gave her head the slightest of shakes to communicate that no apology was necessary. "I'll take a glass of white wine." Candy followed suit.

Steve, however, asked for a tall glass of water with lemon, and said, "I'm the designated driver tonight."

Candy chuckled lightly.

Heather cast her gaze at Candy. "I've heard that same stale line a hundred times. It wasn't funny the first time, and it's aged like milk."

The server scurried away, and Steve went right to work by saying, "The evil characters in your show interest me. Heather already told me about Krampus and I have a mental picture of what the costume looks like. What about the others?"

Candy folded her hands. "I never knew there were so many myths and legends surrounding Christmas. Two of them were too gruesome to incorporate into the show."

Heather said, "If they're worse than the Krampus that attacked me in Munich, I don't want to have anything to do with them."

Steve said, "Let's skip those who don't appear in the show. I'm sure Rasheed would love to know about them, but let's focus on those with a role in your show."

Candy leaned forward. "After Krampus and my first song,

Belsnickel comes on stage. He's said to hail from Southwestern Germany, France, and Switzerland, but it was the Pennsylvania Dutch who brought the legend to America. He is a fur-clad, old, craggy man who comes calling during the Christmas season with a bag of candy in one hand and a switch in the other. Raps on the children's windows lure them outside. Belsnickel then challenges them to recite a poem or a Bible verse. If they stumble, he whacks them with the switch. If they succeed, they get candy."

"Interesting," said Heather. "Who's next?"

"That would be Frau Perchta, the witch of Christmas. The actress wears an elaborate old crone costume with a hooked nose, pointed chin with warts, and rides a broom. She comes with silver coins for good children and young women. She disembowels the unruly and disobedient and replaces their insides with straw and pebbles."

Candy chuckled. "The writers had to change the consequences part of the story to make it Branson and family friendly. In our play, Frau Perchta steals the children's presents and flies off on her broom."

The server returned with drinks and took their orders. When she left, Steve said, "Let's take a break until after we eat. Three bad guys on an empty stomach is my limit."

# 9

The meal lived up to and exceeded expectations. Steve leaned back and gave a quick comment. "A perfectly cooked steak is a rare pleasure."

Heather groaned before saying, "A blazing fire is where that play on words needs to go. Will we still have time to see the water show?"

Candy looked at her phone. "Five minutes. We should arrive right on time."

Heather signed the credit card receipt then hurried to the front door to join the others.

Steve, Candy, and Le Roi set a quick pace. People stared at the sight of the blind man, the singer, and the enormous dog walking fast down the sidewalk that was wide enough to handle the pedestrians heading in both directions.

A crowd had gathered at the fire and water show. Candy raised her voice over the din. "Follow me. There's a place where we can stand on the lower level. It helps that the steep slope of the hill makes it easy for hundreds to have a good view."

It wasn't long before a baritone voice announced the show would start in one minute. The first strains of an upbeat Christmas carol sounded.

Heather leaned into Candy. "Is that a boardwalk running by the river?"

"It runs from the Bass Pro Shop on the south end to the parking lot on the north. There's a couple of fishing piers along the way." She nodded toward the fountain. "The boardwalk splits and goes in front of and behind the fountain. With the northwest wind blowing, you don't want to be behind the fountain tonight. Streams of water blast high in the air and the stiff breeze soaks the back walkway."

Heather asked, "Will those people standing to the right of the fountain get soaked?"

Candy nodded and grinned. "It won't be long before they move."

Heather leaned into Steve, hoping to explain the details of what she was seeing. "There are jets of water shooting up."

"Are the loud booms fire?"

Candy had the answer. "It's a sudden burst of ignited gas. If you're close enough, you can feel the heat. The explosions of fire come out the tops of tall black pipes. They're synchronized with the music and the water forced at very high pressure. I'm amazed every time I see the show."

Le Roi sat placidly beside the other three until the last drop of jetted water fell and the music ceased. Candy gave a benediction of sorts. "That's all, folks. We can either stay until the next show, or ride down The Strip and cross over the dam on the way home."

Steve stated his preference. "My feet are on their way to frostbite. If anyone is taking notes, heated socks would make a nice Christmas present for the rare times I'm in cold weather. If you two are ready to leave, a warm car sounds better than cold concrete and a stiff breeze."

Heather added, "He slept very little last night. It happens every time he goes on a trip."

Steve gave his head a firm nod. "You had an hour and a half flight. I had an eleven-hour drive."

Candy said, "We don't have to ride down The Strip. It's much quicker if we go back the way we came."

Heather's phone buzzed in her coat pocket. She extracted it and looked at the screen. "It's Rasheed. I'll put him on speaker."

"Heather, this will not please you," said Rasheed with an accent that betrayed his frayed nerves.

"Tell me."

"There's broken glass in Candy's entry. Someone hurled a rock through the glass."

Candy let out a gasp and whispered, "Not again."

Heather said, "Let's get to the car. Do you want Rasheed to call the police?"

Steve answered the question before Candy could. "Call them."

The departing crowd made exiting the open-air bastion of commerce slow going. It seemed as if everyone wanted to leave the parking lot at the same time. What should have taken five minutes turned into twenty before they were on the bridge going over Lake Taneycomo. The traffic stayed thick until they passed the College of the Ozarks. Then the hills, curves, and narrow two-lane road kept their speed under fifty.

A sheriff's office deputy with emergency lights activated had stopped at the open gate to Candy's home. Heather rolled her window down as the deputy said, "I'll need to see some ID."

Candy took over. "Leon, let us in."

"Oh, it's you, Ms. Caine. There's been an attempted break in. We have the guy trapped in the house. He's some sort of foreigner. There's also a German shepherd dog with him."

Heather shot back, "The man is an American citizen, and he's the one who called you to report the rock through the front door's window."

Candy added, "Rasheed and these people are all my houseguests."

"He said the same thing, but we didn't believe him. We tried getting in, but the dog had other ideas."

Heather let out a huff. "She's protecting Rasheed and the home."

Steve spoke from the back seat. "You'd better let us through before someone gets hurt."

The officer shone his light on Steve and must have seen Le Roi behind the cage separating the back of the car from the back seat. "Good lord. How many dogs do you travel with?"

"Only two," said Steve. "Believe me, you don't want them mad at you."

"Go on through," said the officer.

Candy was the first person out of the car, followed closely by Heather. Two officers stood on the front porch with the door shut. Heather chose the one she believed was in charge. "Where's my dog?"

Barks from inside answered her question. Heather's response was a quick command for Princess to sit and maintain silence. She then said, "Rasheed, you can open the door."

"Hang on a minute, lady," shouted the officer.

It was too late. The door cracked open, and Princess burst through the opening, going straight for Heather.

The officer drew his pistol and took aim.

Acting out of instinct from years of martial arts training, Heather released a kick that struck the officer's hand, causing the shot to go skyward and the pistol to take flight, landing harmlessly in a holly bush flanking one side of the porch.

"Stop!" shouted Steve.

Princess had other ideas and stood before the unarmed deputy with teeth bared, growling.

Steve spoke in a low tone. "Slow down before someone gets hurt."

The lead deputy got over his initial shock and turned to his partner. "Don't just stand there. Shoot the dog."

Steve faced the second deputy, then did the unexpected. He sat on the second step of the porch and sang the first few bars of "Deck the Halls."

Everyone stared as he completed the fa-la-la-la-la at full volume.

He lowered his voice and spoke in a matter-of-fact tone. "That song got stuck in my head and had to get out. Is anyone injured?"

Heather covered a smirk and played along. "No injuries," said Heather with relief in her voice.

Even Princess tilted her head and stopped growling as Steve kept talking. "I'm a former cop, as is Heather. We're here to help Candy."

"They're my guests, along with Rasheed," said Candy.

"Guests or not, the guy inside is under arrest," blustered the lead deputy.

Steve patted the step next to him. "Why don't you come sit beside me, officer? I'll explain this misunderstanding." He took a breath. "Or, you can stand there making threats and looking like a fool because you lost your pistol. By the way, don't make any sudden moves. The dog still doesn't like you for pointing your sidearm at her mistress."

Heather stared at the lead deputy and said, "Sorry about disarming you, but you were about to make a mistake that would have cost you your job."

"I don't know who you two think you are, but you're going to jail, too."

"No, they're not," said Candy. "The German shepherd wasn't going for you, Matt. She was going to her owner, and that's what my statement will say."

Steve lifted an open hand as if he were asking permission to speak. "I have an idea. It's cold and windy out here. Why don't we all go inside and have something warm to drink?"

"Great idea," said Heather. She shifted her gaze. "If you promise not to shoot our dogs, we'll let you retrieve your pistol."

"By the way," said Steve. "Do you know the detective that handled the robbery and death of the wardrobe lady at Candy's theater this past summer?"

"What kind of silly question is that? I'm a City of Hollister cop. That happened in Branson."

Steve responded to the question he'd posed. "I'll answer your question, so you can learn something. My question about the identity of the Branson detective will help Heather and me solve the wardrobe lady's homicide. That's what we do and why we're here with Candy. There's been one suspicious death, and we don't want another."

"That old woman died of a heart attack."

Heather chimed in, "It's called the felony murder rule. The woman may have died as the result of a separate felony, in this case, a robbery. That makes her death a possible homicide."

"You sound like a lawyer."

Steve grinned. "That's because she is."

"Just my luck," sighed the lead officer, resigning himself to cooperate, at least for the time being. He squared his shoulders. "Lieutenant Douglas worked that case. As far as I know, it's still open."

Heather looked down at Steve, who had worked his magic again. The soft tone helped to distract both officers while making them focus on an unrelated crime. This gave the trigger-happy officer time to still his nerves and bring his emotions under control.

Heather moved to the back of her car and gave a command to Le Roi in French. The enormous black dog moved to Steve's feet and received praise in French.

The lead officer shook his head as if wondering what kind of zoo he'd wandered into.

Heather snapped her fingers and said, "Come, Princess. He's a friend." She then said, "Get your pistol out of the bush." She paused, "By the way, what's your first name?"

"Matt, and my partner's name is Sam."

Candy said, "I can offer you coffee, tea, or hot chocolate. I also baked Christmas cookies, and there's fudge from College of the Ozarks."

Sam rubbed his hands together. "Hot chocolate and cookies would hit the spot."

Steve said, "Don't forget the officer at the front gate."

Rasheed spoke through the hole in the glass. "Is it safe for me to open the door?"

"All clear," said Steve.

"Good. I took photos of the crime scene before I called the police. The rock has a note attached to it."

"Don't touch it," said Matt.

"Of course not," said Rasheed. "Archie Goodwin would never make a mistake like that."

Heather snickered as she looked at Matt's questioning face. "My driver reads a lot of old detective novels."

Steve rose to his feet. "Sam, let's give Rasheed a thrill and have him put up some crime scene tape on the front porch."

With none of the reserve exhibited by his partner, Sam nodded and said, "I'll get it out of my truck."

Heather asked, "Candy, could you lead the way to another door? I'm going to take Princess into the yard so she can pick up the trail of whoever threw the rock."

"I'll need to go with you," said Matt, now on his knees reaching into the sticky bush.

"Look more to your right," said Heather. "I'm sure the rock thrower is long gone, but at least we'll know where he got through the fence."

# 10

Heather watched as Candy and Steve disappeared around the corner of the home while the prickly bush surrendered the pistol. Matt holstered it and joined Heather in the yard, where she retrieved a small but powerful flashlight from her purse. She gave Princess the command to search, and the dog made one looping run to its left and then a sweeping turn back to the right. The dog ran at full speed until she was even with the corner of the home and came to an abrupt stop. With head down, she sniffed the ground then shot into the darkness.

Matt followed her with the beam of his flashlight until they lost sight of Princess. Out of the darkness, they heard her bark and issue what sounded like a cry of frustration.

Thick woods and bushes made for slow going, but the dog's barking yelps grew louder with every step. The ground under their feet suddenly changed, and Heather said. "Shine your light on the ground where I'm looking."

Matt said, "It's an abandoned gravel road."

"Let's follow it."

Bushes overgrew much of the road, but there was still enough gravel for her to follow it downhill to where Princess paced back and forth, looking for a way through the fence.

Heather stated the obvious. "This part of the fence is chain-link and not nearly as tall as the iron fence on the front of the property."

"Yeah," said Matt. "And this looks like it used to be a gate for trucks during construction of the home. The gravel road continues downhill."

"I bet Candy's husband put it in when he built their home."

Matt shone his light on the fence. "Look there. Someone cut the fence and did a sloppy job of putting in a new gate."

"It's meant for one person to slip through," said Heather. "There's only one metal post, a chain, and a cheap lock that looks new. That explains how the person gets onto Candy's property."

Heather scanned the thick woods with her flashlight. "Whoever threw the rock through the window is long gone. Let's get back to the house so Steve, Rasheed, and I can give you all the information you'll need for your report."

They retraced their steps with Heather in the lead. It didn't take long before Matt asked, "What's the story with you and the blind guy?"

"We're former cops and part-time business partners. I was a beat cop and detective in Boston, Mass for ten years. Steve was a lead detective for Houston PD homicide until he lost his sight and his wife to some drug-crazed street thugs."

"Are you really an attorney?"

"I worked my way through law school while I was a detective in Boston."

"What kind of law do you practice?"

"That's a good question, but it's a little complicated to explain. I own a company that acquires, owns, manages, and sells other companies and investments. That means I supervise a staff of attorneys and other executives who interact with their counterparts in the various companies."

His reserve gone, Matt stopped in his tracks. "What are you doing in Hollister, Missouri, looking for a petty criminal?"

"Steve went to high school with Candy. She's been receiving threatening letters. The note tied to the rock that went through her window is likely the latest. We believe this wasn't simple vandalism."

"I still don't understand why you and Steve..."

Heather cut him off. "Steve and I are licensed private detectives. We specialize in solving homicides."

The man was proving his ability to ask questions, most of them worth asking. "From what you've told me, you're a high-powered business executive. At the most, this could be an extortion case."

"Perhaps it's more than that. There's the woman who died after Candy's show this past summer."

The silence indicated he still couldn't reconcile Heather's involvement. She took in a shallow breath and said, "As you can imagine, my job can be a real pressure cooker. Working with Steve to solve crimes is such a change of pace, it helps me maintain my sanity."

She kept walking and broke through the brush and into the side yard. "We'll explain more after we get inside."

He mumbled under his breath, "Something tells me the report I'll write will be a three-pager."

Heather chuckled as motion-activated floodlights came on. A sliding patio door slid open, and Candy stepped onto the back patio. "Come in where it's toasty."

Steve sat in a leather recliner with Le Roi by his side and said, "Candy told us about the old gravel drive. Was that how the rock-thrower got onto the property?"

Heather couldn't help but smile. Steve had already gathered enough information from Candy to discover how the intruder had gained entrance onto the property and had done so in a leather recliner with a crackling fireplace to keep him warm.

The officer answered Steve's question. "The dog led us as far as she could but couldn't squeeze through the gap where a new post butted against an old one. A chain and new lock secured the repair so only someone with the key could get through."

Candy said, "The forest has taken over that old road. Funny. It seems like it was only a year or two ago when we put in the road and started construction. Now someone is using it to get onto the property and send threatening messages through the window of my front door."

Sam stepped into the living room with a cookie in one hand and his mouth grinding away on another in his mouth. Matt looked at his partner and shook his head. "Did you bag and tag the rock?"

The mumbled reply had to wait until at least part of the treat went down the proverbial hatch. "I didn't know if you wanted to take photos or if Rasheed's were good enough."

Matt bit his bottom lip, closed his eyes, and waited three counts before asking. "Take your own photos and ask Rasheed to send you his. Do you have an evidence bag?"

"Yeah."

"Well? Where is it?"

"In the truck."

"Don't you think it would be more useful if you brought it inside?"

"Oh. Yeah. I'll bring some gloves while I'm at it."

Steve took pity on the officer and redirected the conversation. "We'll wait for you to get back before we discuss the note tied to the rock."

Matt waited until it was only him with Heather and Steve in the living room. His earlier arrogance now gone, he moved closer to Steve and spoke in low tones. "I need some advice. Do you think I should call my supervisor or just gather the evidence?"

Steve didn't hesitate. "When in doubt, call your supervisor."

Matt puckered his lips as if he'd popped a super-sour piece of candy in his mouth.

Heather asked, "Don't you get along well with your supervisor?"

A huff of exasperation preceded the reply. "If I call Sergeant Redman, he'll tell me I should have handled the situation myself and shown initiative. If I don't call him, he'll say I should have and I compromised a case."

Steve cut back in. "I had a supervisor like that when I was a rookie cop. He rode me hard and long and dug in his spurs every chance he got. Looking back on it, he made me a better cop." He paused a moment, then continued, "What will you tell him?"

"There's not much to tell. Someone threw a rock through the window of Candy's front door with a note attached to it."

Steve shook his head. "Get out your notebook and write these words: WHERE, WHO, WHAT, WHEN, HOW, WHY, ACTION TAKEN and ADVICE DESIRED, ADDITIONAL PERTINENT INFORMATION. Let me know when you're ready to tell me the answers for each thing you listed."

"That's pretty much how they taught us to write reports," said Matt. He took a small notebook out of his pocket and began writing.

Steve listened and nodded at all the right times as Matt put his mind to work and gave responses.

"Not bad," said Steve, "...but you can do better. You left out the part that you almost shot a dog."

Matt hung his head, then looked at Steve. "There won't be much left of me when the sergeant gets through. Tell me what you'd say."

"All right, I will." Steve pretended to hold a telephone in his hand and spoke in clipped sentences. *Sarge, Matt here. I'm still at Candy's home. There was no break in, but someone threw a rock through the window of her front door with a note attached. No one has touched it yet. The vandalism occurred about forty-five minutes ago. The time is confirmed by a houseguest. Candy has received other threatening letters. Two former detectives, their driver, and two trained police dogs are also Candy's houseguests. They're private detectives investigating the threatening letters. One of the dogs, its owner, and I tracked the suspect to a security fence that has been tampered with. We've*

*secured the crime scene at the front door and in the home's entry way. Do
you want me to process the crime scene, take statements, or wait for you
to arrive?*

*"Oh yeah, one other thing. I pulled my weapon on the dog but didn't
shoot it. One shot was fired into the air to try and scare the dog."*

Steve concluded by saying. "Your sergeant now knows
enough to make an informed decision as to the scope of the
crime, if there's an immediate threat, and how he needs to
proceed."

Heather added, "No one needs to know that I kicked your
pistol out of your hand. That should save you some grief."

Matt rubbed his chin. "Shouldn't I include that?"

Heather leaned into him. "I'm a very good attorney. Nothing
will happen to me if you do, but you may lose your job. Follow
Steve's general outline and forget that you dropped your pistol. I
already have."

Steve added, "Follow the bullet points I gave you and your
relationship with your sergeant will improve."

Steve had another piece of advice. "Talk fast, with plenty of
self-assurance. It will make your sergeant think you know what
you're doing."

"I doubt it, but it will sure get his attention."

"That's what we're counting on," said Heather.

Matt spoke as he walked to the back door. "I'm going outside
to make this call. The sarge likes to holler and use words not fit
for mixed company."

Heather settled into a chair next to Steve and spoke in a low
tone. "Do you think we've stirred the pot enough for one day?"

Steve nodded. "Word will spread from Hollister's cops to
those in Branson by tomorrow morning. If we don't hear from
Branson's detective by noon, we'll stir the pot a little more."

Heather chose hot apple cider while Steve opted for hot
chocolate with two marshmallows. Heather passed on the cookies, but Steve made up for her refusal by taking one shaped like a
Christmas tree plus a piece of fudge. He bit the top of the tree

off as the man with chevrons on his collar made his presence known.

"I'm Sergeant Redman. My officers tell me you two are private detectives. Is that right?"

"That's correct," said Heather.

"What's your purpose in coming to Hollister?"

Heather didn't appreciate his gruff tone nor the way he tilted his head so he looked down his oversize nose at her. She countered his question with an answer that would give him more than he bargained for. Her words came out as if sprayed from a fire hose.

"You posed a question that assumes a singular purpose in our coming to this area. Your assumption is incorrect. My name is Heather McBlythe." She spelled her last name. "One reason I'm here is to explore investment opportunities."

Steve verbally stepped on the last word of her sentence. "I'm Steve Smiley and I'm not here to invest in anything. I am, however, looking forward to going to Candy's Christmas show and perhaps going to Silver Dollar City. We went with Candy to the fire and water display at Branson Landing earlier tonight. It sounded spectacular."

Steve didn't skip a beat and hit the sergeant with a non sequitur. "My dog's name is Le Roi." Steve lowered his voice as if telling a secret. "He acts like a French aristocrat, and understands three languages: French, English, and Dog. He enjoyed the show, too."

Heather followed with, "My dog's name is Princess. She and Le Roi are both trained police and service dogs."

Sergeant Redman held up two hands to a height just below his badge. "Ma'am, you haven't answered my question. Why are you and Mr. Smiley here?"

Heather let out a huff. "I already told you one reason." She gave him a coy smile. "If you wouldn't interrupt, this will go much faster."

Steve hopped back on the fast-moving verbal train. "Did

Officer Matt tell you I went to high school with Candy and her sister, Sugar?" He gulped a breath. "Of course that's not their given names, but with their last name being Caine, the nicknames stuck and they still use them."

It was Heather's turn. "We're expecting other friends and family to join us following our investigation." She turned her head and spoke to Steve. "Should I use the plural of investigation?"

"Stick an 's' on the end of investigation," said Steve. "So far, there's extortion and a possible homicide."

"Stop!" shouted Sergeant Redman. "What extortion and what homicide?"

Steve asked, "Why are you pretending not to know? You spent a long time in the back yard with your officers. They told you about the rock someone threw through Candy's window with the note attached, which isn't the first threatening letter she's received."

Redman's mouth opened to speak, but Heather was tailgating Steve. "We also find it suspicious that a wardrobe worker died last summer during a robbery at the theater where Candy performs."

"We don't like coincidences," said Steve.

Heather added, "It makes us wonder if there could be a link between the two crimes."

"What do you think?" asked Steve. His question, following on the heels of the verbal bombardment, had the desired effect, at least for a few long seconds.

Redman narrowed his gaze and pulled himself up to his full height. "You two are to stay here until I process and clear the crime scene. I'll be back and next time I'll do most of the talking."

Heather said, "We always cooperate when we help the police solve crimes."

Sergeant Redman bristled like an angry porcupine. "I'll make this simple. Don't interfere in police business."

Heather waited until the sergeant left the room before leaning into Steve. "I don't think we'll get much cooperation from Sergeant Redman."

"No matter," said Steve. "It wouldn't be interesting if there wasn't something to overcome. While you were stomping through the woods and Candy was busy in the kitchen, Rasheed put on gloves and untied the note wrapped around the rock."

Heather chuckled and asked, "Where was the second officer?"

"In the kitchen endangering the supply of cookies. Candy agreed to keep him distracted while Rasheed took photos of the note then wrapped it back around the rock and retied the twine. Whoever sent it now wants twenty-five grand. We'll need to set up a meeting with Branson's chief of police tomorrow morning."

Later that night, Heather opened a text from Rasheed containing a photo of the note:

*You're not taking me seriously. Naughty girl. No one from Texas can save you. You've made Krampus mad and you'll be punished. Put 25k cash in an envelope and wait for further instructions. No cops. No private detectives. No tricks. Krampus is watching.*

## 11

Heather cracked open her left eye and reached for her watch on the nightstand. It read 5:27 a.m. She did a quick calculation and determined her night's sleep exceeded her four-hour minimum but came nowhere near the seven hours her psychiatrist recommended. The only time she could recall sleeping over six hours straight was last Christmas during her mental breakdown, when exhaustion and medications conspired to give her body and mind the rest they so desperately needed.

She rose from the warmth of the duvet-covered bed, her toes digging into the thick carpet before they found her house shoes. A nightlight shone the way to the bathroom, where she shut the door behind her and soon had steamy water slowly bringing her body awake. She finished the shower in her usual way, by turning off all the hot water and taking her daily upright polar plunge. This routine was both invigorating and brutal, a discipline that dispelled the last vestiges of slumber and left her alert and excited about what the day might bring.

Her thoughts fixed on the case, and how Steve had outwitted Sergeant Redman to get critical information. A conspiratorial smile parted her lips as she glanced at her reflection in the mirror, but only for a few seconds. She and Steve both preferred to be straightforward with police, but sometimes official policies, procedures, and the hubris of officers and administrators forced them to use alternate methods to solve cases. Last night was one of those times.

With hair dried and pulled back, she dressed for the nippy weather and made her way downstairs as the new day's light brought the world to life both inside and outside the home. Princess had watched her daily ritual play out and was excited to see Rasheed waiting for them at the foot of the stairs.

He bowed and spoke to the dog. "May I have the pleasure of taking Her Royal Highness outside? The squirrels are abundant and very playful this morning."

Heather looked down at the German shepherd. "Go ahead, Princess. A run in the woods will do you good."

No other words of permission were required. The graceful dog waited until Rasheed had the door fully open before she burst forward, spied a furry creature and launched herself off the porch, barking as the squirrel scurried up the rough bark of a hickory tree.

Heather made her way into the kitchen where Steve, Candy, and LeRoi each greeted her. Candy inquired about the quality of her sleep. Le Roi moved to her side and received a good-morning scratch behind his ears, and Steve said, "I spoke with my former captain, who is now one of Houston's assistant chiefs of police. He'll call Branson's chief this morning and give him a heads-up on the phone call you'll make after breakfast. Be sure you ask him to include the detective who handled the robbery of Mabel Grist."

Candy interrupted. "That's the name of the wardrobe lady at my theater who died. She also made all the costumes for the scary Christmas characters."

Steve put down his mug of coffee. "Candy, you never finished telling us about the other characters."

"Ah," said Candy. "Where did we leave off? Of course, there's Krampus..."

Heather gave her head an exaggerated nod. "I don't wish to meet Mr. Krampus again unless it's watching him being arrested."

Candy ticked off two more. "Next is Belsnickel with candy in one hand and a switch in the other. Then, we have Frau Perchta, the first witch of Christmas.

"Then we come to the ones I didn't have time to mention last night. First, we have La Befna who also comes riding on a broom. She hails from Italy and is another who leaves candy in the stockings of obedient children. She's slightly different in that she leaves lumps of coal for those who misbehave."

Heather commented, "Coal in stockings for poor behavior. I never knew that tradition came from Italy."

Candy continued, "The last character in the show hails from France. His name is Hans Trapp. He's a cruel and greedy man who the church excommunicated and kicked out of town. He's depicted as a scarecrow who returns with a sack in hand to scoop up misbehaving children and spirit them away. The child actors confess the error of their ways, escape, and return to their homes and families."

Steve opined, "I didn't know there were that many traditions of evil characters inflicting punishment at Christmas."

"We considered one more from Iceland, but it was too violent."

Steve said, "I'm not sure I'm old enough to hear about it."

Heather let out a sigh. "Don't let him fool you. If it involves crime, especially homicide, Steve can't wait to hear it."

Candy used her theatrical training to put suspense into her voice. "This is the tale of Gryla and Leppaludi, her evil Yule cat, twelve cannibalistic trolls, and her thirteen mischievous children."

"No wonder you didn't use them," said Steve. "There wouldn't be room on the stage for that many."

Candy ignored the interruption. "The thirteen children play pranks for the thirteen days before Christmas. Only well-behaved, industrious children escape the wrath of the thirteen children, the wicked cat, and the two depraved parents who scoop up lazy and misbehaving children. New clothes ward off all bad tidings. Therefore, parents make sure their children receive gifts of new clothes at Christmas."

Steve tilted his head. "What if the children don't make themselves new clothes or the parents don't give them as presents?"

Candy shrugged. "The evil husband, wife, and cat put the children in the family stew pot and enjoy a delightful meal of them."

Heather winced. "There goes the G rating."

"Yeah," said Candy. "But Steve was right. That many characters on the stage at one time would have been a nightmare."

Heather added, "The thought of trying to corral thirteen mischievous children is enough to turn my hair gray overnight. A cat and a dog are all the children I want or need, although I enjoy pretending to be a stepmother to my boyfriend's teenage daughter." She looked at Candy. "You'll get to meet them when they come."

"Do you think your investigation will be complete before they arrive?"

Steve popped back into the conversation. "Possibly. We didn't expect to be working on two investigations. If they're related, it should make things easier."

Heather watched as Candy pulled up the corner of her apron and dabbed her eyes. Steve must have heard the sniffle that accompanied the release of pent-up emotions. "There's no crying allowed until after the new year. That was one of my Maggie's Christmas rules."

Candy half-laughed and half-snorted when she responded. "These are tears of thanksgiving for you two being so kind. I'll never be able to repay you."

"Of course, you can," said Steve. "All you have to do is cook my breakfast. I'd like two eggs over medium, two slices of the bacon I smell cooking, and toast."

"No toast," said Candy. "You're getting grits that were stone-ground by students at the college. They're cooked in whole milk instead of water and served with a full dollop of college-made peach preserves and real butter made at the college dairy."

"I've died and gone to heaven," said Steve.

Candy went to the refrigerator and retrieved a gallon of milk. She measured out the correct amount and transferred it into a large saucepan and carefully adjusted the flame under it. She then turned to Steve. "I did what you told me to do last night and wrote down some names that came to mind. I guess you would call them suspects."

"That's wonderful," said Steve. "I'm always amazed at how our minds work if we don't put too much pressure on them. People can often remember minute details if they stop pursuing answers and allow them to come in their own time." He sucked in a breath and asked, "What are the suspects' names?"

Heather knew Steve was giving her time to activate the recorder on her phone. An exact record of Candy's words might make the difference between solving the cases and missing what seemed to be a minor detail. She pretended to check an email while she turned on the recorder and slipped her phone back into the pocket of her vest.

Candy spoke as she waited for the milk to heat. "There's one I would consider a good suspect. His name is Melvin Bird, the firstborn of three sons." She paused. "I need to tell you the entire story for it to make sense. When Jim found this property, it was nothing but raw land owned by a widower in poor health. Three of his four children had moved from Branson in search of fame and fortune after they gave up on formal education. One son moved to Oregon, one to Chicago, and the lone girl went to Florida. She was the only one who kept in touch with her dad, even though Melvin, the third son, lived in Branson. The years rolled by, and the man's wife died. All four children were here for the funeral."

Steam rose from the milk, and Candy stirred as she poured in the measured amount of finely ground cornmeal.

"Following the burial, the four grown children gathered for a family meeting. Mr. Bird wanted his children to share memories of their mother, but the three boys wanted to discuss the will and to express their opinions of what a fair division of this property would be. Things spiraled downward into a shouting match that turned into a fistfight."

Heather asked, "How much property are we talking about?"

"It's a forty-acre tract, but the prime land is the ten acres on the top where this home now sits."

Steve asked, "How did Mr. Bird react to his sons' squabbling?"

Candy glanced out the frost-outlined kitchen window before returning her gaze to the grits. "He was a man of few words and stubborn as a mule with a sore tooth. The story goes he made no attempt to break up the fight and left with his daughter. When the sons returned the next day, he presented them with a new will that left them nothing. The daughter got everything."

Steve tilted his head. "Is that when you and your husband bought the land?"

"Jim was always on the lookout for land and could smell out a deal. He heard from a janitor at the hospital that three brothers had come to the ER for stitches, broken fingers, and a possible concussion. Jim started asking questions and found out the story behind the injuries."

Steve chuckled. "I wonder if they went to the hospital in separate cars?"

"They were all bruised and battered, but two rode together. Big brother Melvin wouldn't share a cab." She kept stirring. "It's odd. The fight must have cleared the air between the brothers. They all live in the area now and seem to get along."

Candy turned to face Heather and Steve. "This is out of order, but Jim tracked down Mr. Bird after he heard about the fight, made an offer, and had a contract on the property before the boys could talk their father out of it."

Heather asked, "Was the daughter named sole beneficiary in Mr. Bird's will?"

"Yep. The sister got the money from the sale of the land and Mr. Bird's rundown trailer after his death. She moved back to Florida after her father's funeral."

Heather wondered if it was to keep her brothers from pestering her for part of the inheritance.

Steve asked, "Did Melvin or his brothers blame you and Jim for buying the land?"

"They sued us, but it went nowhere. The sale price might have been on the low end of fair market value, but not enough to sway the judge. Every year I receive a Christmas card from Melvin. He includes a dead flower with a tacky note."

"Have you received one this year?" asked Steve.

"Not yet."

Heather asked, "Did you save any of the past cards?"

"I didn't even open last year's. It went straight into the trash."

Candy turned down the burner to a low simmer and retrieved eggs from the refrigerator. "The grits will be done by the time I get the eggs cooked."

"Perfect," said Steve. He then asked, "Who's the second person you think may be a suspect?"

"Her name is Claire Finch, but I don't think she'd ever do anything to me. However, she's a singer who wants to take over my job."

"Is she good?" asked Steve.

"Most people can't tell the difference between my voice and hers. She's younger, prettier, has plenty of curves, and there's no shortage of ambition. I think she's only one good original song away from making it big."

"Yet," said Steve, "she's not headlining a show like you are."

"It's only a matter of time. She makes me wonder if it's time for me to slow down and reduce my performance schedule even more."

Steve quipped, "My advice on that is don't slow down too soon. I was forced into early retirement and almost went crazy. I had to find something to replace at least part of what used to be a frenetic schedule."

Heather took her turn. "I, on the other hand, burned my candle at both ends until there was nothing left of me. I'm still learning how to slow down. This very minute I'm wishing I were in a gym working out until my muscles scream. There's a fear telling me I'll die young if I don't keep my body in perfect shape."

Candy shifted her gaze between her and Steve. "The two of you are no help at all. One of you wants more to do and the other, less." Candy thought for a moment. "The grits are almost ready to eat. Let's forgo the eggs, bacon, and toast and go for a brisk walk at Branson Landing. Heather, you can jog or run if you want while Steve and I walk at a quick pace."

Steve asked, "Is there a coffee shop we can stop at after we walk?"

Candy's eyes sparkled. "You're in for a real treat. PARLOR DOUGHNUTS sits on the other side of the Landing's north parking lot. I'll treat you to a layered maple-bacon donut."

Candy shifted her gaze to Heather. "They also have keto, gluten-free, and even doggie donuts."

"Dish up the grits," said Steve. "This is going to be a great day. Donuts are my favorite food group. With any luck, our meeting this afternoon with the chief of police will be a success, too."

## 12

Heather and Steve agreed they would meet with the Branson and Hollister chiefs of police without Candy. Not that they didn't want her input, but the chiefs might discount the threats Candy had received. This wasn't without merit, but Steve believed the threats were real and needed further investigation. Also, there was the possibility that a woman suffered a heart attack during the commission of a crime. It would be hard to prove criminal intent on a murder charge, but if they found the assailant, they could use the charge to get a confession to the lesser charge of robbery.

They arrived at a new and impressive building, and an officer ushered them into the chief's office without delay. Branson's Chief Noah Fry wasn't alone. With him was a lieutenant with a nametag that read DOUGLAS. Chief Fry looked to be in his late forties, had piercing blue eyes, and was fighting the first stages of a retreating hairline. Douglas, in contrast, appeared built for speed with long limbs, crisp edges to his clothes and a high-and-tight haircut.

Both men stood when the duo entered. Chief Fry smiled and offered a hand to Heather. Douglas did neither.

"It's nice to meet both of you," said the chief in a way that made it sound practiced. "Mr. Smiley, your former supervisor in Houston speaks highly of you. In fact, he says you're the best homicide detective he's ever supervised. That's high praise."

"He's a good man, but I'm not sure I deserve that much praise. After all, I wasn't good enough to sense the danger that cost me my sight and my wife's life." Steve turned to face the lieutenant. "Don't worry about hurting my feelings. If you haven't already said that to the chief, I'm sure you thought it."

Heather noticed a tinge of red creep up the lieutenant's throat. She locked her gaze on him. "You're right as usual, Steve. The lieutenant is blushing."

The lieutenant stiffened and said, "I don't believe private detectives have a place in law enforcement."

"I used to think the same thing," said Steve. "That's why Heather and I do things differently from most PIs. We're more like highly skilled confidential informants who know our place. We collect information and make sure we do nothing that will compromise a conviction. It helps that Heather is not only a former detective but is also an attorney."

Chief Fry held up a hand when his lieutenant opened his mouth for another comment. "Let's all have a seat. You're going to think we're completely without manners if I don't offer you a cup of coffee."

Steve asked, "Is it as bad as the coffee in most police stations?"

"Worse," said the lieutenant.

"Then I'll take a cup," said Steve. "What about you, Heather?"

"No thanks. The lining of my stomach has finally grown back. I don't want to have it peel off again."

This earned smiles from all three men and made the meeting a tad more harmonious.

A knock on the door paused the meeting. A beefy man wearing the uniform of a policeman with extra hardware on the collar walked in. "Come in and join the party, Lewis," said Chief Fry.

"You must be Hollister's chief of police," said Steve as he stood and offered a hand.

The man responded by saying, "Lewis McCloud. You must be Detective Smiley." He turned to face her. "And you're Heather McBlythe." He shook hands with both but focused his attention on Heather. "I may get in trouble for this, but your photos don't do you justice, Ms. McBlythe. I read your bio this morning. Most impressive."

"No offense taken," said Heather. "Unlike most women, I can accept a compliment without making a big deal of it. Nice to meet you, Chief McCloud. Did you have time to read the report concerning last night's excitement at Candy Caine's home?"

"What excitement?" asked Lieutenant Douglas.

His chief explained, "I haven't had time to tell you the details. I'll let Chief McCloud explain."

"Someone threw a rock with a note demanding twenty-five-thousand dollars through the window of Candy's front door last night."

Steve added, "It was the most recent demand for money. Ms. Caine has been receiving extortion notes for months. Heather has another one in her valise, that she'll give to whoever is spearheading the investigation."

Chief Fry cast his gaze to Chief McCloud. "It happened in your jurisdiction, Lewis. It's your call."

"Let's hear what else our friends from Texas have to say. They seem to be several steps ahead of us."

Steve folded his hands in his lap. "I'll start at the beginning, if that's all right with everyone."

Nods and short phrases of acceptance sounded from the two chiefs.

"Our involvement started a week ago," said Steve. He then described how Candy's sister Lola, AKA Sugar, came to

Heather's office with her husband and asked him and Heather to give recommendations for protecting Candy.

Heather reached into her valise and retrieved the plastic evidence bag containing the note Sugar presented to her. Heather added, "You'll notice the chain of custody is unbroken. I asked a friend and former classmate of mine at Princeton to have the letter analyzed."

Lieutenant Douglas took the plastic bag and focused on the names and titles before looking up. "The FBI analyzed this?"

"Correct," said Heather. "It's handy to have friends in positions of authority. The paper and envelope are from common stock. No fingerprints or DNA. What's interesting is that the Branson branch of the U.S. Post Office postmarked it."

Steve added, "Candy thought the letter was another hoax, possibly from a fan, the same as the previous notes she received, which she destroyed."

"She should have come to us," said Lieutenant Lewis.

"True," said Steve, "but she didn't. The letter plus the note tied to the rock are all we have besides our reports of our meetings with Sugar and Candy."

Heather added, "You'll find our reports from our interviews with Sugar and Candy accurate and complete. We'll send those to each department if you want us to."

"Send them," said both chiefs at the same time.

"There's one thing that I find exceptional in the reports," said Steve. "There's a slight chance that this attempt at extortion could be connected to the death of Mabel Grist, the wardrobe lady at Candy's theater."

The lieutenant shook his head and sputtered out a breath of disbelief. "She died of a heart attack. Nothing more, nothing less."

Steve nodded his partial agreement. "There's no doubt that the coroner reached the correct conclusion, but the heart attack could have come during the commission of a robbery. That means..."

"I know what it means," interrupted Douglas. "That's why the case will remain open from now until judgment day. For your information, we have millions of visitors coming to Branson every year, and some of them aren't the most law-abiding souls you've ever met. Besides them, we have our own drug and alcohol problems. Mabel Grist's death had all the signs of a crime of opportunity. She shouldn't have been in the parking lot alone that late at night. Our officers can't be everywhere at the same time. Right now, we're fifteen patrolmen short of where we need to be."

Chief Fry corrected his lieutenant. "It's closer to twenty officers short, but that's not important for this discussion. What is important is that we have an open case that needs a resolution."

"I have more open cases than that one. Last night we added three break-ins of hotel rooms, a serious assault, a new group of pickpockets working the mall, and some guy in a Corvette who outran every officer who tried to catch him."

Chief Fry lifted his eyebrows. "I'm well aware of the number of open cases and the impossible workload you're under. That's why I welcome help from competent people, especially when it comes at no expense."

The lieutenant folded his arms and expelled a full breath through his nose.

Both chiefs ignored the display of petulance and settled the issue at hand. Chief McCloud stated, "I'll keep you advised if Candy reports anything else to my department. I know you're short-staffed, but I only have sixteen officers to cover Hollister."

Chief Fry fixed his gaze on Heather. "You and Steve have free rein to conduct your investigations until I say otherwise. You'll report directly to Lieutenant Douglas."

Steve said, "We prefer to work alone until it's time to make an arrest."

Lieutenant Douglas spoke up. "The way I see things, there's only one minor crime to solve, not two. Proving a murder where one doesn't exist means I'll hear from these two on the third of never."

Steve said, "Would you prefer to hear only about the extortion?"

"You conduct your investigation of the extortion, and I'll conduct mine."

Chief Fry said, "No, Lieutenant. You've already told us you're too busy." He cast his gaze to Steve and then Heather. "I'll give you one week to find out who is threatening Candy. After that, you'll work under Lieutenant Douglas' supervision. Do you have any suspects identified yet?"

"Two," said Steve. "Candy gave us their names this morning. We've arranged interviews with both."

"That's quick work," said Chief Fry.

Steve wagged his head. "Not really. I should have called Candy days ago and asked her to give serious thought to who could be behind this."

"Why didn't you?" asked the lieutenant as his chin lifted.

Steve chuckled. "Some questions are best left unasked until you can share a meal of hot grits with the person you haven't seen since a high school reunion."

Heather covered her smile. "You'll have to excuse Steve. He sometimes gives obtuse answers to questions he doesn't have an appropriate answer for. It's a harmless little game he likes to play. Once you get used to him, he's hilarious." From the look on the lieutenant's face, she wasn't sure he ever found anything hilarious.

The meeting ended, and Heather and Steve went to her SUV where Le Roi enjoyed the cool weather and overcast sky. She guided Steve and said, "We're being followed."

"I hear him. His left shoe squeaks. Get Le Roi out when we get to the car. He probably needs a potty break."

Heather deposited Steve at the passenger's side door. He made no move to enter the car, even though she'd pressed the key fob to unlock the doors.

"Hey Smiley," said Lieutenant Douglas. "I think you and I need to get something straight. I'm in charge of police investigations, not you or your hotshot rich partner. You're on my turf and..."

Steve felt Le Roi brush against his leg. "Lieutenant Douglas, or should I call you Doug or Dougie? I think I'll call you Doug since you didn't tell us your first name. This is Le Roi. He's a dual-certified police and guide dog. He likes it best if you speak French to him, but if you *ne parle pas français,* make sure you don't use any threatening inflection in your voice. Le Roi is very protective of me and Heather. So is Heather's dog, Princess. She's a German shepherd and certified with similar credentials as Le Roi. We rarely go anywhere without them."

Heather arrived and petted Le Roi on his wide head. "So far, Le Roi has crushed only one bad guy's arm who spoke harshly to Steve and pointed a gun at him. Princess had her chance last night, but whoever threw the rock through Candy's window was gone before we started tracking him."

Steve then asked, "Was there something else you wanted to discuss with us?"

"It can wait." The lieutenant beat a hasty retreat.

"Call if you need us," said Heather to the back of the man's head.

Once inside the car, Heather chuckled while Steve remained unsmiling. She then asked, "Did that go the way you expected?"

"Pretty much," said Steve. "I wasn't expecting Chief Fry to give us only one week to find the person threatening Candy."

"Does that mean we won't work on the case if we don't have it solved in a week?"

"Of course not," said Steve. "We're working for Sugar, not for a police department."

"We don't have a signed contract with Sugar or Candy," said Heather.

"I didn't realize we needed one for pro-bono work."

"You know I'm a stickler for having contracts."

"Then draw one up. Sugar will be here in a few days, and we'll have her sign it when she arrives."

Heather asked, "When did you find out Sugar was coming to Branson?"

"This morning after breakfast when you went upstairs to get dressed."

"I have to admit," said Heather. "Candy made a believer out of me. Grits cooked in milk with butter and preserves made a delicious breakfast on a wintry morning."

"It was a good start, but the maple-bacon donut and coffee halfway through our walk was beyond delicious."

"Use the plural of donut. You had at least two. I could tell by the two different sugars on your jacket."

"Busted again," said Steve. "Let's change the subject and talk about the interviews we need to conduct this evening."

# 13

Heather made a quick study of the car's computer screen before leaving the Branson Police Department's new building. Her focal point was Table Rock Lake.

"What are we waiting for?" asked Steve.

"I want to take a different route back to Candy's home, one that goes by the lake."

"Do you have an idea for something to invest in?"

"Not yet, but there's a seed of an idea that's trying to sprout. I think we'll go back a different way. There's a road over the dam that should give me an outstanding view of the lake."

Steve smirked. "Your seed must need water."

"Funny," said Heather in a mirthless tone. She paused. "Now that you mention it, my idea may have something to do with the lake."

"This may spell trouble," said Steve as he clicked his seatbelt into place. "The last lakeside development you tackled was so complex and expensive it almost wrecked your mental and physical health."

"It's also the most successful thing I ever accomplished."

Steve issued a word of warning. "Be sure to count the cost to

96

your mind and body before you launch into something that will take more than you're willing to risk."

"I've already determined the amount of capital I'll invest. It's not that many millions of dollars. My team knows the upper limit, and I've asked my dad to approve anything before I launch into it. There's a time for taking risks and a time to hold back. Whatever I find to do in or around Branson may lose money, but it won't be my financial Waterloo."

Steve took off his sunglasses and rubbed his sightless eyes. "If your father is involved, you're bound to do well. Do you think he'll invest with you?"

"Only if the idea is good enough."

Heather pushed a button, and the car's engine came to life. Steve put his dark-lensed, black-framed glasses back on as they left in search of Table Rock Lake and her next project.

They climbed a steep hill slowly so Heather could take in the view. She made a sharp right turn and pulled into a parking lot. A low whistle escaped her lips.

"What are you looking at?" asked Steve.

"A hotel that looks like it belongs overlooking Central Park in New York, City. It's perched atop a tall hill with a killer view of the lake and the city. I'll look it up and give you more details."

Heather spoke into her phone and put AI to work. In a couple of seconds, her phone flashed back information and photos. She spoke as she read. "This is a stunning hotel, spa, and convention center. The name is Chateau on the Lake Resort Spa, and Convention Center. It's also known as The Castle on the Hill. The hotel has 301 rooms and is ten stories tall. In addition, meeting rooms cover 43,000 square feet. It also has a marina on the lake."

"In other words," said Steve, "it's a swanky joint to spend the night."

"Or get the full treatment at the spa or hold a conference for up to four-thousand people."

Steve said, "It's a shame someone beat you to the land and

the idea. There's also a convention center in downtown Branson, close to Branson Landing where we walked this morning. It doesn't sound like they need another one, but what do I know?"

Heather chose her words carefully. "I'm not looking to duplicate, only to get a feel for the area. From what I've seen of Branson, most of the people who come here are not what you'd call rich, but there's a minority of wealthy ones who want and expect high quality."

"Clean sheets and a television that works are all I need," said Steve.

Heather put her phone in a cupholder and restarted the car. "Let's go over the dam and check out what's on the other side. There's something about the lake that's drawing me to it."

She turned right out of the parking lot and went only a short distance before Table Rock Lake appeared before her. Words flowed from her without effort as she described what looked like a picture postcard. "They couldn't have built the dam in a better location. There are steep hills with homes clinging to them to our right. Because of the sharp angle, everyone should have a killer view of the lake.

"Now we're turning to head south. To the left is the lake's spillway. There's no telling how much dirt, gravel, and boulders they had to haul in to construct the apron of the dam. The dam itself is concrete."

Steve asked, "Do you know how deep the lake is?"

"Candy told me it's over two hundred feet at the deepest point."

"They must have built the dam to plug up a ravine," said Steve.

Heather kept talking. "We're riding over the dam itself now. To our right are miles of water and the main channel of the lake. It goes west as far as the eye can see. There's also an enormous branch of the lake to the south."

Steve kept his head still. "Are we still on the dam?"

"No, there's a US Army Corps of Engineers building on our

right and a large parking lot. There's a VISITORS WELCOME sign. I may come back and do some research."

Steve asked, "Why are you turning right?"

"Another sign caught my eye. It advertises THE SHOWBOAT BRANSON BELLE." She drove through the parking lot until she was close enough to get a good look at the boat. "It's a paddle-wheel boat that would look right at home on the Mississippi River with Mark Twain as its captain."

After parking, she took out her phone again and gathered information. "It's a floating dinner theater with a total capacity of one thousand patrons and crew on board. The cruise lasts two hours, goes to the dam and back, and they change shows several times a year. Groups of up to seven hundred can charter the ship. They prepare meals in the ship's galley."

"It sounds like another great idea that someone beat you to," said Steve.

"It's certainly unique," said Heather. "It's a mini ocean cruise without the bedrooms, and it only lasts two hours."

Heather had left the car running, so all she had to do was put it in gear and return to the main road. She said, "We're less than ten minutes away from Candy's home."

"Good. We need to research all we can about Melvin Bird before our appointment this evening."

The trip back to Candy's hilltop home held one more surprise. Heather slowed as they passed a cluster of identical two-story homes. She thought about pulling into the parking lot but kept going. "On our right is where we'll be staying after we leave Candy's."

"Didn't you call it a reunion home?"

"We're passing a dozen or more of them and big enough to house multiple families. They're designed for multi-genera-tional families to stay in and have room to cook their own meals. Pam arranged for a chef to cook for us." Heather took in a breath. "Did I tell you my father is flying in for a few days?"

"The last I heard, he was coming, but you weren't sure when or how many days he would stay."

Steve then quipped, "How will you react if he brings a future stepmother with him?"

Heather couldn't hold in the laugh. "Good try, but you won't get a rise out of me that easily. I have spies in the Boston press who keep me informed about his social life. He's alternating between three well-heeled socialite widows when he needs a date for special occasions. It will take a very special woman to get him to the altar again."

Steve changed the subject. "I'm looking forward to spending time with Bella and Adam. Even though they live next door to me, I hardly ever visit with them. They have such busy schedules that it's no wonder the stork is staying away from their home."

"Do you think they're trying too hard?"

Steve shrugged. "That's what the doctor told me and Maggie at first. Then he sent us to a specialist, and we found out Maggie needed a full hysterectomy."

Heather spoke in a loud whisper. "You never told me that."

"I didn't? I thought I did. Oh well. It was a tremendous disappointment, but we loved our way through it." He smiled. "I'm one of the few people I know who's never changed a diaper."

"Never?" asked Heather.

"Not one. Never, and now that I'm blind, I have an excuse not to join the poopy-diaper club."

"Don't be too quick to brag. Bella may need you to babysit, and I may not be around to help."

Steve shivered. "I may have to train Le Roi to do it."

"Good luck with that."

They parked in the driveway in front of Candy's home. Heather opened the SUV's rear door, and Le Roi stepped to the ground. He sniffed the clean air then went to Steve's side.

"Do you need a run in the woods?" asked Steve in French.

"Woof."

Steve raised his hand quickly and said, *"Allez."*

The giant schnauzer took off at full speed into the woods as the front door opened and Candy came down the steps to greet them. "Come in. You're in time for hot tea and Christmas cookies."

Steve said, "You're being the perfect hostess when you're really dying to know how our meeting with Sheriff Fry went."

Candy laughed. "Did you take a course in mind reading in college?"

Heather answered for Steve. "He loves to predict what people will ask, even though it's obvious. If he were a true mind reader, he would have known Sheriff Fry would invite Chief McCloud and Lieutenant Douglas to the meeting."

"I also would have known that Heather and I have one week to discover who's been trying to extort money from you."

"Then what?" asked Candy.

"That should be enough time," said Steve. He unfurled his collapsible cane and swept it in front of him until it struck the bottom step of the porch.

Heather added, "We won't quit until we find the person responsible, but Lieutenant Douglas will conduct his own investigation."

"He already investigated Mabel's death and his story is she died of natural causes."

Candy slipped her hand under Steve's arm to guide him up the steps and asked, "What did they say about the Krampus?"

"Nothing," said Steve. "I think they put Mr. Krampus in the same category as the Easter Bunny."

"What do you think?" asked Candy as they walked into the home with Heather following.

Steve waited until he eased onto a barstool in the kitchen before responding. "I believe Krampus will strike again before long. Whoever is hiding under the name and costume wants or needs money. I sense desperation and that they won't stop even if you pay them."

Candy shivered. "That's not very comforting."

Instead of offering platitudes of encouragement, Steve lowered his voice. "I said what I did because I believe it to be true. Hopefully, a healthy dose of fear will keep you on your toes. You may need to react quickly. If you sense trouble, let us know immediately."

"I'm sensing it now."

Steve shook his head. "Does your skin feel like ants are crawling on it?"

"Uh... no."

"Let us know when it does."

# 14

The sun had given up its daily task of providing warmth and light to the eight apartments in an unincorporated area east of Hollister. Heather turned off the main highway, drove a quarter of a mile down a potholed road, and pulled into a parking lot occupied by cars and pickup trucks that bore the marks of use, abuse, and age. A complex of eight decaying apartments stood guard over the vehicles. She looked around and said, "Melvin doesn't live in the lap of luxury."

"I got that impression from his spotty work history," said Steve. "Did you find any photos of him?"

"A few. In the photo from his high school yearbook his head looked too big for his body. There are also a few mug shots of him when he was older. By then his body and head looked a little more proportionate, probably from too many biscuits with gravy. His ex-wife was a pretty girl when they married, but the wedding announcement photo for her third marriage shows that she didn't age well."

"How many children?" asked Steve.

"One from his first wife. Two more after they divorced."

"How many arrests for Melvin?"

"At least a dozen," said Heather. "No violence, three for alcohol, two drug charges, four for failure to appear on traffic violations, and one for failure to pay child support."

Steve opined, "We can probably double that if you count the number of times the police detained him to investigate something and be closer to the truth."

Heather didn't contradict him. When she was a cop in Boston, it wasn't unusual with public intoxication infractions to have the offender pour out their alcohol then have someone take them home. Lack of manpower and resources encouraged officers to exercise discretion for petty crimes.

Steve asked, "There's no record of arrest when Melvin and his brothers had their fight that sent all three to the hospital?"

"I called Chief McCloud about that. It happened before he became chief. An officer made an incident report, but the former chief didn't think the family boxing match warranted any arrests."

"I don't blame him," said Steve. "Cuts, scrapes, gouges, broken fingers, and purple eyes are often punishment enough."

Heather then asked, "How did you get Melvin to agree to talk to us?"

"That was easy. I told him we'd pay a dollar a minute for his time."

Heather closed her eyes and shook her head. "And that was all it took for him to agree to an interview?"

"Not exactly. Melvin said his time was worth two dollars a minute. I hope you brought some cash."

Heather huffed, "This better be worth it."

"There's only one way to find out," said Steve as he unbuckled his seat belt and stepped out of the car.

Heather met him at the front of her car and said, "I'm not used to us going somewhere without our dogs."

"I wanted to make sure Candy felt safe. Rasheed has Le Roi patrolling the yard, and Princess is with Candy. I want her to get used to having a dog by her side."

"When will Sugar bring Candy's dog to her?"

"Soon. Sugar's having a bit of trouble getting time off approved, but should know something in the next few days."

Heather looked up at the door of apartment number 203. "Wooden stairs are in front of us. They look like they haven't been stained or painted since they built the apartments."

"Perhaps you should go first to make sure they aren't rotten."

Heather scoffed, "First you make me pay for the interview, and now you use me as the guinea pig to test the quality of the stairs. Do you want me to test your food for poison?"

"No need," said Steve with a straight face. "My sense of smell has improved so much since I lost my sight that I'm confident in my ability to sniff out most poisons. Le Roi is better, but I'm a close second."

The staircase creaked and moaned but held their weight. Steve leaned on his white cane as Heather gave three sharp raps on the door. A man with stubble covering his face opened the door. He wore a gray sweatshirt under blue overalls with one strap undone. Stained socks, which had been white at one time, covered his feet. No shoes.

"You two don't look like private detectives," said the man with a forehead too wide for his narrow shoulders. His hair looked as if a pack rat had recently moved out.

Heather responded to the man with, "Mr. Bird, I'm Heather McBlythe, and this is my business partner..."

Steve interrupted. "Steve Smiley. I'm the one who called you. Thanks for meeting with us. Can we come in?"

Bird narrowed his gaze. "If you have three dollars a minute, you can come in, and we'll talk all night if you want to."

Heather turned to Steve. "If there's one thing I can't abide, it's a man who tries to renegotiate a deal after it's made."

Bird lifted his chin. "Lady, I can tell by the way you're dressed that you have a wad of money in that designer purse big enough to choke a mule. If you want information I need to see the cash."

Heather interrupted him. "And I can tell by the way you're dressed and the condition of this dump that my partner made a terrible deal. He should have lowered his offer to fifty cents a minute." She narrowed her gaze. "It's two dollars a minute or you can wonder where your next six pack will come from."

"You ought not to talk to poor folks like that."

Heather didn't budge. "And you *ought not* to go back on your word. What's it going to be? Two dollars a minute or nothing?"

Her words hung in the air like cigarette smoke in a school bathroom. Melvin Bird finally waved them in but said, "My words may be a little slow. I've been down on my luck for two months, and Christmas is right around the corner." He then turned his back to her and walked the short distance to a recliner with padding sticking up through the seat.

Heather looked for a place to sit, didn't trust any of the surfaces in the small room for cleanliness or sturdiness, and brought two mismatched wooden chairs from the dining room. Steve settled in the one nearest Melvin, and she sat in the second one after brushing off what looked to be mouse droppings.

Steve took over while Melvin continued glaring at her. "Before we begin, I'd like to thank you for agreeing to meet with us." He reached in his pocket and pulled out a folded stack of bills. "You'll have to excuse Heather's zeal for abiding by contracts. She's an attorney, among other things, and is a real stickler for agreements. You and I are different, but she's my partner, and I've learned how to work around some of her quirky ways."

Heather wondered what Steve was up to. It wasn't long before she found out.

Steve continued, "Melvin, do you know what obsessive-compulsive means?" He didn't wait for an answer. "It's a person-ality trait that causes people to do certain things in a certain way, or it drives them crazy. Regarding written agreements, Heather is over the top. She insists on contracts. In fact, it wouldn't surprise me if she whipped out a piece of paper and started drawing up a contract right now."

Heather followed his lead and pulled a notebook from her purse.

"See what I mean?" asked Steve. "As long as it's in the contract, she's a smiling woman. If it's not, she can be mean as a stepped-on snake. You didn't know this when you tried to renegotiate the agreement, so I don't hold it against you."

Steve leaned forward. "I believe you when you say that you're down on your luck, and I want to do something about it. I'm willing to peel bonus money off this stack and give it to you for suitable answers to my questions."

"What do you consider a suitable answer?" asked Melvin.

"One without a lie or any deception in it." Steve held up a hand. "Before you agree, you need to understand this: I'm blind, but I can tell if what you say is not the truth, the whole truth, and nothing but the truth. If you tell the truth, you get a bill, and the smallest is a one-dollar bill with George Washington on it. There's five ones here and the rest are fives."

"I can agree to that," said Melvin.

"Not so fast," said Steve. "If you lie or don't give complete answers, you lose the last bill you earned from me. Do you understand and agree to the rules?"

"Sure," he said quickly. "All I have to do is tell the truth."

"Good," said Steve. "I'm going to test you while Heather completes the contract and gets it ready for you to write a brief statement that says you agree to take part in this interview."

Heather managed not to smile as she penned a simple contract. Steve had virtually guaranteed truthful answers and scored a way to get a handwriting sample to compare against the extortion notes.

Steve began by asking, "Do you blame your sister and father for you not receiving the inheritance you should have?"

"That ain't none of your business," snapped Melvin.

Steve held up the stack of bills. "If we were playing for keeps, you'd have lost a dollar. You need to realize that I already know most of the answers to the questions I'm going to ask you. I also warned you I can spot lies, deception, and partial answers better that anyone you've ever met."

Heather broke in. "That's true, and you're off to a lousy start. If you want to earn easy money, all you have to do is tell the truth."

Steve then rattled off five inconsequential questions that Melvin answered with no hesitation. With five one-dollar bills in his hand, he had the gambler's gleam in his eyes after winning five straight hands of poker. He wanted more.

Heather presented Melvin with the contract and dictated a short sentence for him to write out. He did so and signed the document without carefully reading it.

Steve then got down to business by giving a preamble to his first five-dollar question. "This past summer, a woman named Mabel Grist died of a heart attack at the theater where Candy Caine sings. Someone robbed her, which may have contributed to her death. Don't pretend you didn't hear of it or you don't have a good guess about who did it. Did you rob Mabel Grist?"

"No."

"Very good, Melvin. Here's five dollars." Steve hit him with another question. "Who told you about the robbery?"

"This guy I know."

Steve said, "That's too vague of an answer, so it doesn't count according to the contract you signed. You can expand your answer or give me back the five-dollar bill."

"That ain't fair!"

Steve straightened his posture. "What isn't fair is that an elderly woman who was working to supplement her income died because someone scared her to death." He paused. "It's your choice: Keep earning money or end the game. If you do, you'll miss out on the easiest money you'll ever earn. Give me a name."

Melvin's eyes darted back and forth twice before he released a sigh and stared straight at Steve. "Nate. I don't know his last name, but he's a harmless man in a wheelchair. They had to amputate both legs above the knees. His rowdy days ended years ago."

Steve peeled off the next bill from his stack and handed it to Melvin as he asked, "How do you know Nate?"

"I go to his place, and we talk about old times. We rode Harleys together until he lost control on an icy road. His accident scared me, so I traded two wheels for four. He's still a friend."

Steve nodded and said, "Losing my sight brought big changes in my life. One thing that changed is how much more attention I pay to the news. Is it the same for Nate?"

"Uh... yeah. Now that you mention it. He's always got that blasted TV on some news channel."

Melvin earned another five dollars, but Steve didn't stop there. He handed the stack to the man who now wore a look of confusion.

Steve stood and said, "That's all the questions we have for you today. We may want to talk to you again before we leave town." He turned to face Heather. "Let's go."

Heather waited until they were in the car before she confronted her partner. "Why did you break off the interview? You had him ready to tell you everything he knows."

Steve said, "I'll tell you as we're driving back to town. I need to think. Most of what he said was true, but not all of it."

Heather eased onto the main road heading back toward Hollister and Branson. They rode in silence for several miles before Steve asked, "What words did Melvin use to describe his relationship to Nate?"

"Nate is his friend and has been for a long time."

Steve drug a hand down his face. "The amount of money we were offering for information wasn't enough for Melvin to betray his friend. The delay in his response told me I'd pushed him as far as he would go. If I'd asked him anything else, he'd have lied."

"Wait a minute," said Heather. "Are you saying Melvin Bird was on the verge of protecting Nate? Are you forgetting that

Nate is in a wheelchair? That doesn't make him an outstanding candidate for the role of a purse snatcher."

Steve nodded in agreement. "All I know tonight is Melvin was on the verge of ending the interview if I didn't do it first."

"Is there anything we are sure of, or did we waste our time?" asked Heather.

"I'm sure we need to arrange things for Lieutenant Douglas to take credit for finishing the investigation and making the arrest."

"Should we pay Melvin Bird another visit and bring another wad of cash?"

Steve wagged his head. "I don't think that will be necessary. Let's focus on Melvin's immediate family, his extended family, and then work our way out to his closest friends. Candy either knows Melvin's family or knows someone who does. After we name the branches on his family tree, it shouldn't take Rasheed long to find a rotten apple or two. As a former university professor, he's a whiz at research. You and I will review his findings and identify the most likely person or persons."

"How does this help us identify the person threatening Candy?"

"It probably doesn't, but it might."

Heather drove for another mile before asking, "What else have you planned for us to do tomorrow?"

"Candy performs tomorrow. We're going to the matinee and evening shows with Le Roi and Princess."

# 15

Overcast clouds gathered by noon and descended on Candy's mountaintop home. It was the type of day that dampened the trees until they gathered large drops that could no longer grip the branches and fell with heavy splats. Heather remembered her mother called these her "tea and a book" days. Dreary winters in Boston helped make her mother a voracious reader and a connoisseur of hot tea.

The morning passed with Heather, Steve, and Rasheed making good progress in identifying Melvin Bird's family and friends. The extended family numbered in the high teens. Not so with the number of close friends. In fact, following the loss of his legs, Nate, a second cousin to Melvin, had become a recluse. Whether this was Nate's choice, or abandonment by his so-called biker buddies, was an open debate. The only things they knew for sure were that Nate rarely left his home and used a wheelchair when he did.

Steve put the investigation on pause when his phone announced the time was twelve noon. Heather looked up as he declared. "Time for lunch. Sandwiches, salads, or both are the choices. Rasheed and Candy have already eaten and will take Princess with them to the theater now. You and I will be there after we have our lunch. We'll leave Le Roi here to guard the property."

Candy spoke as they walked into the kitchen. "Let me tell you again how much I appreciate you being here. I didn't realize how being alone and the threatening letters had negatively affected me. I can now see my shadow and not think I'm being followed by Krampus or one of the other goblins."

"It's our pleasure," said Heather. "I speak for all of us when I say how excited we are to see today's production and to hear you sing. Could you tell us what to expect?"

Candy's face lit up with delight. "The show starts off with an upbeat overture. The lights dim, the announcer introduces me, and I come out dressed as and singing like Dolly Parton. I launch into an upbeat arrangement of *Santa Claus Is Coming to Town*. After singing most of the song, Krampus comes on stage and accuses me of being a bad girl. He then carries me off the stage. The announcer explains the recurring theme of the show: Good versus evil with an explanation of the scary Christmas characters causing mischief with the performers. Different versions of Santa appear throughout the show and save the day."

Candy continued, "You also need to know that this is a variety show with multiple acts, including comedy sketches, a magician, audience participation, a gospel quartet, and a tribute to the veterans. Santa helps me escape the clutches of different evil characters three times right after I sing a song. The comedian and the magician each get help once. Claire, my understudy, impersonates Patsy Cline when she sings her song. In the last scene, all the evil characters try to take us performers captive, but a modern Santa puts them in escape-proof bags, loads them in his sleigh, then tells his reindeer to take them to a deserted island where they can't cause any more trouble. There's a big ending where I lead the audience in singing *Silent Night*, and the performance ends."

Heather said, "If it's half as good as you described, I can't wait to experience it."

Steve asked, "Did you come up with the idea?"

"My Oma used to warn us about Krampus when we were kids, but I never believed it. Like Heather, I once traveled to Germany and learned firsthand about Krampus. The director took my idea, did extensive research, identified the other scary characters, and wove the story and songs together into a complete production."

Heather asked, "Is there a movie in your future?"

Candy quirked a smile. "Not yet, but we've received several inquiries from people on both the East and West coasts. If they ever produce a play or make a movie based on the idea, don't expect it to look like anything you see today. Branson's productions are famous for emphasizing faith, family, and the flag."

Rasheed offered his opinion. "And I'm thankful for each."

Steve closed the conversation by saying, "Heather and I won't be far behind you. Rasheed, keep your head on a swivel. Candy, make sure you keep Princess by your side if you're not on stage."

Heather waited until she saw Rasheed ease Candy's car down the driveway before she returned to the kitchen and asked, "Do you expect trouble today?"

Steve sat at the table with hands clasped in front of him. "It's probably the damp, drippy weather and what Candy said about being afraid that has my antenna up. I value a good woman's intuition, and Candy fits that description."

Steve asked, "What are you sensing?"

"That our investigation isn't progressing fast enough."

"Interesting," said Steve. "Rasheed isn't the only person who needs to keep his head on a swivel." He took in a breath and said, "Slap some meat and cheese on bread and let's get to the theater. Rasheed is good, but given to gab more than look and listen. When we get there, stick with Candy and I'll put my mind to work trying to discover what we're missing."

"Candy's country cooking is making my clothes shrink," said Heather. "I'm skipping lunch."

"That's half of a good idea, so only make me half a sandwich."

"I'll have it ready by the time you get your coat on and retrieve your cane."

Le Roi looked like a painted cement sentinel as he sat on the covered front porch. Heather drove down the steep driveway with the intermittent windshield wipers activated. It occurred to her that her logical mind was doing battle with the part of her brain that emphasized feelings. For most of her life, she lived with logic leading the way. Today was an exception for her and Steve. Something was in the air besides drizzle.

Heather drove and allowed her mind to wander while Steve remained silent. He sometimes withdrew into himself when he sensed danger. One exception to his normal behavior was when a person he cared for was displaying anxiety and could benefit from distraction. She wondered if Steve regretted not leaving with Rasheed and Candy.

They arrived, and Heather announced, "I'll park in the rear of the building. Everyone in the show uses the back door."

Candy, Rasheed, and Princess met them as soon as they entered. Steve asked, "Are the front doors locked?"

Candy had the answer. "They are at night after the last show, but not during the day. You'd be surprised how many people wait until they get to town before they purchase tickets or want them in hand so they don't have to stand in line to purchase them. We open the sales office at nine in the morning."

Steve asked, "Do many people pay in cash?"

"Not as many as once did for tickets, but cash is still king with concessions and merchandise sales. After Mabel's death, we changed our procedures to put all cash in the safe until the next day that our bank would be open. Lieutenant Douglas made that recommendation."

Steve said, "Would you mind having someone show Heather your safe and any other security measures you have?"

"That would be George. He's our fix-anything man who

knows every inch of the building. I'll introduce both of you and leave you in his care."

The mist was changing to fog as Heather, Steve, and Princess followed Candy through a metal door with a sign announcing it was not for public use.

Candy made a brief stop in front of a door and said, "This is my dressing room. It's bigger than necessary, but that's because Jim built the theater for me."

Heather watched as Candy unlocked the door with a bronze key and pulled it open. The key went back to its hiding place under her shirt. "Do all the doors open outward?"

"Only mine," said Candy. "The subcontractor installed the door incorrectly, but I prefer it this way. It makes the room seem even bigger."

Steve asked, "Where do the other performers get ready for shows?"

"In two large rooms: males in one and females in the other, no matter the age. It's mayhem during scene changes, but the performers are used to it. It's all part of the glitz and glamour of live performances."

Steve followed up with, "Are those dressing rooms left unlocked?"

"Yes, but we give each person a salvaged school locker for their valuables. They supply their own locks and keys."

"What about the costumes? Are they kept in a separate locked room?"

"I'd have a revolt on my hands if we did that. The performers handle minor repairs themselves, and who wants to wear someone else's sweat-stained costume? Between the lights, the crowds, and the dancing, our outfits end up damp. There are communal racks for them to dry."

Steve then asked, "Have you ever had costumes go missing?"

"Not until after the last show of the season. We try to recycle as much material as possible after the season ends. Some costumes are so specialized that we know we won't use them again, or they're too worn out to salvage."

Heather took her turn. "What about the Krampus costume? What will become of it?"

Candy laughed, "Are you looking for a souvenir?"

"Hardly. I was wondering if someone else might want it, and could that person be sending you threatening letters?"

Heather's question took the mirth out of the moment.

"Actually, there are two Krampus costumes," said Candy with concern flavoring her words. "Our first actor was a local man who didn't work out. Too short and unable to project his words to the back row. We needed a tall man with a booming voice."

Steve asked, "Are both Krampus costumes in the men's dressing room?"

"I'm not sure what became of the first costume. If it's important, I'll need to check with our seamstress."

Steve said, "Don't bother about it now. I'm more interested in Heather getting with George and doing a thorough security check of your building. Put me in a seat where the sound is good and the view isn't. I'll wait for Heather and Princess to join me."

Candy shifted her gaze to Heather. "George should be at the concession stand. He's our number one popcorn maker."

"Is there any chance I could get a bag?" asked Steve. "Heather made me only half a sandwich for lunch."

Heather said, "That's half a sandwich more than you'll get tomorrow if you spend all afternoon and night munching snacks."

The theater lights were on, but the room remained unoccupied when Candy led them to the third aisle, center section. She slid her hand out from under Steve's arm. "Count off twelve seats and you'll be at center stage. We reserve the best four seats in the theater for special guests who show up unexpectedly. You, Heather, and Rasheed qualify. The show will start in an hour and a half. Doors will open in thirty minutes."

Twenty-eight minutes later, Heather walked down the third

row of the theater's center section. "The first tour bus pulled up. They're expecting six more and several church groups in their own buses, people movers, and vans. George says he expects they'll have less than a hundred tickets to sell to spur-of-the-moment customers."

Steve nodded, but his mind must have been on other things. "I smell popcorn and something else. What is it?"

"I took pity on you and brought a hot dog, popcorn, a small box of chocolate candy, and a medium drink. I'll give them to you one at a time to reduce the chance of stains on your jacket. Which do you want first?"

"The hot dog and the soft drink. There's a built-in holder on the armrest, so I can handle the drink and main course with no problem. After that, the chocolate. I'll save the popcorn for later."

Heather sipped a Diet Pepsi as Steve polished off his hot dog. He took a drink and leaned into her. "Did you see the safe?"

"Yeah. It's barely adequate. One very strong person, or two normal-sized thieves, could carry it away. It's not anchored."

"Anything else?"

Heather whispered as the sound of conversations spilled down the aisles. "George will give me the full tour after the first performance."

# 16

The standing ovation finally ended. Heather remained seated with Steve as satisfied patrons exited the building after the matinee. Many gave voice to their favorite performer or their most despicable Christmas character. Krampus took the early lead, but Belsnickel was a close second, especially among the people from church groups. Getting whacked with a stick for not perfectly reciting Bible verses seemed much too wicked a thing to do, especially with all the translations and paraphrase versions available today.

Yet, good triumphed over evil in the end, veterans were honored, the children in the audience were each given a gift, Candy performed incredible impressions of Dolly, Loretta Lynn, and Tammy Wynette. She also sang in her own voice the Christmas song she made famous. Claire also did an outstanding version of Patsy Cline singing "White Christmas." So good that she and Candy took bows together to thunderous applause at the close of the show.

Steve summed up his impression of the production with a simple. "Wow. Candy has gotten better with age." He let out a sigh. "She and the other performers will be busy signing autographs and merchandise for quite some time. I guess I'll stay here."

"No, you won't," said Heather. "You've been in that chair too long. Get up and come with me. Let's go backstage for a few minutes. George needs to restock the concession stand and put money in the safe, so he won't be available for quite a while."

Steve stood, stretched, and yawned. "If the other shows in Branson are anywhere near as good, you may need to build a big, swanky hotel so I could have a place to stay for about three months out of the year."

Heather shook her head, even though he couldn't see her. "You have plenty of money if you want to take a long vacation. You could even buy a condo or apartment and rent it out when you weren't here."

Steve countered with, "I'd better stay where I am unless we're working a case. Bella and Adam are trying to get into the baby business, and I need to make sure you don't blow another head gasket by working too hard. Besides, I'm liking the taste of freedom with my self-driving golf cart. I don't think it would like the steep terrain of the Ozark Mountains."

They reached the dressing rooms. Doors to both the men's and women's stood wide open. "I can tell which one is the men's," said Steve. "When we passed the door to the women's, it smelled of a dozen brands of perfume. The guy's dressing room reminds me of a football locker room." He stopped and listened. "I don't hear anyone. Go in and look around. Count the costumes and make sure all the ones for the Grinches are there."

Heather did so and came back with her report before anyone joined them. "All the costumes are present. Some of them must be blood-boiling to wear; they're turned inside out, and fans are drying them."

Heather asked, "Why did you want to make sure all the costumes were there?"

Steve answered with a dismissive, "Just a hunch."

Heather didn't press him but followed his instructions to

check the lock on Candy's door to make sure it showed no sign of tampering. She soon delivered another negative report and asked, "Anything else?"

"That's all for now, other than there's a long break between shows. Candy says she usually has a salad delivered. We may want to do the same. You should have time to do that and complete the building's security check."

Heather wanted to say something tacky, but a noisy group of entertainers passed them without breaking stride or paying any attention to them. She'd save her banter with Steve for a more opportune time.

It turned out that Heather had plenty of time to call in salads, accompany George, and eat the light meal with Steve, Candy, Rasheed, and Princess.

The sheer number of patrons delayed the start of the evening show by ten minutes. There were enough seats for tickets sold, but a few customers who didn't pre-purchase before arriving at the theater didn't like the idea of being separated from their group. Candy had to make a special appearance to placate the last-minute planners. Heather, Rasheed, and Princess surrendered their seats and stood at the back of the theater, pretending to be ushers. George found a seat for Steve in the sound booth.

Lights dimmed and, as in the first show, blaring prelude music set the stage for what was to come. Heather turned to Rasheed following Candy's first song. "I thought the first performance was good, but Candy's first song tonight was positively electric."

Rasheed nodded in agreement. "I must bring Junani to experience this. I could watch this show many times and not tire of it."

"That reminds me," said Heather. "Junani will be here in about a week. They're flying up in my plane with the acquisitions team."

"What wonderful news! I'll count the minutes until..."

Heather shushed him with a finger over her lips and whispered, "I'll give you details at the intermission."

The play progressed as actors and singers fed off the audience's positive reactions. The intermission did nothing to quell the mood. Muffled sobs came from the crowd when the veterans stood and saluted the flag. Heather knew Candy had left for her final costume change.

Heather leapt to her feet as the muffled sound of an explosion sounded from somewhere in the back of the building. Ear-piercing screams of the theater's fire alarm sounded as the former soldiers, sailors, airmen, marines, and coast guardsmen remained standing at attention.

Heather grabbed Rasheed by the arm and jerked his jacket hard enough to propel his first three steps. "Get Steve out of here."

By this time, Heather and Princess were sprinting down the outside aisle, headed for the curtain that separated the crowd from the backstage areas. The detective and her dog were almost at the curtain when the house lights came on. The baritone voice of the announcer spoke in a strained voice. "Please make your way to the nearest exit and move away from the building. Do not block the fire lanes with your vehicles."

It wasn't long before Heather got her first whiff of smoke, but where was it coming from? Wide-eyed performers streamed from the two large dressing rooms, but no visible smoke came from either door. She pushed her way past the fleeing cast and came to the door of Candy's dressing room. Wisps of smoke came from the top of the backward-installed door.

Heather's right hand pounded on the door as her left hand tried to turn the doorknob. "Locked," she whispered.

"Help," came the sound from the other side of the door. "Get me out of here."

"Lay flat and crawl toward my voice," shouted Heather.

Coughing came and then a raspy voice. "I'm locked in." More coughing. "Help me, Lord."

Heather looked for something, anything, to attack the lock with. She then realized she'd worn her crossbody purse. She unzipped it and poured the contents onto the floor. From the pile she grabbed what looked like a manicure case and soon had two metal tools that looked like they belonged at a dentist's office. She took a precious second to still her nerves and then thrust the first crooked instrument into the lock. She tried to listen, but the wailing fire alarm made that impossible. With her left hand, she slid the other instrument into the locking mechanism and hoped she was right about the type of lock she was dealing with.

Seconds raced by as Candy's cough replaced words. The staccato, high-pitched bleeps from the fire alarm had a three long beeps, then rest, pattern. Heather didn't know how many times the pattern repeated itself before she heard a faint click during a rest and felt the lock release its grip. She threw open the door and received a blast of hot smoke in her face. Without thinking, she issued a command. "Fetch!"

Heather then leaned forward as far as she could without falling over and went into a coughing fit. She was still coughing when she crawled forward, keeping as low as she could as billows roiled over her head. Princess was on her stomach with her teeth latched onto the white collar of Candy's Mrs. Clause costume. The seventy-pound German shepherd made slow progress in dragging Candy toward the door.

Heather stayed low, took a firm grip of the soot-stained collar and pulled with all her might. Between woman and dog, they pulled Candy into the hall and shut the door behind them.

Delirious and coughing, but alive, Candy spoke a single word between gasps. "Krampus."

George arrived with a fire extinguisher, but he didn't reopen the door. Instead, he scooped Candy in his arms like she weighed less than a stuffed bear and headed for the rear exit. Heather and Princess caught up with him in the parking lot. Thick, cold fog muffled the wails of approaching first responders and the voices of concerned performers when they noted the identity of the limp woman being carried by George.

Instead of stopping, George set off at a quick pace, carrying Candy up a steep hill, to the front of the theater. Heather and Princess followed, even though she had to stop once, catch her breath, and try to clear her scratchy throat. Princess also breathed more heavily than normal.

Two firetrucks and three police cars had arrived by the time George surrendered Candy to a woman who identified herself as a doctor and was using a corner of the covered driveway as a temporary triage area. Blankets came from who knows where. One generous soul offered her oxygen concentrator when she exited the building and saw Candy's labored breathing. The doctor accepted the generous offer and promised to return it as soon as EMT's arrived.

A shiver coursed through Heather, a sure sign her adrenaline rush was waning. She then remembered Steve and Rasheed. Looking down on Princess, she said, "Find Steve."

The dog didn't delay. She trotted toward the entrance, looking back now and then to make sure Heather was trailing. With stragglers leaving, and more first responders arriving by the second, the scene was somewhere between chaotic and total bedlam.

Princess was undeterred. She wove her way around patrons and police with no problem. Once in the theater, Heather lost sight of her, but not for long. Princess was sitting in a chair next to Steve, looking like she was ready to make changes on the soundboard. Steve stroked her head and asked her questions in a way that made her think her dog would answer them.

Heather approached the trio and, between coughs, had a pointed question for Steve. "Don't you know you're supposed to evacuate a building when there's a fire?"

He replied, "Both you and Princess smell like smoke, but this room doesn't. That tells me the fire was confined to the dressing rooms."

"Only Candy's dressing room," said Heather. "It was a close call."

Steve's voice lowered. "Where is she?"

"Outside, under a doctor's care, waiting for an ambulance to take her to the hospital. She may already be gone."

Steve was silent for an uncomfortable length of time. She'd seen him like this before and knew he was prioritizing what to do next. He then said, "When you say gone, do you mean gone to the hospital or..."

"Hospital."

He nodded and mumbled something under his breath. After straightening his spine, he asked, "Was she able to say anything?"

"Only one word. Krampus."

Steve let out a deep moan. "I was afraid something like this would happen. After all, it's December fifth. In Germany, this is the day Krampus strikes."

Heather could have kicked herself for not remembering the importance of the day. She put her self-loathing on hold when Steve said, "Let's get to the hospital. The firefighters and police won't want our help until after they gather evidence from the arson and attempted murder."

Heather tried to clear her throat but started coughing again. Once the coughing subsided, she said, "Uh... you and Rasheed will need to go without me."

"Do you need to get checked out? It sounds like you took in some smoke."

"No, I'll be fine, but my purse and everything in it are on the floor outside Candy's dressing room."

"So? Rasheed can drive. They'll gather everything as evidence, and we can get it back tomorrow morning."

"I wish it were that easy," said Heather before more coughing interrupted her. Finally, she said, "I had to use my lock-picking tools to open Candy's door. I left them at the scene. They'll want to ask me questions."

"You're right," said Steve. "Oh well, you're a clever lawyer, and you saved the life of one of Branson's favorite stars. Talking your way out of this shouldn't be a problem for you."

Steve tilted his head. "I wonder which will be the hardest to explain. Will it be the tools, or the existence of a Krampus?"

"Both," said Heather.

Steve snapped his fingers as if suddenly remembering something. "That reminds me, before you leave tonight, find out what you can about the actor who was first selected to play the Krampus."

"Anything else?"

"One more. What happened to his costume?"

Heather took a deep breath, which triggered another round of coughing. Steve waited until she caught her breath before asking. "I think you need to get checked out."

She waved a hand back and forth. "You two try to find a back way to the hospital. I'll be fine. Don't worry about coming to get me. It's going to be a long night for all of us."

"Long and miserable for Candy," said Steve. "What a lousy way to end such a good day."

# 17

Heather stayed out of the way until a clutch of firefighters carried empty cylinders of flame suppressants out of the building. She believed it to be a good sign that they didn't stretch hoses from the street to combat the blaze with water. Perhaps closing the door to Candy's dressing room had kept the flames from spreading. She hoped so.

The reduction of adrenaline in her system also reduced her racking cough to occasional muffled ejections of air. She tested her lungs by leaving the sound booth and taking slow steps to the concession stand. George met her there and said, "I thought you left. EMT's are still here. Do you want them to check you out? I don't like the sound of that cough."

"I'm good as long as I talk softly." She took a shallow breath. "And don't use long sentences." She looked around. "Do you know if Chief Fry is here?"

"By the looks of things, every cop in town is here, was here, or is on their way. Someone used the fire as a distraction to steal our safe. The only thing they didn't get was the cash from my final round through the concession stand. The chief is in the sales office with the crime scene people."

"Thanks, George," said Heather with a touch to his arm.

"Steve and Rasheed are at the hospital. They'll keep me posted on Candy's condition as soon as they can."

"That's good. I was the first person Candy hired when her husband built this theater for her. You'll not find a better woman than Miss Candy."

The crackle of police radios filled the lobby. Chief Fry finished responding to whoever he was talking to and turned to face Heather, Princess, and George as they made their way to the sales office. He stopped them before they reached the door leading into the office and fixed a hard gaze on her. "George tells me we have you to thank for Candy's life."

A tickle in her throat caused Heather to delay her response until the cough reflex passed. She whispered, "It took me too long to get the door open." She felt for her dog's head and gave it several strokes. "Princess was the first to reach Candy and began pulling her out."

Princess sneezed, and the chief knelt beside her and took her head in his hands. "Her eyes look rheumy. You both must have taken in too much smoke."

"Not nearly as much as Candy did. Have you heard any updates from the hospital?"

"Not yet. I've placed two officers there to guard her and keep me posted on her condition. The only thing suspicious they've reported so far is a Mid-Eastern man and a blind guy."

"That would be Steve and my driver, Rasheed. Don't be surprised if you get a complaint concerning Rasheed. Steve and I are training him to think like a detective. He's naturally inquisitive, sometimes to the extreme."

Heather cast her gaze toward the office. "Did George tell you I examined the safe earlier today? You'll find my fingerprints on it and on the doorknob of Candy's dressing room. In fact, my prints are all over. I did an evaluation of the building's security earlier today."

"Thanks for telling me. I'll let Lieutenant Douglas know. He's in Candy's dressing room." The chief quirked his head to one side. "What deficiencies did you find?"

"The biggest one concerned the safe. I recommended she either get a much bigger one or anchor what she had to the concrete foundation."

"There's nothing like telling someone to lock the barn after the horse is already gone," said the chief. His radio came to life, and he mumbled something about talking to her later as he walked to the front door.

Heather told George she was going to find Lieutenant Douglas. He responded by saying, "I guess Claire will take Candy's place for the foreseeable future."

Heather scanned the lobby. "Did Claire leave?"

"I don't think so. She may be in the women's dressing room."

"I'll head that way. If you see her, tell her I'd like to talk to her."

Heather was almost to the curtain separating the aisle on the left side of the theater from the backstage area when a uniformed police officer pushed the thick cloth aside. He took one look at her, lifted his chin and spoke in a terse tone. "Good. I won't have to chase you down. Lieutenant Douglas is looking for you."

Heather didn't like his tone, but couldn't respond like she wanted to. She said softly, "Thank you for telling me. I was on my way to see him."

While walking past him, the officer grabbed her arm and said, "He told me to put you in cuffs if you gave me any trouble. Put your hands behind your back for my safety."

Heather slammed on the proverbial brakes and froze the officer with a stare. She shifted her gaze to his hand and then back to his right eye. By this time, Princess was in full attack mode, with teeth bared, emitting a throaty growl. Heather whispered, "I've just come from speaking with Chief Fry. He didn't see a need to handcuff me." She smiled. "If you don't remove your hand, you'll soon be on your way to the hospital. If you're lucky, my dog will only crush your hand."

The officer seemed to weigh her softly spoken words, dropped his hand and took three steps back. As he put distance between them, Heather kept talking. "It so happens that I'm an attorney." Her words were cut off by a deep cough.

After she caught her breath, Heather continued in the same quiet voice. "At no time did I say or imply by word or deed that I wouldn't voluntarily follow you to Lieutenant Douglas. Yet, you grabbed my arm. I can only conclude that you took it upon yourself to detain me. What crime do you suspect me of committing?"

Looking away from her intense gaze, he seemed to gather his thoughts, then said, "You'll have to ask Lieutenant Douglas."

Heather shook her head. "Your response tells me you don't know whether he gave you a lawful order or not. Not only do you not know the inciting incident that led you to make assumptions about my past and future actions, but you exceeded his instructions."

"Huh? What inciting incident?"

"Exactly!" said Heather, then wished she hadn't raised the decibel of her voice when another coughing spasm hit her. Taking a shallow breath to avoid more coughing, she said, "You don't know, but you assumed I committed a crime that warranted the use of force and detaining me in handcuffs."

The officer swallowed hard as Heather kept talking. "If you still insist on handcuffing me, I'll not resist."

"That won't be necessary," said the officer. "In fact, I don't see any reason Chief Fry or Lieutenant Douglas need to know about our talk. You'll find the lieutenant outside what's left of Candy's dressing room."

"I know the way." She looked down at Princess and said, "Friend."

Princess gave her a look that asked, "Are you sure?"

"Oh, yes. He's a good friend now that we understand each other."

The officer stood to one side and said, "That's some dog, ma'am."

"Woman's best friend," said Heather as she passed.

She walked down a hallway, turned a corner, took several steps, and waited for Lieutenant Douglas to speak. He looked up from a pile of plastic evidence bags, said nothing, and sorted through the bags, ignoring her obvious presence. She knew the game he was playing and decided he could play it by himself.

Instead of waiting for Douglas to speak, she took a step forward and spoke in a raspy voice. "Good. You found my purse and its contents. Thank you for gathering it for me."

He stood, which gave him a height advantage. "This is now evidence. It will need to be processed."

Heather shrugged. "It's a good thing I have a driver to take me anywhere I need to go. I have a copy of my license and a spare credit card, too."

The lieutenant smirked. "I'm trying to decide if I should arrest you now or wait until you have a sleepless night in an interview room."

"That's not a friendly thing to say to someone who's helping you solve some very serious crimes."

Douglas bent over and picked up a bag containing Heather's lock pick tools. "How do you explain these being in your purse?"

"You found those on the floor, not in my purse."

"Are you denying these are yours?"

"Of course not. There wasn't a crowbar or acetylene torch, so I used what I had to unlock the door." She gave him a smile that was as real as a plastic banana.

"In case you didn't know, using these to pick locks is illegal."

"Not if there are exigent circumstances."

"I think you used them to gain entrance to the room, planted a firebomb, waited until Candy was changing costumes to detonate it, and came back to save her from a fiery death."

Heather glared at the haughty man. "If this police gig doesn't work out, audition as a stand-up comic."

Lieutenant Douglas narrowed his eyes and returned her glare with one of his own. "I know you'll weasel your way out of this, but not before you spend an uncomfortable night in an uncomfortable interview room. Unfortunately for you, Chief Fry will be here with me until he goes home sometime around dawn, and I go home to get some sleep. It may be tomorrow afternoon before I interview you. If that's not enough to keep you, that has-been blind detective, and your dogs away from my investigation, I'll think of something else." He issued a toothy grin. "It's called having the home-field advantage."

A snappy comeback germinated in Heather's mind, but didn't have time to drop from its pod before Douglas reached behind his back and pulled out a set of handcuffs.

It was a combination of training and panic that caused Heather to command, "Stay," as she took a step to her right and blocked Princess from what was sure to be a battle with a dog that Douglas would lose.

"Call off your dog and put your hands behind your back," said Douglas.

Heather looked at a distant spot on the ceiling behind the lieutenant. "I noticed you're not wearing a body camera." She focused on the spot. "You should check out the new security camera filming you."

Heather had to admit it was one of her better off-the-cuff lines, because it worked. Douglas jerked his head to look at a water stain and was too late to catch her step, reach, grab one end of the handcuffs, and slap it over his wrist.

His first instinct was to reach for his pistol, but she'd already found the dangling end of the cuffs and attached it to her own wrist. Princess used more restraint than Heather thought possible, but her bark reverberated off the walls of the hallway.

Heather and the lieutenant went in circles, both jerking their arms, him trying to pull his pistol from a shoulder holster, and her keeping him from doing so. "It's your lucky day. If Steve's dog were here, you'd be missing body parts," she panted, then tried to suppress the cough she felt coming.

A look that combined fear and surprise replaced the rage in Douglas's eyes as he looked past her.

Heather knew she'd read him correctly when she heard Chief Fry's voice behind her.

Heather spoke before Douglas had a chance. As she spoke, she kneeled, and wrapped her free hand around her dog's neck. "Dougie bet me I couldn't slip out of his handcuffs. I got one hand free and he slapped it on his wrist. That made it more of a challenge to slip the other one." She drew her fingers together, turned her arm to a specific angle and pulled her hand free.

A quick nod and the hint of a smile came from the chief of police. She doubted the fairytale fooled him, but he played along. "That's the type of cooperation and camaraderie I expect from all my officers, especially the supervisors. Good work to both of you. I had my doubts, but now I'm convinced our combined forces will lead to quick arrests and solid convictions."

Heather tried and failed to tamp down a cough from her tight lungs. The likely cause was the laugh that almost passed her lips.

"That does it," said Chief Fry as Heather's cough intensified. "You're going to the hospital if I have to take you there myself."

Heather waved him off. "You're needed here." She coughed again. "I'll get a taxi and go now." Another cough. "Do you have an update on Candy?"

"Nothing yet, and an officer will take you."

Heather nodded and squeaked out, "I'll try to weasel something out of the nurses."

The lieutenant snorted. "That should be no problem for you."

She placed her hand on his forearm. "Thanks, Doug, but I bet you'll get the information faster than I will. Would you mind calling me or Steve if you hear anything?"

"Of course."

The words didn't fit the man's snarky tone, so Heather continued the saccharine-infused conversation in a soft voice. "Thanks again for processing my property. I'll send someone to retrieve it tomorrow." Another cough erupted as she turned her head to face Chief Fry. "Princess and I will wait in the lobby for your officer."

# 18

Princess yelped for joy when Heather and the officer put her into the back seat of the patrol car. The officer looked on with something between admiration and covetousness painting his face. "What a great dog. I've thought seriously about going through the training and having a dog like her as my partner."

"It's an enormous commitment, but worth it. Her name is Princess. She completed her training and certification to become a police dog in Houston. She loves the smell of patrol cars. I think it's the computers and radios that give off the unique scent."

The officer chuckled. "More likely the vomit I have to wash off the hard plastic seat in this unit."

Heather nodded but didn't respond with words. Instead, she wedged herself into the passenger seat. The onboard computer was just the beginning of what encroached on her space. The officer directed her to "throw the junk on the floor," but she held most of it on her lap.

As they turned into the hospital parking lot, she saw Rasheed had parked her SUV away from any entrance, near a narrow strip of grass with a lone spindly tree. She spotted movement and told the officer where to drop her off. She thanked the officer and reminded him to unlock the back door so she could retrieve her dog. Once free from her literal solitary confinement, Princess greeted Rasheed with a quick sniff and a wagging tail.

Rasheed explained his being parked so far away from the hospital. "They showed me the door. I tried too hard to extract information from a nurse. I don't understand. I used the same technique and words as Bogart did."

The frosty night air felt as if someone were scrubbing her lungs with steel wool. A deep cough shook her frame. "I promised Chief Fry I'd get checked out. Load Princess after she waters the tree and drive me to the emergency room doors."

Deep concern filled Rasheed's eyes. He spoke with actions and words. "Get in the car and out of the fog." He waited until he had Princess in the back of the car before speaking again. "Does Steve know you're here?"

She answered with a side-to-side swivel of her head and asked, "How's Candy?"

"The nurses seal their lips with superglue. Steve said he'd keep me posted, and not to bother him by sending texts. I've never seen him so despondent."

The car moved. In mere seconds, the sliding glass doors to the emergency room opened, and a duo of scrubs-clad people came out into the cold air. A beefy man pushed a wheelchair. The woman met Heather with a question. "Heather McBlythe?"

"Yes."

"Chief Fry told us to expect you. We were looking for a police car."

Rasheed took over as Heather eased into the wheelchair. "They had to drop off her dog." He turned to Heather. "Do you want me to call your father?"

"No, I'll call him tomorrow morning." Another spate of coughing overtook her.

"I'll call Steve and tell him you're here."

Her first inclination was to tell him not to bother Steve, but that bit of foolishness blew away on the north wind.

Heather surrendered herself to the indignities required and was soon wearing only a gown and a name tag on her wrist. She thought the barrage of questions were a little much, but not worth the energy a complaint would require. Heather tried to relax as the technician wheeled her gurney down the corridor and around the corner to the radiology department. As expected, things moved fast to begin with, then slowed, and then seemed to come to a complete stop. If it weren't for the cannula in her nose pumping oxygen, she was sure she could go to sleep and be fit as a fiddle when she woke up after dawn.

She was on the verge of passing through the gates of La-La-Land when the emergency room doctor returned. She was a wisp of a woman who looked like the Asian girl Heather had in her freshman English class. Not college. Finishing School.

The raven-haired sprite spoke in short sentences. "X-rays show minimal damage. You're staying overnight. Primary cause for concern is pneumonia. Rest. Stay inside for a week. Drink hot green tea and plenty of water. Ice chips help soothe a sore throat. Use a scarf over nose and mouth if you must go outside. No strenuous exercise. If no problems in the next twelve hours, you'll go home."

The door to her room was swinging shut before Heather could offer an objection or even a word of thanks. "That's just great," she whispered. "I'm sidelined when Steve needs me."

Time again moved slowly. When she was sure the hospital gods had forgotten about her, a smiling attendant came in and took all the steps needed to move her to a room. A click, clang and whoosh sounded, and off she went down a maze of hallways to the elevator, then upstairs to a private room. A nurse was waiting, gave her the low-down on how to adjust the bed, operate the television, and showed her the red call button.

The nurse completed the tutorial with, "There's a handsome blind man wanting to see you. Are you ready, or do you need to use the potty first?"

"Show him in and plant him in the recliner. He's my business partner. Don't be surprised if he stays the night."

"You're supposed to rest. Do you promise not to talk very long?"

"He's a man of few words, and I have a sore throat."

"Ah... a man who's a good listener, and a level-headed woman. My favorite type of guests."

The tap of the metal tip of Steve's cane sounded from down the hall, growing ever closer. The door opened, and Steve appeared in the doorway with the nurse guiding him. His first words were, "I hear you blow smoke when you cough."

Her voice raspy and feeling the strain of talking, Heather responded, "I can also breathe fire like a dragon. Don't get too close."

The nurse chuckled and said, "Don't stay up throwing one-liners at each other. Sleep is the universal cure for many ailments."

"Don't worry about me," said Steve. "I specialize in long naps, and I get downright testy if someone interrupts me."

"Put him in the recliner," said Heather. "He'll be asleep in no time."

Steve said, "Nurse, even your squeaky shoes won't bother me when you come to check on Heather."

Another chuckle came from the nurse before the door shut behind her.

The hissing of oxygen flowing through her nasal cannula sounded loud in the quiet of the room as Steve extended his hand to Heather. She took it and gave it a firm squeeze. Trying to speak above a whisper, she asked, "Have you heard anything about Candy?"

"No, but I bet you have. Spill it... if you can."

"Tongues are wagging in the ER. They said she inhaled a lot of smoke, and it may be a long time before she can perform again."

"How long?" asked Steve.

She coughed lightly, then said, "Weeks at least. Perhaps months."

Steve dragged a hand across his face. "Your father is sending a specialist to see her."

"You called my father?" Heather squeaked.

"It was the only way I could get information about your condition. You know the rules excluding non-family members from learning anything of value. While he was speaking with the hospital administrator, he asked if you needed a specialist. He then asked about Candy. It was the way the administrator answered that told your dad her case was serious." He paused. "By the way, your father is flying in."

Heather shook her head. "Not necessary. All I need is sleep and stay out of the cold wind."

Steve spoke through clenched teeth. "It's my fault that both of you are in the hospital. I knew it was December fifth. Legend says that Krampus commits his mischief the night before St. Nicholas comes. The notes warned us, and I didn't take them seriously."

"Me either. I should have known better." Heather shifted in the bed then coughed again. "Krampus. That's the only word Candy said when Princess and I pulled her out of the room."

Steve asked, "Are you as mad as I am?"

"More. Lieutenant Douglas tried to arrest me tonight."

Steve sat upright in the recliner. "You're here, so that tells me he didn't succeed. What did you do to him?"

Heather spoke in a soft voice. "I handcuffed myself to him and then told a whopper of a story to Chief Fry."

Steve erupted in laughter and followed it with, "At least you didn't shoot him."

"I thought about it."

Steve leaned back. "You'd better tell me the story, if you can without straining your voice too much."

"I'll give you the short version, then you can tell me what actions you've taken."

"You know me too well," said Steve. "Talk softly and stop as often as you need to."

Heather gave the abridged version of her unpleasant encounter with the man they were supposed to be working with to solve crimes.

Steve took in every word before making a pretend church with most of his fingers interlocked, his index fingers forming the steeple which he tapped lightly against his chin. More than a minute passed before he said, "Your exploits may work to our advantage. It's obvious the lieutenant wants nothing to do with us, and we'd be fine not working with him. That leaves us clear to start fresh with our investigation. I called Leo and gave him the names of Candy's sister, Sugar, and her husband, Randy. I still like the idea of having a homicide detective on our side, even if he is in Houston. This case started in Texas and..."

Heather finished his thought as revelation dawned. "It might end there. Now that you mention him, Randy tried to minimize the notes Candy received, and he was very vague about his work."

"Another reason for me to blame myself," said Steve. "It was a sloppy investigation from the first day, and now Candy's paying for my laziness."

"Stop it!" said Heather with enough force to trigger a deep coughing spell. A few sips of ice water helped tamp down the reflex.

"Sorry," said Steve. "Let me tell you what Rasheed and I are going to do tomorrow."

"Do you mean today?"

"Yeah." He took out his phone and asked it for the time. The voice said, "One-o-six, a.m."

Steve picked up where he left off. "Rasheed and I are surfing the net this morning and starting fresh. We're backtracking to the people we've already spoken with. I want to re-interview them and do a more thorough job of finding out about their pasts."

Heather said, "I have one request."

"Make it."

"I'll go crazy sitting here with nothing to do but watch the clock. Have Rasheed bring my laptop this morning by nine and give me some names."

"One name only," said Steve. "But I expect an exhaustive report. No more sloppy work from any of us. Are you good with that?"

"More than good. You can go home now."

"I can't."

"Why not?"

"I told Rasheed to take Princess home and not come back before tomorrow morning. You're stuck with me for the rest of the night."

"I'm good with that, too."

# 19

Heather reached for her nose and whatever was making it itch. She then opened her eyes, surveyed her surroundings and located the hospital bed's control. The bed groaned and popped but performed its task of raising her upper body.

Steve's voice sounded to her right. "Good morning. I was wondering if you would sleep all day."

She tried to speak, but it felt like she'd tried to swallow a lit match. "Need ice water," she whispered. After taking multiple sips, she tried her voice again. "Much better," she said.

"Good. You have a busy day ahead of you. You're scheduled for another X-ray, a visit from an inhalation therapist, a more thorough exam by the specialist your father located, and Rasheed will be here in a few minutes."

"I thought you were going to sleep," said Heather before taking another sip of throat-soothing water.

"I'm surprised you slept through my snoring. It was loud enough to wake yours truly after several hours of deep sleep. That left me a couple of hours to think, plan, extract information from the nurses, and send texts." Steve lifted his head. "Rasheed will come through the door in three... two... one, now."

The door swung on its hinges, and Rasheed entered carrying a cup of coffee, a paper bag, and her valise. "Greetings to both of you. Princess and Le Roi send their warmest regards, which is a good thing because the temperature is in the mid-twenties."

Heather continued to sip through a straw but raised her hand and waved him in.

Steve sniffed the air. "Coffee and maple-bacon donuts. What a perfect way to start the day."

"That reminds me," said Rasheed. "I have a new proverb for both of you to critique. It came to me in the pastry shop." He took a breath and spoke as if he were on stage. "The early riser satisfies his bank account with prosperity, and his stomach with tasty delights."

"I've heard worse, but not lately," said Steve.

"Needs work," whispered Heather.

Instead of deflating Rasheed's ego, he said, "Honest criticism from a friend brings joy to the poet."

"Much better," said Heather in a stronger voice. "Worthy of inclusion in your future book."

"I agree," said Steve. "Hand over the items that inspired you this morning before the coffee cools and loses its creative power."

"After that," said Heather, "put the valise on the bed so I can reach it, then step out of the room while I powder my nose."

Steve teased her driver. "I'm exempt. That drafty gown she's wearing could fall on the floor and I'd be none the wiser. Heather never has to worry about what she's wearing or not wearing in my presence. It's one advantage of spending time with a sightless person."

"And it comes in handy more often than you'd think."

Rasheed held up both hands. "Please say no more. I'm leaving and will fix my thoughts on a YouTube program I began this morning. It was about neuroplasticity, the brain's ability to change how we think."

The door shut, and Steve asked, "Did you hear what Rasheed said?"

"Yeah. What about it?"

"That's what we need to do. Change how we've been thinking about this case. It started last night when I knew we needed to start over. What I didn't realize was that when we start over, we'll repeat ourselves with the same procedures and get the same lousy results."

Heather threw back the covers. "Hold that thought. Some things can't wait." She swung her legs slowly off the bed, allowing herself a moment of standing to be sure she was steady. Reassured, she grabbed the IV stand and pushed it into the bathroom with the back of her gown flapping.

She returned to find a breakfast tray on the over-the-bed table. The selections included green Jell-O, pale-yellow broth, and pink yogurt, the liquid diet trifecta of hospital torture.

Heather pushed the table away from the bed and said, "Where were we?"

"Rewiring our minds to get better results."

"Right," said Heather. "I guess you realize that while we slept, someone likely used an acetylene torch, chisels, and big hammers to open the safe. It only took one giant man, or two regular-size men, to carry it."

Steve followed her train of thought. "They used the fire as a distraction to pull off the robbery. The timing had to be perfect. The getaway vehicle needed to be large enough to carry the safe. I'm guessing a pickup truck." He stopped and said, "How are we doing so far?"

"Good, but why harm Candy?"

Steve had an answer, but she could tell it was a guess. "Perhaps they mis-timed the fire. If they'd waited a few more minutes, Candy would have been on stage."

"That's possible."

Steve scooted back from the edge of the recliner and spoke

to himself in a gruff voice. "Think, Smiley. Consider new ideas, no matter how crazy they sound."

Heather's mind was like a black hole in outer space, a one-way opening where everything, including light, disappeared. Silence prevailed until Steve said, "Let's back up and consider the crimes that were committed last night. The first is the attempted murder of Candy. The second is the robbery, and the third is the fire. Let's pretend these are separate crimes."

"Are you saying they're not linked?"

"I don't know what I'm saying other than there was no reason to murder Candy if all the thieves wanted was money in the safe."

Heather asked, "Which crime do you want me to focus on?"

He delayed answering her question by asking one of his own. "Would you agree that someone was genuinely trying to kill Candy last night?"

"Uh... no. Not definitely, but there must be a reason she didn't use her key to get out."

Steve drummed his fingers on the recliner's arm. "Call George from the theater and have him come talk to you this morning. Get names of anyone he can think of who has a grudge against Candy or anyone who would benefit from her death."

Heather quirked her head to the right. "Why me? I'd have thought you'd want to grill any suspects."

"I'm too emotionally involved to work on the attempted murder case today. Two women I care deeply about are in hospital beds. I'll take the robbery today. I have a hunch, but we'll discuss both tonight. Hopefully, you'll get out of this torture chamber this afternoon."

Heather tried to swallow the lump in her throat but needed water to accomplish the simple task.

Rasheed came back into the room and explained his prolonged absence. "I brought Le Roi with me this morning and thought he needed a break from the back of the car."

"I'm glad you're here," said Steve. "We're starting over with everyone associated with the case. We interviewed Melvin Bird, but I'm not satisfied with the job I did. Something's been bothering me, but I can't put my finger on it."

Rasheed voiced a suggestion. "Perhaps if you talked to me as if I were a ten-year-old boy with no knowledge of Melvin Bird, something new would occur to you. Sometimes we assume things, and at other times we overcomplicate them."

Heather gave her voice a rest as Steve launched into a quick tutorial about Melvin Bird. "Melvin is the eldest son of the man who owned the hill that Candy's house sits on. A family squabble between Melvin and his two brothers so angered their father that he left nothing to the sons and all he owned to his daughter. After that he sold the land to Jim, Candy's late husband."

Rasheed interrupted. "Were the transactions legal and equitable?"

Steve looked at him. "I don't believe a ten-year-old would use those words, but yes, everything was on the up-and-up, at least according to the law."

Heather jumped in. "Melvin felt cheated by everyone involved, including Candy's husband."

"Ah," said Rasheed. "We have a motive for the robbery of Candy's theater. The fire could be a distraction, and an attempt to harm Mrs. Candy. In my adolescent mind, I think he would want compensation for not receiving his inheritance."

"Let's move on," said Steve. "Heather, we called Melvin and scheduled an appointment with him at his apartment. Describe the location, the apartment complex, and Melvin's apartment."

She closed her eyes and pictured the route. "We drove east from Branson on a winding two-lane road for about twelve minutes, then turned right, drove a quarter of a mile and turned into the parking lot of a two-story cluster of apartments. The vehicles look like they'd outlived their usefulness. Rusted, faded paint, one had a flat tire. There was nothing about the cars or apartments that could win a contest for looks or safety."

Steve stopped her. "Were all the vehicles old clunkers?"

Heather closed her eyes tighter. "All but one. There was a late-model black pickup parked away from the others, not near the cluster of apartments."

"That's new information," said Steve. "Take us upstairs and into the apartment."

Heather complied and closed her eyes again. "The stairs and porch need a fresh coat of stain or paint. The railings wobbled. We knocked and then entered the apartment. I had a bit of trouble finding chairs I felt safe sitting in. The furniture was junk with enough stains to make any self-respecting rat choose a better place to live."

"Wait," said Steve. "Tell us what you see in the kitchen."

"I see nothing out of the ordinary. There's a refrigerator, a sink, countertops, cabinets, an avocado-green stove with oven, and a table with chairs."

Steve moved forward a bit in his chair. "I would have remembered the avocado-green stove. That tells me you never described the kitchen to me."

"There wasn't anything worth mentioning."

"Exactly," said Steve as excitement trickled into the single word. "What was on the counters? Were there dishes in the sink, or pans on the stove?"

Heather squeezed her eyelids closed. "Now that you mention it, no."

"I didn't think so. After focusing on it, the apartment didn't smell bad, and neither did Melvin."

"You're right," said Heather. "He was dressed like a homeless vagrant, but there was no sweaty odor coming off him."

Steve stood, unfurled his cane and said, "Rasheed, let's go. I doubt he's home, but that will be important to know, too."

---

LE ROI GAVE A SINGLE "WOOF" OF GREETING AS SOON AS STEVE clicked his seat belt. "*Bonjour, mon ami,*" replied Steve. He switched to English and asked if Le Roi wanted to visit a criminal. The response was a moaning yawn, a bit of latent rebellion for not asking in French.

Heather had texted Melvin Bird's address to Rasheed while the two men walked to Heather's car. After Rasheed told the car's computer their destination, they drove past Branson Landing, onto the bridge spanning Lake Taneycomo, around a traffic circle and headed east.

Highway noise told Steve they were making good time, but the westbound traffic going into Branson was slow-going. A quick question to Rasheed confirmed his observation. He nodded his approval and said, "If Melvin really lives in that apartment, he should be there. He didn't impress me as an early riser."

The trip went as Steve expected, with Rasheed doing most of the talking and him mumbling an answer now and then but not paying much attention. His thoughts rested on Candy and if the fire had ended her singing career. He knew about career-ending injuries, and they weren't his friend. The therapist who counseled him after losing his sight told him what to expect. Fears thrived in darkness, but the rising of the sun brought hope. He'd need to overcome life without sunrises. He wondered if a singer could live without songs.

A bump in the road brought Steve out of his thoughts. "I remember that pothole. We're almost at the apartments." The car slowed, turned right, and before long, turned again. Rasheed asked, "What am I looking for?"

"Anything unusual, especially a vehicle that looks out of place."

"There's a small motorcycle with the back tire missing."

"Keep looking."

"All I see are cars and small trucks like the ones in my home country, only these don't have bullet holes in them." He paused, "Wait. That one has a few."

"Nothing like a full-size, late-model pickup?"

"The only large pickup is on jack stands, and it was new four decades ago."

"Park near the stairway, go up, and bang on the door of 203. Make something up if anyone answers."

"I sense you are sending me on a journey to look for pomegranates in the middle of the ocean."

"You have keen senses, but it's a task that must be done. It's possible that someone other than Melvin Bird occupies the apartment. If so, they'll describe you to Melvin when he returns and not me."

"Very shrewd of you, my friend."

"Besides," said Steve, "I'm warm, comfortable, and you're learning what it means to be a junior detective."

"Working with you and Heather is far superior to the years I spent as a professor's assistant. That was slave labor."

The driver's door opened and closed with a quiet click. Steve thought about his next step as he waited for Rasheed's return. The report was as Steve expected. No one answered the door.

Rasheed brought the car to life, "Are you satisfied with the negative outcome of our efforts so far?"

"I don't count not finding a suspect in a place he should be as a negative outcome. In fact, it's positive. We now need to find out why he's not here, where he is, and who he's with. Take us to Candy's home. The next phase of our investigation will take place on computers. We'll also make some phone calls, send emails, texts, and, most importantly, we'll do it in front of a fire while drinking hot chocolate. We'll work hard *and* smart."

## 20

Heather looked to her left. The nearness of her father's face and his concentration on driving on unfamiliar roads meant she could allow her gaze to linger. How long had it been since she'd really studied his profile? She focused on his chin and the wisdom-creases caused by half a century of amassing a fortune. It was a strong face: sure, confident, wise, not prone to show emotion, but loving in a non-verbal, non-tactile way. She realized this was a rare opportunity to stare without him asking why.

Allister McBlythe, the flesh and blood man sitting next to her, started life with generational wealth and breeding. He married a beautiful young woman with a similar pedigree and financial standing. Two small fortunes combined to form a large one, then grew exponentially under his leadership. This was the same man who, hours before, had received Steve's phone call, pushed all business aside and rushed to her bedside.

"What are you looking at?" he asked.

"My dad."

"It's not polite to stare." He shot a mischievous smile her way. "But under the circumstances, I don't blame you. I'm a little nervous myself."

149

"What circumstances are you talking about?"

"Me driving. My license expired thirty-seven years ago. I can't remember the last time I got behind the wheel of a car."

"How did you rent this SUV?"

"Rent? My PA purchased it from a local dealership this morning. I'll have no use for it after I return to Boston, so you can have it. It would make a nice Christmas present for whomever you want to give it to."

The special moment didn't last long. They approached a traffic circle, and her father came to a complete stop even though the sign said yield and there was plenty of room to merge with traffic. A horn blared from behind them. He looked at her. "Why are they honking?"

"You didn't need to stop. Look to your left, wait for an opening, and merge between the cars."

"I remember these from Paris, or was it Rome? No one stops, they only pause, honk, and drive like mad."

The driver in the truck behind them laid on the horn and didn't let up.

"He's a rude so and so. I have a mind to stay here and make him wait."

"Please don't. It might lead to a road-rage incident, and you don't have a license to drive."

"As you wish. Here goes."

The rapid acceleration threw her back against her seat while centrifugal force pressed her against the door. All the while, her father's left hand mashed against the steering wheel, causing the vehicle's horn to scream its warning. Tires squealed and screeched as the one-lane roundabout expanded to two. Not more than an inch separated the new SUV from the car they'd cut off. More blaring horns.

Heather held on for dear life as her father failed to take the first right. A woman's voice from the car's computer announced, "Recalibrating."

Her father, calm and collected, spoke above the noise. "Where do I turn?"

"Slow down, and I'll tell you."

"Speak up. I can't hear you above the horns and that silly woman who keeps saying, 'Recalibrating.'"

They completed the first trip around the circle and pressed on to the second. Heather gathered herself, leaned to her left and tried to speak in a calm voice. "Slow down, wait until I tell you, then exit the circle to the right."

"Can you turn off the computer? It must be malfunctioning. It keeps saying the same thing, and the map is going in a circle."

"Turn now," said Heather.

They were almost past the exit before her dad jerked the wheel clockwise and they shot onto the road leading to down-town Hollister. Heather breathed a deep sigh of relief, which caused a coughing spasm.

He looked at her. "The doctor warned you about taking deep breaths. You really should be more careful."

They passed over a bridge with a sign that read Turkey Creek. "I want to show you something that will remind you of a country village in England. When the road turns to the left, we'll go straight." She pointed, and he slowed. "Park the car in the first open spot."

"I see one on the left side of the road. How authentic, and what fun! I get to drive as if we were in England."

She didn't correct him.

Once stopped, they faced traffic. Heather announced, "I'll drive the rest of the way to make sure the navigation computer works properly. Sometimes all it takes is turning the car off and restarting it. That reboots everything."

"If that doesn't work," said her father with emphasis, "I'll have the dealership come get it and take my business elsewhere. I'm most disappointed. If you'd like a different make or model, say the word and we'll return this one."

"Let's see if restarting it works before we decide. The car is perfect in every other way."

"It's your call and your car. Do with it as you please."

They both exited the car and stood on the sidewalk admiring the classic Tudor style of the buildings.

Allister said, "You weren't kidding about this looking like an English village. Who would have thought you'd find this in the middle of the Ozark Mountains."

"Yes, it's unique from the rest of the Branson area architecture. We should have dinner at the restaurant down the way one evening."

Her father gave her a side hug and said, "But first, it's time to get you home and resting. I don't want to get in trouble with Steve, or the doctor."

It did not surprise Heather that the car and its navigation system performed perfectly all the way back to Candy's house. Princess sat on the front porch, a one-dog welcoming committee with her tail in full motion when she recognized the unfamiliar car's occupants. Le Roi rounded the corner and went directly to Allister. He appeared to nod a greeting, and her father did the same, but added. *"Bon soir, mon ami."*

"Woof."

The front door opened, and Rasheed hurried into the night air. "Greetings, Mr. McBlythe. Your arrival inspired me to write a proverb about a father coming to aid and comfort his child in a time of trouble."

"I look forward to hearing it. How's the book progressing?"

Heather interrupted. "You two can stand out here in the cold. I'm going in where it's warm." She looked beyond Rasheed before casting her gaze back to him. "The new front door looks good. Did it take them long to install it?"

"Not long at all. The workers stormed the house as if it were a castle under siege and completed their work with skill and speed." He moved toward the back of the car. "I'll take the luggage upstairs to your room."

Heather and her father entered the home and found Steve waiting in the entry area. He exchanged greetings with Allister and said, "The home office is on your right. Consider it yours. I can tell you're carrying your leather valise with your laptop in it. Leave it there then come sit with me by the fire. I'll take your coat and hang it in the closet on your left."

"Thank you, Steve."

Heather asked, "Is that hot cider I smell?"

"The smoke must have affected you," said her father. "That's *gluhwein*, the perfect drink for a bitter December night."

It wasn't long before Rasheed had rearranged the furniture. Four two-legged people and two four-legged dogs soon sat looking at sparks flying upward from a crackling fire.

Rasheed consumed no alcohol, so he sipped tea from a Christmas mug. Heather, Steve, and her father used similar mugs, but Allister insisted they fortify the mulled wine with rum.

Steve raised his mug and said, "To Candy. May her recovery be quick and complete."

"To Candy," said the rest.

Heather added, "The prognosis for a long recovery wasn't what I'd hoped for, but it came as no surprise. She inhaled much more smoke than I did."

Rasheed sounded more upbeat. "The human body has remarkable rehabilitation capabilities. I believe she will sing again, and it will come sooner than the six months the doctor predicted."

Steve approached the subject from a different angle. "She has someone who can take over the Christmas show, and she told me earlier she wanted to slow down with off-season traveling performances. In an unwelcome way, she's getting what she wants."

Rasheed said, "The protagonist in a book I read last year spoke with a Chicago dialect and said, 'Yous got to hit a curveball if you're going to make it in this racket.' Candy impresses me as a dame who can hit a curveball."

"Amen to that," said Steve. He leaned toward Heather. "Did Allister talk to you about Candy's sister?"

"What about her?"

"He sent his plane to bring her here."

Allister flipped his hand. "They had nothing better to do, and Steve said that he, you, and Rasheed would be busy for the foreseeable future."

"My plane is sitting in Conroe. We could have used it instead of flying yours all the way to Texas and back."

Steve said, "Allister insisted."

An impish grin pulled up the corners of her father's mouth. "I'm finding that the older I grow, the more I enjoy looking for opportunities to celebrate Christmas by giving. Besides, the decision needed to be made, and you were getting a CT scan."

Steve added, "Rasheed will leave soon, go to Branson's airport, pick up Sugar, and take her to the hospital."

Her father added, "I'll relieve Sugar in the morning and sit with Candy. That will leave Rasheed and Steve free to catch the person or persons responsible for attacking her and harming my daughter."

Heather cast her gaze over everyone assembled. A feeling of surrender flowed into her. "I should have known you three would cook up a conspiracy to cut me out of planning how to move forward with the investigations. No more clandestine meetings without me, and I'll be part of the brain trust that solves these crimes."

"Agreed," said Steve.

Both dogs shot up from their prone positions and raced to the front door. Steve was the first person to react. "*Ami*," he said in a firm voice. Le Roi stopped in his tracks, but kept his gaze on the front door, his ears up and alert.

Heather followed him by speaking to Princess. "You heard Steve. It's a friend. No barking."

Princess glanced over her shoulder before turning toward the door, quivering with anticipation.

Rasheed answered Heather's unasked question. "Our supper has arrived. Steve and I had no time to cook, so we took the easy way out and phoned in an order for fried chicken with all the trimmings."

Steve elaborated on Rasheed's comment about supper by saying, "We already set the dining room table. Heather, I know you must be close to starving after your liquid diet. This meal should hasten your recovery."

"Or harden my arteries."

"Do like me and practice moderation."

A snort came from Heather's nose. "You and moderation are very distant cousins."

Steve grinned. "I've always appreciated you being a quick healer. It's a good thing we have much to discuss tonight and even more to do tomorrow."

The young man making the delivery handed off some of his load to Rasheed and carried the rest past Le Roi and Princess. "Awesome dogs, but they look like they'd rather take a bite out of me than the chicken."

"They'd like nothing better," said Rasheed, "but you should be safe as long as you don't pet them."

The young man didn't tarry long enough for Heather to retrieve cash from her purse.

"Don't worry about the tip," said Steve. "I included it in the order."

The meal progressed with minimal conversation for several minutes. Heather then asked, "Steve, what did you mean when you said we have much to discuss tonight and even more to do tomorrow?"

"Our conversation will depend on what you learned from George, and I need to tell you about Rasheed and I going back to see Melvin Bird."

"Was he home?"

"That depends on how you define his home. He wasn't at the same place you and I went to."

"Are you saying that's not his permanent address?"

Steve put a half-eaten chicken leg on his plate and wiped his mouth with a paper napkin. "The apartment east of Hollister is his permanent address, but he doesn't live there, at least not all the time."

"Do you know where he lives?"

"We'll know for sure tomorrow morning when we pay him a visit. Rasheed and I had a productive day working from home."

"And I had a productive interview with George."

Her father spoke up. "I find the way you two tease each other with hints of information interesting. Is it common for police officers and private detectives to do this?"

Rasheed answered, "As an aficionado of the noir detective genre, I'd say it's not only common, but essential. Steve and Heather do it as well as any I've read and studied." He tilted his head. "I must add, I've tried the same with Junani and it is not appreciated."

Steve changed the subject. "Someone at this table is about to be late for an important meeting. Does anyone want to guess who that person could be?"

"I do," said Heather.

"Me too," said her father.

Rasheed looked at his phone. "A man who loves the sound of his own words is late for many appointments." He rose. "My apologies for not being available to clean the kitchen. The airport beckons me."

Her father said, "And a man who doesn't budget his time wisely washes dishes when others go to bed."

Rasheed grinned. "As I am often told concerning my proverbs, 'It needs work.'"

Heather's laugh brought on a tickle in her throat, but she controlled the cough with her second helping of *gluhwein*.

## 21

Heather snuggled under a fleece throw on the couch as a log shifted in the fireplace. Muffled voices came from the kitchen, but they were too distant for her to make out the conversation between two of the three most important men in her life. The only one missing was Jack, her long-time romantic interest. She allowed her thoughts to take her to a happy place, somewhere between what had been, what was, and what might be.

Her thoughts shifted to business, and she wondered why. It might have something to do with her father's proximity. In the next room was a man who represented a world that she'd tried to replace by becoming a cop, but she'd ended up like him, at least most of the time. She took a sip from her mug and whispered, "That's not completely true. He's all business, all the time."

It then occurred to her that her assessment of him wasn't accurate either. He used to be all business, but here he was in Branson, Missouri, washing dishes with Steve, teasing Rasheed, practicing generosity, and sending his jet to pick up a stranger so Candy, a woman he'd never met, could be with her sister.

Was it possible that her father was becoming more like her?

She had certainly become like him, and it cost her a mental breakdown. Perhaps they could meet in the middle. She had an inkling of an idea for a new business in Branson, but it wasn't far enough along to mention to anyone but her acquisitions team. Her father would want to know specifics, but there weren't any yet. Best to wait until she had an initial feasibility study.

Voices approached, and she put her thoughts into a mental file folder and closed out that section of her mind. There was a complex case to solve, and she needed to focus on it. Growing her business must wait.

Steve came in and settled into a recliner next to where she sat on the couch. Her father was passing through on his way to the office. "I have some calls to make, and there's talk of an airport worker's strike in Spain."

"Another?" asked Heather. "Didn't they come to an agreement in July?"

"That was a stopgap contract. The chances of it happening now are slim, but not out of the realm of possibility. I believe the union is bluffing and setting the stage for next summer's negotiations of a long-term contract."

Her father bent over the back of the couch and kissed the top of her head. "Good night. You can stay up for forty-five more minutes. Any longer and I'll call your doctor."

Steve said, "I'm only good for thirty more minutes. It's always fascinated me how nurses know when to check on patients. It's as if they're trying to minimize the sleep of everyone in the room."

Heather waited until the door to the home office clicked shut before saying, "We now have twenty-nine and a half minutes. Start talking."

"Rasheed and I had a busy day. I believe Melvin Bird, his brothers, and possibly one of their sons committed the robbery of Candy's theater and started the fire as a diversion. I also believe they use the apartment east of town as a place for distributing drugs."

"What makes you think that last part?"

"The smell. Remember when we were talking this morning and I asked you to describe the inside of the apartment? You said you didn't smell anything significant, either in the apartment or even on Melvin."

Heather cast her thoughts back again. "Yes, that should have been some sort of flag. Even a halfway clean bachelor apartment will have a distinctive odor to it. For most middle-class bachelors, it would smell like sweaty clothes."

"Think back again to the kitchen. There were no dirty dishes, no half-full coffee pot, no pans on the stove?"

She closed her eyes in concentration, then they flew open. "Now I get it. I don't remember dirty dishes because there weren't any. Melvin's clothes were old, worn out, and stained, but I don't remember him smelling bad. The same goes for the furniture, but there was no clutter. I've never been in a bachelor apartment that didn't have an empty pizza box or beer can on a kitchen counter and the trash can filled to overflowing."

Heather threw in a word of caution. "But selling drugs out of an apartment is bound to draw the attention of his neighbors. Eventually, they'd notify the police."

"Not necessarily. I want you to do some research at the county courthouse and see who owns all the apartments."

Heather caught up with Steve's thinking and excitement coursed through her. "You spent the day thinking like a criminal. It will be easy to check the license plates on the junk cars in the apartment's parking lot."

"I had Rasheed go back to the apartments this afternoon and compile a list. It contains descriptions of the vehicles and their license plates. No one came or went while he was there. Your buddy at the FBI can run them without raising flags with the local police."

Heather stared into the fire. "If you're right, that setup allows them to give the illusion of occupancy with no one living there. No tenants mean no calls to the cops."

Steve issued a word of caution. "I hope you realize that we'll need to verify all my suppositions about Melvin Bird not living there, his brothers and a son being involved with him, no tenants living there, and the place being involved in some sort of criminal activity."

"If I had my tools to pick locks, I could go tonight and come back with some of your answers. I used them to open the door to Candy's dressing room so Princess and I could get her outside. Unfortunately, I left them, along with everything else in my purse, in the hallway. By the time I could return to the crime scene, Lieutenant Douglas was bagging and tagging it all. He was particularly interested in my locksmithing tools. It may be days before he gets around to returning everything, and I have a feeling I'll never see those tools again."

"Can't you order more?" asked Steve.

"Sure. Amazon carries complete sets of lock-picking tools. Anyone can order them, just like you would a hammer or a screwdriver. They're not illegal to own, but Douglas found them at the scene of a crime."

Steve rubbed his chin. "I like the idea of you and Rasheed finding the doors to the apartments open, but that's not possible tonight."

He paused for a tick of the clock. "Still," he said in a way that drew out the last two letters of the word. "I think it's necessary to find out what's going on at those apartments. If you ordered the tools, when would you get them?"

"I get next-day delivery on most items. Sometimes, same day."

"Order them now. Tomorrow is soon enough to verify my suspicions. We don't need you skulking around those apartments at night, but we need to know what is or isn't going on there."

"I'll get my laptop and be right back." The trip to her room gave her time to poke holes in Steve's plan. She returned not only with her computer, but with questions.

She ordered an upgrade to the set of tools that was in the Branson Police Department's property room and closed her computer.

"So, you believe Melvin Bird stole the safe from Candy's theater?"

"I'm leaning that way, but we have no proof. All I have is my gut instinct at this point."

"Do you think he's smart enough to plan something that complicated?"

Steve pursed his lips and waited a few seconds before saying, "I've been asking myself that same question. I'm leaning heavily toward saying 'No,' but there's an outside chance one of his brothers might be."

"Hmm," said Heather. "There wasn't much conviction in that answer."

Steve said, "The mental picture I have of them is they're the hillbilly version of The Three Stooges. The research I did on them today reinforced those images."

Heather pulled in a shallow breath and asked, "You think the fire, harming Candy, and stealing the safe are part of the same crime."

"I'm not sure."

"If yes, why did they try to kill Candy?"

Steve chewed on his bottom lip before saying, "That's the question that kept me awake last night and will probably do the same tonight."

Silence and fatigue prevailed. The fire in the fireplace had gone from tall tongues of yellow flames to a bed of red shimmering embers. Steve raised the footrest on the recliner. Heather kicked off her fur-lined boots and drew her legs and sock-covered feet under the fleece throw. Princess joined her at the end of the couch and curled into a tight ball. Sleep had Steve in its grasp and she didn't feel like moving.

Heather cracked open an eye when Rasheed came through

the front door but didn't let on that she heard him. He retrieved another throw from a basket and covered Steve.

The sound of steady breathing from the master detective and the two dogs ushered in her last conscious thought of the night. Steve was wrong about one thing. He'd not stay awake on this cold December night, and neither would she.

# 22

S oft footsteps, the smell of coffee, and daylight easing into
the living room greeted Heather the next morning. Muffled
voices came from the kitchen as the expectant eyes of her dog
stared at her. Her hand moved on its own to reach out and pet
the head of her companion. Her voice came out raspy. "Good
morning, Princess. Have you been awake long?" She cleared her
throat and said, "We have much to do today. I'll skip yoga this
morning, but let's go upstairs to make ourselves presentable. I
brought a new Christmas bandana for you to wear."

Thirty minutes later, Heather and Princess made their
appearance in the kitchen where Steve sat at the bar and her
father wore an apron over his version of informal clothes, no
coat and tie.

"Someone's missing," said Heather. "Where's Le Roi?"

"Outside, patrolling the grounds, like I wanted him and
Princess to do last night. The recliner had other ideas
concerning me giving instructions. It sucked me into its warm
arms and held me captive until six this morning."

"The couch did the same to me."

Her father joined in. "You were both so deep in sleep that I
didn't dare wake you."

Rasheed made his appearance with his usual smiling greeting and a spring in his step. "The day abounds with possibilities and opportunities. I spoke with Junani and she sends her warmest regards." A shadow seemed to cloud his countenance. "Heather, I must apologize. In my conversation this morning, I let it slip that you were injured in a fire. My beloved chastised me severely for allowing any harm to befall you. Upon reflection, Junani is correct. I hope you will forgive me."

"There's nothing to forgive."

"I wish that were true."

Steve interrupted. "Rasheed, Heather has a dangerous assignment to complete today. She'll need a competent man to stand watch and come to her rescue if needed. Do you feel up to the task?"

"More than ready."

"Good. Grab your coat and hat. I need you to take me to the hospital. I'll stay with Candy while you bring her sister here to rest."

Heather added, "You and I won't leave for our mission until this afternoon. We have to wait until my new set of lock-picking tools arrives."

Rasheed's eyes shone with delight. "That is a skill I've yet to master, but it's on my to-do list. Perhaps you could recommend where I should start."

"We'll talk about it later today. For now, take Steve to the hospital and bring Sugar back."

Rasheed took a step and stopped. "There's something about Miss Sugar you should know. She brought only a small carry-on bag and a light jacket."

"She can borrow anything she needs from Candy for the next day or two. I'll pick out a coat, hat, and gloves for you to take to her."

Steve joined her at the coat closet in the home's entryway. "While you're handing out coats, hand me mine. Enjoy your time alone with your father."

"He'll probably go back into the home office and stay there all day."

"You underestimate him. Ask him to go with you and Rasheed today."

Instead of dismissing the idea, Heather stopped and considered it. "Is this a dare?"

Steve shrugged. "I look at it as an opportunity."

"Yes, it's an opportunity for him to be arrested."

"They might detain him for an hour or two, but they won't arrest him with his hotshot attorney daughter there to defend him."

"I wouldn't do him much good wearing handcuffs myself."

Steve flipped away her response. "Dual arrests would be like both of you getting identical cuts that required stitches or matching tattoos."

"I'll ask, even encourage him to come with us today, but I have no intention of getting caught, let alone being injured or putting ink into my skin."

Steve nodded in agreement. "A shared experience suits both of you better." He shrugged into his coat. "You should also talk to him about that business idea that's rattling around in your head."

Heather didn't ask how Steve knew what she'd not mentioned to anyone. "I'll take that under advisement," she said, and handed him his gloves.

---

RAISED EARS ON BOTH DOGS ALERTED HEATHER TO RASHEED'S return with Sugar. The dogs remained on full alert until Heather assured them in English and French that the visitor was a friend. The woman appeared road-weary, sleep-deprived, and as if she'd aged ten years, even though it was only a couple of weeks since she and her husband had come to the corporate office in The Woodlands, Texas.

What Heather didn't expect was a patch of yellow peeking out from under her makeup, the telltale sign of a bruise under her left eye.

Instead of reacting, which would signal Sugar's secret was now out of the bag, Heather busied herself by hanging up the borrowed coat and asking a question while her eyes focused on the task at hand. "Are you hungry? There are biscuits and sausage patties from breakfast."

A meek voice answered, "No, thanks. The nurses gave me a breakfast tray. They said it was extra, but I think they heard my stomach growling during the night. All I want is a hot shower and a bed."

"Your sister's bedroom is all yours. You'll have the house to yourself until around dark. Did you and Steve work out a time when you'd go back to the hospital?"

"Around seven tonight, but he said he's flexible."

"That's Steve. He makes plans, but he leaves plenty of room in the margins for changes. My downfall is not leaving enough time to react to unexpected events." Heather turned and faced the closed door of the home office. "Speaking of unplanned things, my father flew in when he heard I was in the hospital. He's a charming gentleman. You'll meet him later."

Heather knew she was babbling and continued to do so. It was much better than saying, "Who's responsible for that bruise on your cheek? Are there any more signs of abuse you'd like to show me or talk about?"

Sugar made a point of keeping the bruised side of her face away from curious eyes. Heather reciprocated by taking the carry-on bag from Rasheed and leading the way upstairs. She delivered the bag and left the bedroom as quickly as she could, without making it look like she had a tale to tell.

Heather looked down at Princess and noticed that Le Roi had stayed downstairs. She whispered, "Good girl," and turned her attention to Sugar. "Do you like dogs?"

"I'd give anything to have a dog like yours."

"Good. I'll be busy most of the day. She can stay with you up here. She'll let you know if she needs to go outside."

"Can she sleep with me?"

"She'd love it."

Rasheed and her father met her at the bottom of the staircase. The three retreated to the kitchen. Keeping his voice low, Allister went first. "How's our latest addition to the impromptu hotel?"

"Not as good as I'd hoped. The bruise on her face tells me Candy is correct in not having a high opinion of Sugar's husband."

Rasheed asked, "How should I treat her? It's hard not to stare."

"Staring is the one thing you shouldn't do. She's dealing with a mountain of shame and hopelessness. I believe she'll need professional help, but in the meantime, she doesn't need to know the details of our investigation."

Rasheed asked, "What if she asks?"

"Make your responses vague. Make up or quote one of your proverbs."

"Clever," said Rasheed. "Proverbs convey general truths, but nothing too specific."

Her father asked, "Should I stay here today?"

"I left Princess with her. That dog has more training in dealing with emotional problems than the three of us put together. We'll each keep to our plan with one exception."

Heather cast her gaze at Rasheed. "You and I are going shopping. Sugar's carry-on suitcase didn't weigh over fifteen pounds."

"Junani calls that kind of binge shopping *retail therapy*."

"Exactly," said Heather. "In this case it will boost the spirits of the giver and the receiver."

Her father grinned. "Does that include the pack mule to carry all your purchases? After all, that's why you're taking Rasheed."

Her driver responded with, "The mule of a generous master dines on the finest oats."

Allister stroked his chin. "Sorry, Rasheed, but that proverb should stay in the barn."

---

It was mid-afternoon before Heather and Rasheed returned from their marathon shopping spree. Instead of overwhelming Sugar with everything at once, Heather divided the trove into seven days' worth of outfits, including shoes or boots, to be doled out over a week's time. The exception was undergarments and a new winter coat.

Heather credited Candy for the gifts, so Sugar wouldn't balk at receiving them from a stranger.

Sugar wasn't the only one to receive a present. Heather opened the package which had been waiting for her at the gate and examined her replacement lock-picking tools. She practiced on the front door and found them to be superior to those that were somewhere in the bowels of Branson's police department.

Rasheed drove, Heather surrendered the front passenger seat to her father and she had the back seat to herself. Le Roi took up much of the back, caged-in area.

The two men chatted incessantly as they made their way east. They were approaching the turnoff when Heather noticed a familiar-looking late-model black pickup. It had parked in the driveway of an abandoned building, about fifty feet past the road they were to turn on.

"Don't turn. Keep driving straight," said Heather.

Rasheed did as instructed, but her father asked, "What's wrong?"

Heather waited until they'd passed the truck before answering. "That truck parked at the abandoned store is the same one Steve and I saw at the apartments."

"Are you sure?" asked her father.

"The license plate confirms it."

Her mind raced, and in a matter of seconds she'd formulated a plan. "Rasheed, I have a special assignment for you. Pull into the next driveway and trade places with me."

Heather waited until she was in the driver's seat to speak. "I believe the person in that truck is Melvin Bird."

Rasheed said, "There was more than one person in the truck. I counted three."

"Three? That's two too many," said Heather as she thought out loud. "All it takes is one person to cover the road from both directions." She puffed out her cheeks then blew out a huff of air. "Now I'm sure something is very wrong."

Her father whispered, "To paraphrase the Bard, 'There's something rotten in Southwest Missouri'."

"Well said, Dad."

She sucked in a full breath. "Here's the plan. There are thick woods on the north side of the road from here to Bird's truck. Rasheed, I'm going to get you as close as possible without being spotted. Get out as fast as you can. I'll turn around and drive several miles before looking for a place to stop. Hopefully, there's a store or a restaurant. Look for evergreen trees or bushes to hide behind. Get close enough to see what they're doing, but don't let them see you."

"It will be a lead-pipe cinch, sweetheart," Rasheed said in a mock-gravelly voice.

"What did you say?"

"Sorry. I was channeling Bogart."

Her father chuckled as she put the SUV in gear.

Tension rose as they drew close to a curve that hid their approach. Heather slowed before placing two wheels on the grass. Rasheed was out and running for cover before she could caution him not to slam his door. She performed a three-point turn around and headed east without squealing the tires. Le Roi whimpered his frustration at not being invited to go with Rasheed.

Her father looked at her. "Do you really believe a crime is being committed as we speak?"

"It may have already happened, it is happening, or it will happen soon."

"No wonder you enjoy this life so much. My heart is racing, and adrenaline is coursing through my old veins."

"This is nothing," said Heather. "Staring at a knife or gun will really get the juices flowing."

"No thanks. My cardiologist wouldn't approve of that much excitement."

They drove four miles before spotting a barbecue restaurant. "This will do nicely," said Heather. She parked and looked at her father, who asked, "What now?"

"We wait for Rasheed to text me. If you're hungry, thirsty, or need to use the facilities, now's the time and place. There's no telling how long it will be before we hear anything."

Her father scanned the parking lot and the building. "Are we on a stakeout?"

"You could call it that."

He looked left and right again. "How long do we wait to hear from Rasheed?"

"As long as it takes."

Fifteen minutes passed, then thirty more. Her father shifted in his seat. "Are all stakeouts like this?"

"Pretend you're fishing."

"I never had the patience to watch a cork for over a minute before checking the bait."

Heather let out a huff. "If you want something to do, call Steve. Tell him where we are and what we're doing. Ask if there's any update on Candy."

"Excellent idea."

"Put your phone on speaker so I can hear."

Steve answered the phone on the fourth ring. "Hold on, Allister. I'm going into the hallway." A few seconds passed before he said, "I can talk now. How is the investigation proceeding?"

"I'm on my first stakeout. I liken it to watching paint dry. Heather and I are waiting for a text from Rasheed. We're outside a barbecue restaurant four or five miles east of the apartments."

"I can't think of a better place to wait for a text, but why so far from the apartments, and what's Rasheed up to?"

Heather took over. "I spotted Melvin Bird's truck near the road leading to the apartment. Two other men are with him."

Her cell phone pinged with an alert of an incoming text. "Hold on. Rasheed sent a text. It's only one word, *DRONES*."

Steve went silent for several seconds before asking, "Did you say drone or drones?"

"Drones. Plural."

Steve's voice lowered to a tone he only used for no-nonsense conversations. "Rasheed is in grave danger if any of the three men spot him. Abort today's original mission. Eyes in the sky are watching the road in both directions and the apartments. Send a text to Rasheed and tell him to stay hidden until they recover the drones and the truck has been gone for at least fifteen minutes. Thirty would be better."

"Anything else?" asked Heather.

"Treat your father to a plate of backcountry barbecue and take Rasheed a brisket sandwich and a big to-go cup of sweet iced tea. He's earning it."

"I'll get Rasheed two sandwiches." She sucked in a quick breath. "How's Candy?"

"She can't talk yet, and her hand is too shaky to write. Lieutenant Douglas tried to interview her, but didn't have any luck. She's sleeping now, but I'll get some answers from her after she wakes up."

Allister asked, "How will you do that?"

"By holding her hands." Steve told his phone to end the call.

Heather dictated a rather lengthy and stern message to Rasheed, instructing him to lie low and quiet if he wanted to experience a honeymoon with Junani. She sent it and said, "That should do the trick. Let's follow Steve's advice and treat ourselves to a late afternoon meal."

On the way inside, her father asked, "Why did Steve tell us to abort our mission? I was looking forward to watching you pick locks and us discovering a hoard of illegal substances."

"Steve always has his reasons. He also likes to keep a few secrets during an investigation. You can ask him tonight why he told us to stand down, but there's no guarantee he'll tell you."

## 23

Le Roi led the way to the front door as voices came from the front porch. Heather twisted the silver knob on the deadbolt and stood back. Steve, with a hint of a grin on his lips, entered first with his white cane sweeping a path in front of him.

"You find humor in my pitiful plight," said Rasheed. "How was I to know what poison oak looks like? That plant does not curse the rocky hills of my native land. At least it's only my left hand, and the other place I mentioned that cause me such discomfort. My jeans, boots, coat and hat protected me."

Steve countered with, "I squatted on poison ivy once when I was almost thirteen. I didn't know what misery was until that day. To make matters worse, my mother insisted on slathering the affected area with calamine lotion. That was an indignity no boy should endure, especially one whose voice was changing."

Heather joined the conversation. "As fascinating as this conversation is, my father and I would like an update on Candy's condition. We also need to discuss drones, Sugar arriving with a bruised face, the theft of a safe, arson, attempted murder, interviewing other suspects, and what Candy needs us to do to keep her theater running."

Heather's father opened the office door and stepped out. "Welcome home, Steve. Have you eaten supper?"

"Not yet, and I've been thinking about barbecue all evening. The aroma reached all the way to the front door. I knew Heather wouldn't forget me. Barbecue is one of my biggest weaknesses."

Heather whispered loudly enough for all to hear, "Along with a dozen other things."

"That's true, and you're right to mention the ever-growing list of issues we're facing." He then said, "Let's address the most obvious item first: The use of drones to keep an eye on what appears to be a drug distribution operation. I wasn't sure if you should first call your buddies at the FBI, or others you know at the Drug Enforcement Administration. They'll both want to be involved. Since you've already involved the FBI, let them decide when to contact the DEA."

He took a breath. "You can do that while I'm chowing down on supper. Tell me everything the three of you saw and did today when scouting the apartments."

Allister asked, "Why didn't you want us to go to the apartments? I was looking forward to seeing Heather in action with her lock-picking tools."

"I needed time to think," said Steve. "If I'm right about those apartments, we'll know soon enough, and you'll be glad you didn't go there today."

Heather patted her father on his arm. "Remember what I said about Steve keeping secrets?" She turned and walked into the office, closing the door behind her.

Heather made the call, gave details, and answered a volley of questions. Following the interrogation, she received a sobering response to her father's question.

After promising not to go back to the apartments, the call ended, and she walked into the kitchen where Steve's fork hovered over a piece of pecan pie.

"Steve was right to abort today's mission. Using a small,

isolated apartment complex to serve as a drug distribution center isn't a one-off thing."

Steve nodded his approval. "Tell your father more while I finish my meal."

Heather turned to face her father. "This is highly confidential, so what I'm about to tell you stays in this room." She paused for a tick of the clock then began her explanation. "This is one way a sophisticated drug operation distributes large quantities of products. A shadow corporation buys a rundown property, cleans out any remaining tenants, creates false leases to nonexistent people, puts worthless cars and trucks in the parking lot, and makes the complex appear occupied."

Steve swallowed a bite of pie. "The apartments look lived in, but there are no occupants, just junk cars in the parking lot and used furniture in one unit. Melvin doesn't live there but wanted us to believe he did. We made an appointment with him and met him there. Our questions to him involved a land transaction that occurred long ago when his father denied the three brothers an inheritance. We had Melvin pegged as a suspect in trying to extort money from Candy, not as a drug dealer."

Heather continued, "Using drones as an early warning system isn't a new wrinkle for the FBI. What is new is the use of incendiary devices to destroy the apartments if they're raided."

Her father sat up straight. "Are you saying the people behind this operation will destroy their own property?"

"Why not?" asked Steve. "They picked up the property cheap and laundered some of the drug money through bogus rent payments. Besides, fires have a nasty habit of destroying evidence."

"And people," said Heather. "A raid on a similar setup last month resulted in two officers receiving serious injuries when they forced entry into an unoccupied apartment."

Rasheed exclaimed. "I can see it. They forced open a door and BOOM. A booby-trap!"

Heather took her turn. "That's why Steve told us to abort our plans. He sensed danger."

Her father's widened eyes spoke of concern. He puffed out his cheeks and asked, "What happens now?"

"We stay away from the apartments," said Steve.

"Right," said Heather to add emphasis. "Federal agencies with almost unlimited resources and technology will take over."

"Not completely," said Steve.

Heather tented her hands on her hips. "I've heard that tone before. What are you up to?"

"We came across something that may or may not relate to our investigation, and Heather has reported it to the proper authorities. But don't forget, we came here to find out who was sending threatening notes to Candy. That's still our primary mission." He paused. "I'll be the first to admit that our investigation has become more complex because of the fire, the injuries, the robbery, and how Melvin Bird and his family fit into any or all of it. There are a lot of coincidences, and there may be more. But..."

Heather broke in. "Here it comes. I can't tell you how many times I've heard him say what he's about to."

Steve lifted his chin. "I'll let you do the honors this time."

Heather quoted Steve. "A coincidence doesn't prove guilt. Dig deeper and verify everything."

"Excellent," said Steve. "It's still early and we have much to discuss."

Her father said, "I recommend we put on a pot of coffee and retire to the living room. First, I'd like to hear an update on Candy's condition."

It wasn't long before Heather delivered a steaming mug of coffee to Steve. The fire crackled, and the dogs sat beside their owners. Steve said, "There are unfamiliar smells in here. What changed since I left this morning?"

Allister had the answer. "Sugar slept a solid eight hours and awakened with nervous energy. She located a closet dedicated to

Christmas decorations and transformed the living room into something Norman Rockwall would have enjoyed painting. The tree may be artificial, but you must examine it closely to tell. Her goal is to complete all decorations by the time they release Candy from the hospital."

"And speaking of Candy," said Steve. "She still can't speak. In fact, the doctor doesn't want her to. That frustrated Lieutenant Douglas to no end. He locked horns with a nurse who must have received her training in the Marine Corps. She knows how to follow orders and how to handle people who think she should do otherwise."

Rasheed asked, "Does that mean you weren't able to question Candy about her attacker?"

"It meant I asked the nurse's permission to hold Candy's hand and speak to her. She asked me how I lost my sight. I told her about the attack in a Houston parking lot and what happened to me and Maggie. She likened it to a battlefield injury and told me several ways she communicated with wounded soldiers who couldn't speak. Candy and I started with simple yes-no questions. By the time I left, we'd worked out a rudimentary ten-letter shorthand alphabet with our fingers. If anyone came in, it looked like we were holding hands."

"Brilliant," said her father.

Steve shrugged off the compliment. "Candy told me there wasn't a person in her room wearing a Krampus costume, but she saw him near her door going toward the men's dressing room."

Heather then asked, "Why didn't she use her key to get out?"

"The explosion knocked her loopy and the lights in her dressing room went out. She tried to pull it out of her shirt under her costume, but it zipped up the back."

Heather thought hard and worded her next question carefully. "Are you sure she remembered everything the way it really happened?"

"I know what you're asking, and my answer is, I don't know. It was a very high-stress situation. She remembered coming into her dressing room and closing the door behind her. There was a sudden whoosh that blew the drawers of her dressing table open, and the fire grew quickly. I've told you the rest."

Heather sipped her coffee before saying, "We don't know if Krampus was involved or not."

"It has me scratching my head," said Steve. "It's possible she doesn't remember the events as they happened."

"Or," said Heather, "it's possible that there's nothing wrong with her memory. If that's the case..."

Steve took over. "The arson and robbery at the theater are related crimes. The attempted murder may not have been intentional. That leaves the attempt to extort money from Candy as the fourth crime."

Heather concluded her part of the discussion by saying, "Then again, all four crimes plus the drug distribution could be part of the same criminal enterprise.

The room fell silent until Steve asked, "Let's get our focus off drugs. Who stands to gain the most from Candy's injury?"

Rasheed said, "When you don't know what your next step should be, follow the money."

"Well said," said Allister.

"I agree," said Steve. "Heather, I want you to have a talk with Claire Finch tomorrow. Candy wants her to take over her spot in the Christmas show. I'm wondering what she's capable of doing to get that big break."

Rasheed added, "Bogart was always leery of good-looking dames."

Allister spoke up. "May I go with Heather?"

"I don't see why not. I'll go back to the hospital and stay with Candy. That will give me time in a recliner to unravel this tangled web of crimes we've fallen into. Rasheed can stay here with Le Roi to guard the house."

Heather added, "Princess will keep watch over Sugar."

Rasheed raised a hand while asking a question. "May I make a suggestion?"

"Of course," said Heather.

"At your convenience, could you schedule an appointment for Mrs. Sugar to go to a salon? I believe it would give her a much-needed psychological boost."

"Of course. That's a wonderful idea."

Steve said, "I agree, but let's make this a learning experience for you, Rasheed. A private detective must get out of their comfort zone from time to time. Do research and find the best salon in town. Schedule the appointment for late in the afternoon. Heather will write off the charge to your credit card as a business expense, so don't let Sugar skimp on the services. Make sure she gets the works."

Heather cast her gaze toward Steve. "Is there anything else we need to cover tonight?"

"I don't, but you do."

"Oh? And what's that?"

"You and Allister need to discuss your idea for a new business. Get it out in the open so he can help you and you can more fully concentrate on the case."

With the proverbial cat out of the bag, Heather had no choice but to look at her father and say, "Would you accompany me to the office? There's something I'd like to discuss with you, and Steve won't stop pestering me until I do. My consolation is that he doesn't know what I have in mind."

"Lead the way, favorite daughter of mine."

"If you don't mind," said Heather, "I need to schedule an appointment with a possible arsonist before we get started."

"I can honestly say I've never heard that before attending a business meeting."

Heather carried her laptop into the home office, settled into the leather executive chair behind the desk and opened a file that contained information on Claire Finch, including her contact information. "Claire, this is Heather McBlythe. Would it be possible for you to come to Candy's hospital room early tomorrow morning?"

"Of course. I tried to get in to see her today but was told she's not receiving visitors."

"You're an exception."

"Name the time and I'll be there."

"Seven-thirty, and don't eat breakfast."

## 24

"There's thick fog this morning," said Heather. "We need to leave ten minutes earlier than I told you last night."

Steve nodded, issued a grunt, and continued to sip from the day's first cup of coffee. He settled his mug on the bar and asked, "How did your powwow with your father go last night?"

"I'm cautiously optimistic that I may have hit upon something that pleases him." She poured herself a cup of coffee into a disposable travel cup and gathered her valise.

More time passed in silence than should have. Steve checked his chin to make sure he'd not missed any stubble while shaving. "Is there a reason you won't tell me what the next multi-million-dollar idea is? I may want to invest in it."

"It's a long shot, and I couldn't get a good read on what Dad thought of it." A mischievous tone infiltrated her next words. "Besides, it's Christmas, the season of secrets."

Steve pushed his mug away. "Ah-ha! It's a game of secrets you want to play. All right, count me in. I say I can guess what your next big idea is before Christmas."

Heather shook her head. "You cheat. I'll give you three days."

Steve pushed his lips to one side as he considered. "If it

weren't for the case we're working on, I'd say that was a fair bet. I want six days."

"Four," said Heather.

Steve shot back, "Five, and the time starts at noon today."

"Deal," said Heather, as she took Steve's empty mug and placed it in the sink.

Steve slid off the barstool, looked down at Le Roi, and told his dog to stay and guard the home... all in French, of course.

Heather looked at him and said, "I thought Dad was coming with me today."

"I changed my mind. I spoke to Allister and he was good with staying here. He said something about looking into doing some local research."

Heather shrugged. "Fine by me."

Once in the car, Steve said, "Let's see what secrets Claire has for us to discover today."

The thick blanket of fog didn't reach all the way to the top of Candy's hill, but when they dropped in elevation, it was like driving inside a frosted light bulb. Heather scooted as near the windshield as she could without her chest touching the steering wheel. The only navigation tools she had were a white line on her right, the center stripes on her left and the computer's map that identified streets.

By maintaining a cautious pace, the white-knuckled trip ended in the hospital's parking lot, where she breathed a sigh of relief. Steve quipped, "I didn't know you could drive that slowly."

"Don't complain. I kept it between the ditches and out of the lake."

"Can you find the door or do I need to lead the way with my cane?"

Heather wasted a hard stare on him. "If I have to drive through anything that thick again, you'll need to ride on the hood and use a longer cane."

Despite allowing more time for the journey, they arrived in Candy's room only seven minutes later than they had planned.

Rasheed rose from the recliner while Sugar stood by her sister, dabbing her mouth with a napkin.

Heather asked, "Are you still on a liquid diet?"

Candy nodded her head while Sugar said, "Her appetite is coming back. She ate some of everything."

"That's excellent progress," said Steve. He moved to Candy's bed and asked, "Can you put up with me for twelve more hours today?"

A firm nod of her head came next, as well as a wide smile.

By this time, Rasheed had vacated the recliner. Heather cast her gaze at him and asked, "How long have you been here? You left only a minute before we did."

He shrugged. "I arrived five minutes ago."

"How could you see in that thick fog?"

"I grew up driving in sandstorms. Fog is not so different, except blowing sand is grittier and gets in your teeth." He paused. "Is 'grittier' a proper word?"

"If it wasn't, it is now," said Steve. He changed the conversation by asking, "How did our patient do last night?"

Sugar was ready with an answer. "She slept much better last night. They still don't want her to talk, but all the vitals are good except her blood-oxygen count. Even that is getting better."

Candy held out both hands to Steve. He grasped her hands and squeezed, then moved his hands to her wrists. She did the same to his. If Heather hadn't known about the ten-finger code Steve invented, the twitching fingers would have meant nothing to her.

Because Sugar didn't ask why Steve and Candy were holding each other's wrists, Heather wondered if they intended to keep some things to themselves. It wouldn't surprise her, especially in the middle of an investigation.

Another thought came to Heather. Steve and Candy had known each other in high school and had fond, perhaps wistful, memories of what might have been. Combine a lonely widower and an equally lonely widow with the nostalgia of Christmas, and gently stir in a crisis. Could this be a recipe for romance after all?

"Heather," said Steve with force. "Didn't you hear Rasheed? He and Sugar are leaving."

"Oh. Sorry. I was thinking about Christmas presents, and what to give Jack."

"Give him more time alone with you. That's all he wants."

Heather wondered if he was projecting his own desires. "You may be on to something. I'll give your suggestion serious consideration."

Rasheed and Sugar left, and Steve said, "Move to the other side of the bed. I told Candy that Claire would be here soon. She asked if Lieutenant Douglas was coming early, too. It seems he came after I left last night and tried to question her. Sugar told him that Candy still couldn't speak and needed to rest. He didn't like it, but he didn't press her."

Heather shifted her gaze to Candy. "Your sister loves you very much. We don't want to wear you out, but we need to know what you want to do about the show. Do you want to cancel the Christmas show entirely?"

A firm shake of her head answered that question.

"Do you want your producer and director to find a replacement?"

She tapped out a message on Steve's arm.

Steve said, "C l r. Do you want Claire to take your place?"

A firm nod.

"Do you want Claire to communicate your wishes to your producer and director?" asked Heather.

Another firm nod came from Candy.

Steve asked, "Now that you've thought about what I asked you yesterday, do you remember anything else about the fire?"

She shook her head.

Heather asked, "Is there anything we can get you?"

Candy's grasp stayed on Steve's wrists as she typed out a

message in their code. Steve smiled. "She wants her sister to have a dog like Princess. Sugar can't stop talking about her."

Heather smiled and gave an answer that fit the season. "You'll need to write Santa a letter and tell him what you want."

Candy's fingers pressed into Steve's wrist. Steve smiled and said, "She wants you to write the letter for her."

Taps on the door preceded its slow opening and Claire's tentative entrance. "I wasn't sure this was the correct room."

Heather moved out of the way, and Claire took her spot. Steve stayed on the other side of the bed from Claire, but he and Candy released their grip. Candy held out both hands for Claire to take.

"It's so good to see you," said Claire. Heather took a long look at the young singer and made a few mental notes. She was more petite in person than she looked on stage, which meant she had a powerful stage presence. The damp, nippy morning air had placed a tint of pink on Claire's cheeks. Her hair was the color of ripe wheat, and there was a bumper crop of it. It fell softly down her back, clasped at the base of her neck by a brown leather strap with a wooden peg running through it. The one-word descriptor that came to Heather was *wholesome*.

The looks they gave each other communicated that something more than friendship existed between the two singers. Claire whispered, "I'm so glad to see you. Please get well soon. I don't know what I'd do without you."

It could have been a sappy line in a melodrama, but Claire delivered it with conviction. If this was an act, it convinced Heather otherwise.

Steve took over. "Candys not supposed to talk yet, but she and I have worked out a way to communicate."

"Oh? How do you do that? Can I learn it?" asked Claire.

"Sure. All it takes is ten fingers and practice." He held up both hands and wiggled his fingers. "The English alphabet has twenty-six letters. Five of them are vowels, sometimes six if you count Y. Since Y and I make the same sound we replace I with

Y. That leaves five vowels and twenty consonants. We don't use vowels." He paused. "Are you following so far?"

"I think so."

Steve pressed on, holding up both hands again and wiggling his fingers. "That leaves twenty consonants to spell out words. Don't worry, your brain will fill in the vowels for you." He stuck out his left thumb and said, "B." He then stuck out his index finger and said, "C." On he went until all ten fingers had a corresponding letter.

Heather watched as Claire's eyebrows knit together in concentration. "What about the next ten letters?"

Steve said, "Pressure is how we solved that problem. Heavy pressure acts as a cap lock for the last ten letters. Give me your hand and I'll show you."

She complied, and Steve pressed harder with his left thumb. "That's *N*." He then tapped her wrist with his left thumb. "That's *B*."

Candy picked up a sheet of paper from her nightstand and waved it before handing it to Claire. Steve either heard it or felt the breeze and said, "I had Candy draw two sketches of a left and right hand. She labeled each finger with the letter that went with it. It's a cheat sheet, or I guess you could call it a written code."

Steve said, "It's not as burdensome as you'd think. Candy taps out messages to me, and I respond with words. She still uses her cheat sheet, but she won't need to by the time she can talk again."

Heather entered the conversation. "It's a simple but effective solution to a temporary problem."

Steve grinned. "Heather's right about it being simple. Try learning to read Braille. There's nothing easy about that." He paused. "As for ditching it after Candy gets her voice back, I'm not so sure about that. We sort of like talking to each other and Heather not knowing what we're saying."

Heather shifted her gaze to Candy as she pointed at herself and held up two fingers to signal *me, too.*

Candy beckoned Claire to come closer and motioned for her to look at the code she'd placed on her lap. She took Claire's wrists, then tap by tap and press by press gave her a message.

Claire spoke each corresponding letter until she understood Candy wanted her to take over as the lead in the show. If that wasn't enough, Candy kept tapping and pressing letters that said she wanted Claire to take over her off-season tour.

Claire cried.

Heather explained to Claire that she would need to call the producer and director that morning.

Steve rose from the hospital recliner and took Candy's hand. "You're a good woman, Candy Caine." He continued to speak in a soft voice. "Heather and I are going to steal Claire for a while. She has a big day ahead of her and will need to eat breakfast. If I'm not mistaken, there will be a full rehearsal today. Do you need anything before I go?"

She shook her head.

"I'll be back in less than an hour. Heather won't, so she'll tell you goodbye now."

Heather shot him a questioning glance. He deliberately made plans for her without telling her first, which was his way of getting back at her for not sharing what she and her father had discussed. She let it pass without comment because she'd find out soon enough, and after all, it was the season for secrets, be they little or big.

# 25

Once in the hospital's elevator, Heather asked Steve where he wanted to go for breakfast. He responded with a question, "Has the fog lifted?"

Claire answered for Heather. "It won't lift until mid-morning at the earliest. It has something to do with the temperature inversion of the water coming from the bottom of Table Rock Lake and flowing into Lake Taneycomo, which is only a few blocks from here."

Steve shook his head. "If it's all the same to you two, let's take our chances in the hospital's cafeteria. The thought of poking along at the speed of a drugged turtle doesn't appeal to me."

Heather said, "That's fine with me. I'm in no rush to tempt fate."

The elevator bumped to a stop and the door opened. Claire led the way. "The cafeteria is this way. The food is usually pretty good, especially at breakfast."

"Do you visit often?"

"Not anymore. A friend recently delivered her twins here. Her husband claims an allergy to hospitals. Of course, it isn't a real allergy. He's addicted to fishing." Her head wagged from side to side. "I promised myself I wouldn't judge him and now listen to me. Oh well, I got to hold her babies before he did. The blessing went to me."

Steve said, "I like the way you think, Claire. It's no wonder that Candy has taken such a shine to you."

"She's a truly amazing woman. I can't believe she's letting me take over the lead *and* giving me her bookings for the off season."

Steve announced, "We've arrived, and it smells good. Find a table out of the way and plant me there. Heather knows what I like, and she'll bring it to me."

Heather leaned into Claire and whispered, "Steve likes everything, so I can't make a mistake."

"That's not true," said Steve. "I'm not fond of liver, brains, or anchovies for breakfast."

Claire shivered and Heather said, "Don't let him spoil your appetite. Steve's sense of humor sometimes leaves much to be desired. The best thing to do is fight fire with fire."

Claire played along. "Steve, they have boiled mountain oysters with turnip greens. Would you like a serving?"

"If it were lunch, I'd go for it."

Heather said, "I'll get you a to-go serving for your lunch."

"We're wasting time," said Steve. "Take me to a table where we can have a nice, normal breakfast."

Heather delivered him to the table in a far corner while Claire filled her plate and joined him. Heather returned with scrambled eggs, a sausage patty, two strips of bacon, biscuits, gravy, and a waffle on a separate plate. She looked at Claire. "Would you mind buttering his waffle and pouring a modest amount of syrup? I'll get coffee for everyone and then get my food."

"No coffee for me," said Claire. "If I drink more than one cup a day, it makes me jittery, and I flub my lines and lyrics."

Steve was halfway through his meal when he asked, "Claire, do you know a local man named Melvin Bird?"

"I don't know him personally, but I know his son. Everyone calls him Jay."

Heather sputtered, "Jay Bird. I guess a name like that goes with Branson's mountain humor."

Steve said, "It's almost as good as Candy and Sugar Caine, but they brought those from Houston. Tell us how you know Jay."

"He works at the theater when we need extra help and he's not busy doing his other job."

"Do you know what his other job is?" asked Steve before he popped in a bite of waffle.

"No. I never asked. Is it important?"

Steve used the waffle in his mouth as an excuse to shake his head.

Heather asked, "What's his job at the theater?"

"Covering for whoever calls in. He can work at the concession stand, help with parking, or fill in for an usher. He used to work more often than he does now."

It occurred to Heather that Steve already knew that Jay Bird was Melvin Bird's son, and he'd expect her to find Jay and interview him after the fog lifted.

Steve took a drink of coffee, swallowed, and asked, "Do you know what kind of car or truck Jay drives?"

Claire waved her fork like a conductor's baton. "Funny you should mention that. He used to drive an old cargo van but upgraded to a new Camaro this past summer."

"Is that when he got the new job?" asked Steve.

"I think so. That would make sense."

Steve asked, "Have you ever met his father?"

"No, but that doesn't mean he hasn't come to see a show. Locals get significant discounts. It's always better to have seats filled, even if you almost give them away."

Heather was looking at Claire when she looked up and her whole countenance came alive. Whoever she spotted had to be someone special.

Steve gave the answer before Heather could turn around.

"Hello, Lieutenant Douglas. I hope you don't mind us kidnapping Claire this morning. She has big news to tell you."

The lieutenant bent over and kissed Claire on the cheek. He tried to hide the displeasure and suspicion in his voice by playing along. It was a sure bet that Steve caught the tinge of satire in the Lieutenant's voice when he said, "What a pleasant surprise to see you two."

Douglas shifted his gaze to Claire. "What's the big news, sweetheart?"

"Candy chose me to take her spot in the Christmas show."

"That's wonderful, but everyone knew she would because you were her understudy. It only makes sense that she'd choose you."

Claire held his hand. "That's only half of the good news. She wants me to take her place on her off-season tour. I'll be traveling all over the Midwest and South. That much exposure is how I can introduce songs I wrote. It only takes one big hit, and there's no better way to test audiences than with live performances."

Douglas shot a quick glare at Heather then wasted one on Steve. They lasted only a second each before returning his gaze to Claire. "That's wonderful. You're finally getting the break you deserve."

Heather suspected the lieutenant's words were as real as Monopoly money, but he voiced them all the same.

Claire rose. "If you'll excuse me, I need to call the director and producer."

"Why?" snapped Douglas.

Claire laughed. "Because Candy asked me to. That showed me that Heather and Steve have earned Candy's total trust." She gave her head a sharp nod and said, "And after spending time with them this morning, they have my trust, too."

Steve asked, "Lieutenant, if you're not too busy today, call me or even better, come by Candy's room. I'll be there until about seven tonight."

"I'll be busy all day," snapped Douglas.

"Too busy to stop in to see Candy?"

"Can she talk?"

"No, but..."

"Forget it. I'm busy."

"Honey," said Claire. "Listen to what Steve has to say."

He spoke over his shoulder as he made for the door. "I'm too busy for idle talk."

Heather delayed her departure until Lieutenant Douglas's fast footsteps had taken him out of the cafeteria.

Claire watched him and dipped her head. "Please forgive him. He's under so much pressure to solve the robbery and find the person who tried to kill Candy. All his other cases are piling up."

Steve pushed his coffee cup away. "I'll get him back to talk to Candy today. Perhaps he knows a trick or two to get her to remember more of what happened to her."

"How will you get him to come back?"

Steve leaned forward and whispered, "I'm sneaky."

Heather directed her head nod toward Claire. "I can testify to Steve's sneakiness. I've learned not to ask too many questions when he says he can do something. He either won't answer, or he'll give you an answer that's so absurd you'll be sorry you asked."

While Heather was pacifying Claire with an evasion of her question, she changed the subject. "There's no reason you can't make your calls here. You need to finish your breakfast and we want to hear their reaction. I've never included entertainment in my business portfolio. This is an exciting opportunity to learn something new."

Claire said, "I don't have an agent. I've always trusted Candy to take care of me. Do you think I need one?"

"We'll talk to Candy about that. For now, sign nothing."

Steve pushed back from the table. "You two don't need me here to conduct entertainment business. I counted the steps and turns from the elevator to this table so you don't need to show me the way. I'll go tell Candy to expect a handsome policeman to visit her today."

Steve unfurled his cane and took one step before his phone announced a call from Leo Vega.

"Good morning," said Steve. "Did you get the information I asked for?"..."Good. I'm not in a place where I can talk. I'll call you back in five minutes."

He slipped the phone back into the pocket of his jacket and tapped his way out of the cafeteria.

Claire was polite enough not to ask who Leo Vega was, but she communicated her interest with raised, questioning eyebrows. Heather answered the unasked question. "That was Steve's former partner in Houston. He helps us gather information from time to time. I'll have to wait to find out what Leo said."

"How long will you have to wait?"

Heather couldn't help grinning. "Normally, Steve tells me right away, but I'm not so sure this time."

The conversation shifted again as Heather asked, "Are you ready to take the giant step to becoming a star?"

Claire typed in the number of the show's producer. "I'm as ready as I'll ever be." She hit the send button. Following a brief explanation, Claire suggested a three-way conversation that included the director. The upshot was nothing short of elation and a promise that the Christmas show would hold a rehearsal that afternoon and would reopen the next day.

After Claire departed, Heather sent a text to Steve.

*Show reopens tomorrow. Going home to work with Dad & tell the acquisition team when to come. Anything for me to work on with the case?*

The ping of an incoming text sounded as she climbed into her car. She started the engine, watched the windshield wipers sweep mist off the glass, and checked her phone.

*No assignment for you today. That could change. Expecting
Douglas back by 10. Making progress on Krampus but not
there yet.*

Heather wondered what Steve meant by *progress*. Did he
know who sent the threatening letters? Was that why Leo
called him?

Other questions floated through her mind. She sensed Steve
had the answers to these questions and others and had confidence that he'd tell her soon. Perhaps there were pieces of information he still needed to complete the picture.

She was almost out of the parking lot when her phone
chirped the notification of another text message from Steve.

*Call FBI. Tell your buddy we need complete forensic report on
fire.*

"Another piece of the puzzle," Heather said to herself. She
then spoke as if Steve were sitting in the car with her. "Detective
Smiley, you're not the only one who can add and fit pieces into a
puzzle."

She drove back to Candy's home and found Rasheed sitting
in the living room, reading. She settled onto the couch and
asked, "How would you like to do some real sleuthing today?"

"Will it involve crawling through the woods or coming into
contact with plants that bring misery?"

"It shouldn't, but it might."

Rasheed straightened his spine. "Count me in. A good detective must follow the trail, no matter where it leads."

"Well said. Steve and I trained you how to find where people
live. I'm giving you the names of several persons of interest. I
want you to find them, go to where they live, and take photos of
the dwellings and the vehicles parked there. You'll need to
complete this assignment in time to take Sugar to the hospital
and bring Steve home."

A broad smile parted Rasheed's lips. "That's a challenge worthy of a true detective."

Heather issued a warning. "You must complete the challenge without being detected or raising suspicion. This is a pass-fail test."

Rasheed said, "Send me a text or email with the names. I'll be in my room on my computer. Once I locate them, don't expect me to return until I have completed the mission."

# 26

Heather looked out her bedroom window as headlights from her car danced their way up the black driveway. She watched as Steve and Rasheed walked to the steps leading up to the front porch. It had been a busy day for her and her father, and the day wasn't over yet.

She descended the staircase in time to greet her driver and Steve while they were taking off their coats, scarves, and gloves. Rasheed also wore a fedora with the front brim pulled down, the Middle-Eastern version of Sam Spade. "Have you eaten supper?" she asked.

"Sort of," said Steve. "Supper at the hospital cafeteria isn't nearly as good as their breakfast. I may need some Christmas cookies."

"Food had to wait today," said Rasheed. "It took me longer than expected to find the homes of the people. It turns out two live together in one house and the other two in a much nicer home next door. Both are in Kimberling City. It's only eighteen miles west of Branson, but it took me over thirty minutes to get there. Silver Dollar City amusement park is on the way, and heavy traffic delayed my arrival and journey back to Branson."

Rasheed added, "You'll have my full report tonight. For now, the kitchen is calling me. No food has passed my lips since this morning."

Heather led Steve into the living room where she settled him on the couch and sat next to him so they could talk in hushed tones.

Steve rubbed his hands together. "I'm glad you took the initiative and gave Rasheed an assignment today. You saved me the time and trouble of having to tell him what we needed. So, the brothers all drive new trucks."

"And motorcycles," said Heather.

"There's also a three-wheeled motorcycle."

Heather growled. "The next time I give Rasheed an assignment, I'll have him report to me before he calls you."

"Why?" asked Steve. "I always tell you what I'm working on and keep you informed."

Heather let out a snort. "It's not that you don't tell; it's *when* you tell that gives me heartburn. You usually wait until the last minute."

"That's for your own good. It makes you work harder to think through all the possibilities. Besides, you play the same game. You planned not to tell me you gave Rasheed an assignment until after I shared my conversations with Lieutenant Douglas and Leo."

Heather knew Steve was a step ahead of her but didn't want to back down. "You're guessing."

Steve came back with, "You put the entire case in jeopardy. We can only hope no one spotted Rasheed."

"You're upset because I did what you planned to do. I bet you had it planned for tomorrow."

Rasheed had eased into the living room unnoticed, carrying a chicken leg. He backtracked from the fray and said, "It is a wise man who leaves when two lions roar."

Steve gave a poor impression of a roaring lion.

Heather followed with the same.

Steve's belly jiggled, and Heather lost her composure.

Rasheed said, "That's better. You are wise to clear the air from time to time. It releases tension. Junani is especially skilled at this. I'm still learning to limit my words when my kitten growls. So far, I'm up to saying, 'Yes, dear.' Assertiveness is a skill I've yet to master."

Heather said, "That reminds me, Junani called and asked why you didn't return her call. That was over an hour ago."

"Oh, dear," said Rasheed. "My lioness will roar tonight. I'll be in my room trying to explain why a private detective has to turn off his phone when casing a joint. Unfortunately, I forgot to turn it back on."

Steve waited until Rasheed was halfway up the stairs before he asked, "Is your father in the office?"

"He and I have been on conference calls with our acquisition teams all day. The team from Conroe will be here the day after tomorrow. His team will stay in Boston for now, but that could change."

Steve held up a hand. "That's all I need to know. Are you ready to add another log to the fire and put our cards on the table?"

She asked, "All our cards?"

"Of course not. This case reminds me of what Maggie and I thought would be a simple water leak around the toilet of our newly purchased dream home. I pulled the toilet and discovered the leak had traveled under the bathtub and rotted the floor and some of the floor joists. What I thought would be a one-day project turned into a two-month tear out and rebuild by a handyman who wasn't that handy."

Heather came back with, "I thought you were going to tell me you have everything figured out."

"Not yet, but what Rasheed did today helped. It surprised me you sent him out on his own to find the Bird brothers."

Heather retrieved a medium-size log and placed it in the fireplace. While she had her back turned, Steve said, "I guess I should tell you about my phone call with Leo. I asked him to do deep background checks on Sugar and her husband, Randy. He found what we both suspected. They're hurting for money in a big way."

Heather stared at the fire. "I could tell that by the way they dressed when they came to my office and the lack of clothes Sugar brought with her. What about their jobs?"

"Job," said Steve, then he corrected himself. "That's not accurate, there are two jobs, but Sugar works both, or at least she did before Candy went to the hospital. She worked at a dollar store and spent the rest of her time altering dresses from home. From what Leo could find out, she's a skilled seamstress. Randy could be a successful salesman, but he has two weaknesses."

"Whiskey and women?" asked Heather.

Steve corrected his previous statement. "Make that three weaknesses: women, whiskey, and gambling. It's the trifecta of personal and marriage destruction."

"How broke are they?" asked Heather.

"No money in the bank. Ruined credit. Up to their necks in debt. Leo heard a rumor that a loan shark is closing in on Randy."

The fire popped sparks that the metal screen caught. Heather continued to stare at the flames and said, "He'd be safer in prison."

Steve drew a large breath through his nose and released it. "I wonder how desperate he is."

Heather shot him a quick glance. "Are you thinking he might be desperate enough to kill Candy?"

"The thought crossed my mind. Sugar is Candy's only living relative, and Candy will leave almost everything to her."

"How did you find that out?"

"I asked her today," said Steve as he shifted in his chair. "Don't worry, I phrased it in such a way that Candy didn't think I was pumping her for information. We were discussing the fire, and I told her about the guy who wants to see me dead. That led to me telling her who gets what if he succeeds.

That's when Candy told me Sugar will get almost all of her estate."

Heather asked if Candy had helped Sugar and Randy over the years.

"Many times," said Steve, "but last summer Candy realized she was causing them more harm than good, so she cut them off. She called it shock therapy. Not giving Sugar money when she begged for it was the hardest thing Candy had ever done."

Heather kept her gaze on the fire and thought about the hundreds of requests her company receives every year for charitable contributions.

Steve also seemed lost in thought when he said, "There's going to be lumps of coal in a lot of stockings this year."

"Are we still talking about Sugar and Randy?"

"Yeah. Let's change the subject. Did you hear anything from your buddy at the FBI?"

"Not yet. I'm not sure if that's good or bad."

"It's good," said Steve. "There's a lot of logistics his special agents will need to work out before they make their move. Be sure you send him a copy of Rasheed's report along with your notes."

"Do you want me to send him everything in our files?"

"Not yet. Let's not show all our cards until we're ready to bring all aspects of the case to a close. I'm holding back what Leo told me."

Heather asked, "Are we looking at days, a week, or longer?"

"Days."

"That's good. Dad will move out to stay with my acquisitions team and give them guidance while I'm busy with this case."

Steve's head wagged from side to side. "He's an amazing man. His idea of a relaxing vacation is doing what he always does, but not wearing a tie unless he goes out in public."

Heather asked, "Are there any more secrets you want to disclose to me tonight?"

"It's not a secret, but Candy is getting better."

"Is there any talk of her coming home soon?"

"Not yet, but you know how doctors are."

Heather nodded even though Steve couldn't see her. She thought about adding a disparaging remark, but the fire took her thoughts elsewhere. "The fireplace mantel needs stockings. Rasheed and I will do something about that tomorrow."

"Good idea," said Steve. "Make this home look and smell like Christmas. I bet Candy has scented candles somewhere. That would be nice. I sense hard times ahead for Sugar and Randy."

# 27

The day started before dawn with Steve making noise in the kitchen. He heard Heather's approach and let out a huff of disgust. "I give up. Where does Candy hide the coffee? I found the maker, filled the reservoir with water, located her stash of mugs. The only thing missing is coffee."

Heather went to where he stood. "It's right in front of you."

"I checked those cabinets."

"Try the top shelf of the lower cabinet."

Steve let out a groan and mumbled, "Who keeps coffee in a lower cabinet?"

"Short people like Candy."

"Oh... yeah... I should have known."

Heather gave him a pat of sympathy on his arm. "Your brain will kick in after you've had a slug-from-the-mug."

"As fuzzy as my brain is, I'll need multiple slugs and a long nap in the hospital's recliner." He continued speaking as he measured out one more scoop than Heather would have. He then said, "Come show me what all these buttons mean."

She gave him a short tutorial and the machine came to life. Following this, she asked, "How did you get Lieutenant Douglas to come back and question Candy yesterday morning?"

"I had Candy write a note and give it to a nurse. She called Douglas and told him how Candy could communicate and that she had things to tell him."

"Good thinking," said Heather. "You must have been fully caffeinated when you thought to do that."

"I was, and I left the room so he could ask her anything he wanted in private."

Heather then asked, "What's on your agenda today?"

"Waiting for the phone to ring, resting my mind, taking a walk, and enjoying a two-hour nap. I might have slept for thirty minutes last night."

"Does that mean you solved all the crimes?"

"Some are still hiding in the shadows. What about you?"

"The same," said Heather as the coffee machine delivered its last full squirt then sputtered steam. "Thanks to Rasheed's report, I'm confident I know who stole the safe. What I'm lacking is hard evidence. Why they tried to kill Candy is one of those shadowy things."

Steve responded with, "I think I know, but there's a layer that I haven't broken through yet."

Heather filled two mugs and set one in front of Steve. He found the handle but didn't pick it up. "What does your day look like?"

"Waiting to hear from my buddy at the FBI, reviewing everything in our files, putting the finishing touches on the Christmas decorations, enjoying my father, and making sure my acquisitions team and pilots are ready for tomorrow."

"Do you want to give me a hint about what your newest project will be?"

"Certainly not," said Heather with emphasis. "We have a bet."

"Good," said Steve. "We're too close to the end to lose our focus. There's still a chance I could be wrong about a couple of things."

Footsteps approached from the office. Steve spoke over his

shoulder. "I understand you're leaving us tomorrow."

"That's correct," said Allister. "I'm trading in my hilltop view of the bright lights of Branson for something overlooking Table Rock Lake. Both are refreshing changes from my office in Boston. It's amazing how a change of scenery activates the creative juices."

Steve waited until her father took his seat before asking, "Why are you renting a holiday home on the lake instead of hotel rooms?"

Heather punched Steve in the arm hard enough to get a squeal out of him. "Say nothing, Dad. It's a trick. Steve thinks he can guess the project we're working on. He and I have a bet that he can't."

"Ah-ha!" said Allister. "You're accusing him of industrial espionage?"

Heather pointed a finger at Steve. "He may look innocent with his dark glasses and white cane, but he cheats every time we make a bet."

Steve held up his hands. "You exaggerate. I don't cheat every time we bet."

"Did you hear that? He admits to cheating at least some of the times."

"Nonsense," said Steve. "It's my finely tuned powers of observation, attention to detail, and superior deductive reasoning that give me the edge."

"Prove it," said Heather. "What have you observed so far?"

A sly smile came to Steve's lips and left as quickly as it appeared. "You're assuming the role of a prosecuting attorney. Therefore, it's up to you to supply evidence beyond a reasonable doubt that I'm cheating."

"Objection," said Heather. "This isn't a criminal complaint, because the bet doesn't involve any threat of incarceration." She spoke under her breath. "Even though a few hours in time-out would be my recommendation."

She kept talking. "Because we're not looking at a criminal

offense, this will be a civil trial. I need only to show a preponderance of the evidence, not proof beyond a reasonable doubt. I submit as evidence your blatant attempt to extract information from my father by asking him such a leading question."

"You call that evidence? You're assuming motive. There's no proof of intent in my asking a simple question. I've yet to inquire of either you or your father about anything related to your project."

Heather sensed the mock trial tilting in Steve's favor. Her father confirmed her fears by saying, "It sounded like an innocent enough question to me, and Steve hasn't asked what I'm working on. We've had no electronic communication since I arrived. As far as I can tell, he's working solely on your case, whereas your thoughts and actions are divided between our project and the crimes you're trying to solve."

Steve asked, "Would you like to hear the random bits of information that I've picked up concerning your latest scheme? These are guiding me to discover your project."

Her father's eyebrows lifted. "I'd certainly like to hear them."

Steve took his first sip of coffee and lowered his mug before speaking. It was a subtle but clear signal he believed he'd won the first round of their battle of wits. His voice took on a tenor of confidence. "Heather, multiple things have impressed you greatly since you arrived in Branson. The first was the water display at Branson Landing. The second was the CHATEAU ON THE LAKE RESORT SPA AND CONVENTION CENTER."

"Of course it impressed me. It's a magnificent facility with stunning views of Table Rock Lake and the city."

"Ah, the Lake," said Steve. "That's the third thing you've raved about. Whatever your project, it's something related to water. That leads us to consider the Branson Bell, a floating dinner theater."

Rasheed bounded down the stairs and into the kitchen, cutting Steve off from saying anything more. "My beloved sends her warmest regards. She's so looking forward to flying here tomorrow."

Steve said, "That's new. I thought she was coming with the next group."

Heather explained, "Dad suggested the acquisition team could use a top lawyer on site."

"It never hurts," said her father.

Heather leaned in Steve's direction. "What happened to those finely tuned powers of observation, attention to detail, and deductive reasoning? You didn't know Junani was coming."

"I was distracted by a drug ring, a fire, a robbery, an attempted murder, an attempted extortion, a marriage on the rocks, and a Krampus. Old age must be sneaking up on me. I used to work on multiple complicated homicides at the same time."

"You make my head spin," said Rasheed. "I'll warm up the car by driving down the hill to check the mail."

Heather directed her attention back to Steve. "You forgot to add a delightful singer to your list of distractions."

Steve didn't question or object to her addition of Candy to the list of things taking up space in his head. Instead, he said, "There's something else bothering me."

"Only one more thing?"

Steve grinned. "Just one that I want to mention before Rasheed and I leave. It's Lieutenant Douglas. We need to play nice with him."

"Why?"

"He's a good cop with a bright future, he's local, and he has excellent taste in women."

Heather quickly added, "And he dislikes us."

Steve shook his head. "We haven't earned his trust. He's overworked and worried about losing Claire to bright lights and applause. He overreacted to the news that she would take over Candy's tour."

Heather puffed out her cheeks and asked, "How do you do it?"

"Do what?"

"Look at people, situations, and crimes from all angles."

Steve shrugged. "You and your father do the same with business deals."

Heather asked, "What's the next thing we need to do to solve the crimes?"

"Three things," said Steve. "The first is wait for a phone call from the feds. Next, get Lieutenant Douglas involved in the case, and finally, discover who's the brains behind the drugs and the robbery. It's certainly not any of the three stooges."

"Who?" asked Heather's dad.

"The three Bird Brothers." Heather shifted her attention back to Steve. "I'll take the first and last of those things. You get Douglas involved in the case."

"What about the Krampus trying to kill Candy?" asked her father.

Steve dismissed the question with a wave of his hand and a simple statement. "That can wait. Sugar is safe for now, and Candy has either me or Sugar with her almost all the time in the hospital." He paused. "Now that I hear my words out loud, that's not much security. Let's tell the nurses to report any suspicious people hanging around the hallways. I'll also call Chief Fry and see if he has any officers looking to earn some off-duty Christmas money."

Rasheed burst through the front door and rushed to join the gathering. With clipped words he said, "A cell phone. Also a letter that looks like the others from Krampus are in the mailbox."

Heather sprang from her seat, went to the coat closet, and grabbed her coat. Rasheed was hot on her heels and shouted, "I'm responsible for driving you and keeping you from harm. I left the door to the mailbox open and saw no wires."

Heather and Rasheed were in the kitchen in less than ten minutes. "I left the cell phone and brought the letter."

"Good," said Steve. "Let's see what Krampus has to say."

Heather used a thin blade kitchen knife to open the letter. Rasheed delivered a plastic bag from his coat pocket and said, "A good detective always carries evidence bags."

"Same paper, envelope, and handwriting," said Heather. "The letter says: *Krampus warned you and now you're responsible for a broken Candy Caine. Have the blind guy deliver a hundred grand. I don't care who pays. The phone is for the rich woman from Conroe. Keep it on you at all times. Instructions will come.*"

Steve was the first to speak. "If Chief Fry can't provide officers, we'll hire armed security to sit outside Candy's door around the clock."

Heather asked, "Do you want me to add anything to my list of things to do?"

"Get the phone out of the mailbox and make sure it stays fully charged. I need to spend much of the day rethinking who Krampus is."

# 28

Heather sat looking at the cheap burner phone and the fire she'd built to take the chill off another frosty morning. Her day started later than yesterday's early morning sparring match with Steve. In fact, she didn't appear in the kitchen until after he and Rasheed had left for the hospital. Two mugs in the sink of the otherwise clean kitchen signaled they intended to eat breakfast in the hospital cafeteria. The coffeepot still contained three-quarters of hot brew for Heather and her father.

The flames mesmerized her to the point she wasn't aware her father had entered the room until he said, "Good morning, my favorite daughter."

Her response came attached to a yawn. "Good morning, Dad."

He gave her a sideways look. "Yesterday at this time, you were ready to conquer the world. Aren't you feeling well?"

"I couldn't sleep last night. It seems Steve and I are taking turns battling insomnia."

"You must be getting close to the end of the cases."

Heather shrugged. "I hope Steve is."

"I suggest you stay in your robe and keep looking at the fire until it puts you to sleep."

Heather couldn't think of a snappy comeback or a reason not to follow his advice, but she didn't want to appear lazy. "Are you going to check the markets?"

"You know my habits. I'll get a cup of coffee and spend the first two hours in the office. Do you want me to wake you when I make breakfast?"

Another yawn delayed her response. "Yes, please. You'll need to pack, so I'll cook. I doubt the fire will put me to sleep."

The quiet home, the dancing flames, and the leather couch had other ideas about her inability to sleep. Two and a half hours later, her father's noise roused her.

Following a light breakfast, she and her father discussed market trends, their proposed project, and which stocks to invest in if they progressed with her idea.

By the time she had completed her yoga routine, showered, and dressed, it was almost time for her father and Rasheed to leave for Branson's airport. She couldn't remember how long it had been since she had begun a day after 11:00 a.m.

Her car, carrying her father and Rasheed, was winding its way down the hill when her phone rang. She answered it as she walked into the office and sat behind the desk. "Hello, Skip. How are things in DC?"

"Busy, thanks to you and Steve. Last night, we had a special ops team do a late-night recon of the apartments. They came back with everything you told us to look for. You were right about the place being wired with booby traps. The basic components are the same recovered from the theater. They disarmed them but did so in such a way that made them look untampered. We now have samples of the accelerant to match against the substance used in the theater fire."

"That was a foregone conclusion. How long before you move in?"

"It may take a while to gather enough evidence to get a warrant to the homes you gave us. We can link only one suspect to the apartments."

This wasn't what Heather wanted to hear. She said, "They're probably using cell phones. Burner phones, if they're smart. We believe at least one of them to be very cunning. You may need someone local to put bugs in the homes and vehicles."

"We need a warrant from a local judge for that."

"Yeah, you're right." She took a breath. "What's your next step?"

"Set up a task force of federal, state, county, and city officials."

An audible moan came from Heather. She sensed the case slipping into a mire of delays.

"That's risky," said Heather. "They may have someone on the inside with big ears and a bigger mouth. All it would take is one person to ruin the bust."

"Do you and Steve have a better plan that won't jeopardize the convictions?"

Heather recognized the opportunity and went for it. "Of course we do. I just don't know what it is yet. How much time can you give us to come up with a quick, legal solution to getting enough evidence for a warrant?"

"One day. I'll give you and Steve twenty-four hours to submit a plan."

"Midnight tomorrow," countered Heather.

"Ten o'clock, and that's my last offer."

"Done," said Heather. "Ten o'clock tomorrow night, central time."

This brought a booming laugh from Skip. He settled himself and said, "As always, you win. I'll give you an extra hour but after that it's a multi-agency task force."

Heather wasted no time calling Steve, who answered on the third ring. He asked, "Did your buddy at the FBI call you?"

Heather responded positively and launched into an explanation of what Skip had said.

"Let me get this straight," said Steve. "We have a day and a half to come up with a plan to solve a bulging basket of crimes, and do so in a way that gives Lieutenant Douglas the credit. Is that correct?"

Heather responded, "You're the one who decided Lieutenant Douglas needs to get the credit. It would be easier if you weren't so concerned with his feelings."

Steve countered with, "Do you want the press hounding you for an explanation of how and why a businesswoman from Texas and a blind former cop became involved in solving a series of crimes in Missouri? I know I don't."

Heather said, "Thank you for that rhetorical question. If I've painted us into a corner, I apologize. I thought the master detective could come up with a simple, effective plan. If not..."

Steve accepted the challenge. "Give me a few hours to think. I'll have something to present when I get home."

Heather hoped to have at least the germ of an idea by the time Steve arrived home that night. Two hours passed lost in thought with nothing of value coming to mind. A mechanical ringtone brought her back into the present. Her phone's screen identified the person calling as Steve. She placed the phone to her ear and asked, "What's your plan?"

"It's a longshot, but it might work if all the stars line up, we both carry a rabbit's foot, and cross our fingers for luck."

Heather responded, "Why don't I feel encouraged?" She gulped a breath. "Two questions: Is it legal, and will it work?"

"I'd say it's somewhere between almost legal and legal enough. As for working, we'll have to wait and see. Do you want details, or would you prefer I not tell you?"

Heather rolled her eyes. "If this could cost me my law license, I'm not sure I want to hear it."

"I'll phrase my plan in such a way that keeps you out of trouble. After all, this will be privileged communication between me and my attorney."

"Tell me, but I reserve the right to reject your plan."

"Suppose," said Steve, "someone smeared mud on the license plate of a car belonging to a young man suspected of being involved in a serious crime. Also suppose the police pulled over this young man for having an unreadable license plate and the routine traffic stop turned into the police finding a reason to bring the young man in for questioning."

Heather groaned. "The last time I checked, planting drugs is illegal."

A tinge of offense flavored Steve's response. "Who said anything about planting drugs? Besides, I haven't told you the complete plan. The person with the unreadable license plate is the weakest link in a family of criminals. The police choose not to arrest him but give the young man a good scare.

"Soon after, a pair of highly skilled private detectives interviews the young man again. They have enough leverage over the young man to get him to talk. They record the conversation and feel obligated to report their conversation to the proper authorities."

Heather folded her hands on top of the desk. "I can think of only a dozen ways this plan could fail."

"I agree," said Steve. "Do you have a better idea to wrap the case up quickly?"

Heather considered Steve's words until she matched names and faces with the players. The weak link was Jay Bird. The trusted sources were Candy and Claire, while the skilled detectives were Steve and her.

This was Steve at his finest. His plan involved stretching but not breaking the boundaries of ethics and legality to achieve a greater good. Smearing a license plate with mud was the only criminal offense, and it was barely a misdemeanor. Most people would look at it as a harmless prank. Heather reconsidered the legality of the entire plan. It could work if all the pieces came together quickly.

Heather then looked inside herself in relation to the ethics of Steve's plan. She had no qualms about picking a lock and committing a burglary if it meant keeping drugs off the streets. Smearing mud on a license plate wouldn't cause her to lose sleep.

She estimated her chances of getting caught as less than one in ten thousand and her chances of being arrested for it as even less.

Heather took a full breath and said, "What's our next step?"

"I'll call Chief Fry. His main concern is finding out who set the fire and stole the safe. You call Skip at the FBI. His priority is halting the interstate delivery of drugs. With any luck, we'll interview Jay Bird at the theater after tomorrow night's performance and please both the locals and the feds."

"What plan do you have for Chief Fry to follow?"

"I'll suggest if Jay has an open container or a small amount of marijuana in his car, the officer could detain him a few hours, but he needs to be released in plenty of time to make the evening show for the rest of the plan to work. If there's no pot or alcohol, you and I will need to be creative when we interview him."

After ending her call with Steve, Heather called Skip who agreed to go along with the plan as long as it was Steve and Heather conducting and recording the interview with Jay Bird.

Following their conversation, Heather said to herself, "I'll take Princess with me after it's dark. She and I will look like twins in our matching black vests and no one will be the wiser."

# 29

The standing ovation for Claire and the rest of the cast waned as Heather, along with Steve, waited to add their congratulations to Branson's newest headliner. From the line that stretched from the lobby back into the theater, they'd be waiting a while. The Candy Caine Theater was back in business.

All the while, Heather kept watch over Jay Bird as he sold merchandise to fans. His red-rimmed eyes gave evidence that his previous night's time in jail for suspicion of driving while intoxicated had taken its toll on him. Heather described the young man's condition to Steve, who simply nodded and said, "Good."

Heather leaned into Steve. "Nate pushed ahead of people in his wheelchair to cut in line. He's shaking Claire's hand like he may not give it back. Now she's squatting beside him to get into the frame of a selfie." Heather kept watching and listening as Melvin Bird, Jay's father, pushed the wheelchair into the night air, and spoke louder than necessary. "Candy was good in her day, but Claire has her beat by a country mile."

The last patron left fifty minutes after the show's finale, and Claire motioned for Jay to join her where Steve and Heather stood. "Jay, you remember Mr. Smiley and Ms. McBlythe, don't you?"

"Yeah."

"They need to talk to you again."

Jay looked at Heather and asked, "Does it have to be tonight?"

Steve nodded. "I'm afraid so, Jay. It shouldn't take long, but it's important. In fact, it will be the most important conversation you'll ever have."

Heather added, "He's not exaggerating."

Jay's Adam's apple rose and fell as he swallowed. "Am I in trouble?"

"Let's find a quiet place to talk," said Steve.

Claire said, "The sales office is open. I'm going to get out of this hot costume. Doug's waiting for me backstage. Call if you need me, or him."

Heather held out her hand toward the business office. "After you, Jay."

He didn't move. "What did Claire mean when she said, if you need 'him'? She was talking about Lieutenant Douglas, wasn't she?"

Steve snapped back, but in a muted voice. "Jay, you're an inch away from going back to jail, and if you do, you won't get out until you're an old man. Heather and I are your last and only chance. Don't test our patience."

Jay took his first tentative step to travel the short distance. Once in the office, Jay stared at the three chairs that were already set up in a triangle in front of the desk. Heather pointed at a chair that sat slightly lower than the other two. Steve tapped his cane until it hit the base of his chair and settled into it. Heather followed suit, and three sets of knees almost touched.

Heather spoke in her lawyer's voice. "Jay, we came to Branson to investigate a case of someone trying to extort money from Candy."

Steve broke in. "It didn't take long before we learned about the suspicious death of Mabel Grist, which is still an open case. What do you know about her death?"

"Nothing."

He'd barely gotten the word out when Steve erupted. "That's a lie." He stuck out his thumb. "One: You know she had a heart attack." He unfurled his index finger. "Two: Her purse was missing." Steve's middle finger made a trio out of a duet. "Three: Someone stole her purse."

"I had nothing to do with that."

"Save it for someone who isn't so gullible," said Steve. "You said you knew nothing right before I proved you knew at least three things. I have seven more fingers. Start talking."

Jay's gaze darted left to right, as if he were looking at the spread feathers of a peacock for the first time. "Uh... I know some people think someone scared her to death."

Steve didn't let up. "Your words have already betrayed you. You know more than you're telling us and more than you told Lieutenant Douglas."

Heather sighed and looked at Jay with what she hoped was her best look of pity. "Start over, Jay. Mr. Smiley was the top homicide detective in Houston. He can tell by the tone of your voice every time you're trying to hide the truth."

Steve leaned back. "Do you want to know what I think?" He didn't wait for an answer. "I think someone planned to steal the safe a long time ago. They had leverage over a young man named Jay Bird and told him to get the keys to this theater. You followed orders and did what you were told."

Jay's eyes darted again from side to side, so Heather said, "You're right again, Steve. Jay looks like a worm trying to wiggle off a hook."

"I like Heather's analogy of you being the worm that's trying to get free. What you haven't realized yet is we're the fishermen who will put the hook in you from head to toe."

Steve took some of the menace out of his words. "Have you ever heard the phrase, *The truth will set you free?* It's true, so start talking or you'll go back to jail and explain to Lieutenant Douglas why you held back information from him."

"I can't. They'll kill me."

Steve didn't contradict Jay. Instead, he put a ray of sympathy in his voice and said, "I can tell that's what you believe, but it's not true."

Heather played good cop and asked, "Isn't there something else you can ask Jay that will help him beat a murder charge?"

Steve pushed out his lips and said, "Let's start with an easy question. What happened to the extra Krampus suit? The one that went missing after the first actor didn't work out?"

Jay wouldn't budge. "I can't tell you about that either."

"For the same reason?" asked Heather. "Someone will kill you?"

Jay nodded an affirmative response, so she said, "Yes," for Steve's benefit.

Steve allowed a few seconds to pass. It was like watching silent gears fall into place and mesh with others. "You don't want to say because *you* took the costume." He held up a hand to blunt a reply. "Don't deny it. You took it, wore the costume to the theater, put on the mask, and used it to scare Mabel Grist to death."

"No!" shouted Jay. "I took the costume, but she died on the way to her car. I never even put the mask on."

Steve said, "And then you took her purse, which held the keys to the theater. The others were going to use them to steal the safe."

"I never touched Mrs. Grist. I watched her clutch her heart and fall, but she never saw me."

Steve shrugged. "I like my version better. I bet Lieutenant Douglas will too."

Heather gave him a sly smile. "I'm a very good lawyer. Good lawyers make deals with prosecutors. But before they will do that, they need all the truth. Did you take the purse?"

His head dipped. "Yes."

"Who did you give it to?"

"Nate."

Steve fired another verbal salvo. "Was that when the others cut you out of the money from the drug deliveries?"

Jay sucked in a full breath and held it. The action gave Steve the answer to his question and time to say, "That explains why you had to get rid of your new Camaro. Your family turned against you."

"There's nothing new about them doing that," said Jay. "My daddy and uncles would sell out anyone, including me, if it meant more money in their pockets."

Heather said, "Explain what you mean."

Jay looked at Steve, then at Heather. "It's simple. They were making money hand over fist but wanted more, so they cut their labor expenses by one." He paused. "That's not really true. My family isn't known for being the sharpest hoes in the garden shed, if you know what I mean."

Steve nodded and asked, "What about you? Are you smart enough to know a good deal when you hear one?"

Jay lifted his head and stared at Steve. "This past summer I thought I was the smartest person on the face of the earth. I had money, girls waiting in line to ride in my new car, and I only worked a few days a week. Two months ago, I learned there are people you can't trust, my daddy being one of them."

"That sounds like a true statement." Steve massaged his chin. "What about the fire that almost killed Candy? There's arson and an attempted murder someone has to answer for. Who had brains enough to plant the device in her dressing room to create a diversion while they stole the safe? It wasn't your father or your uncles. They don't possess that level of creativity."

Jay took in a breath and released it in resignation. "You're right Mr. Smiley, but they're smart enough to follow orders. Nate is the mastermind behind everything. I don't know for sure, but I bet my old man planted the firebomb. He's got a bad back, but my uncles are plenty strong."

Jay volunteered the next bit of information without prompting. "Nate has Mrs. Grist's purse and the Krampus costume in the basement of his house. He said they were his insurance policy against me ever going to the cops. All it would take would be an anonymous tip telling them where to find evidence of my involvement in all their schemes. He called me his sacrificial lamb."

Steve rubbed his cheek. "You say Nate is the mastermind. Maybe he is and maybe he isn't. No one is smart enough to remember all their business transactions. Where does he keep cash, computer, Mrs. Grist's purse, and the Krampus costume?"

"Like I said, in the basement. The stairway to it is under the kitchen's cooking island. The top is granite to match the other cabinets, and there's even a working sink in it. The top hinges up, and cabinets open to reveal the stairway. Who would think to look twice for the stairway to a basement in the house of a man in a wheelchair?"

Silence blanketed the room. Steve leaned back and relaxed as Heather took over. "How would you like to live in Florida with your aunt?"

Jay sat up straight and jerked his head back like a chicken. "Huh?"

"You heard me. If you come through with telling all you know, I have it on good authority that someone very high in the FBI will speak with your aunt about the possibility of you living with her until you get a good job and can get out on your own. If she won't take you in, I'll personally see to it that you get a fresh start."

A light of hope flared in his eyes. "I thought I was going to prison, and I was bargaining for a lesser sentence. Mr. Smiley scared ten years of life out of me."

Heather smiled, but there was no levity in her words. "Prison is where you'll go, and you'll stay a lot longer than ten years if you don't tell Lieutenant Douglas and some nice federal agents everything you know."

Steve took out his phone and told it to call Lieutenant Douglas. "Jay's ready for you. Come get him. Heather and I will give you back your wires. I never did like wearing a tiny microphone."

On the way back to Candy's Heather asked, "Are you pleased with the outcome of tonight's meeting with Jay?"

"So far, so good. Now we can focus on what brought us to Branson."

# 30

Heather sat behind the desk in Candy's home office reflecting on the previous night. Steve and Rasheed had left for the hospital on time, and Rasheed had already returned with Sugar. Between yawns, she related that Candy's breathing seemed much improved and the doctor had ordered an upgrade to her dietary restrictions.

Princess walked alongside Sugar up the stairs and resumed her duties of bringing comfort to a woman damaged by years of misfortune and abuse.

It came as no surprise when Rasheed asked if he could go to the reunion home with the pretext of checking to see if her father had any needs he could help with. Of course, that was a complete ruse. He and Junani had some catching up to do. She pictured them taking a long lakeside walk. It also occurred to her that she and Jack needed to put another log on the fire of their romance. But first, there was a list of things to accomplish that didn't include hand-holding strolls by the lake.

Rasheed returned in time for lunch with a spring in his step and a smile parting his lips.

Later, an unfamiliar dark blue minivan snaked its way up the driveway. Heather called for Le Roi, who was already standing at attention, looking out a window by the front door. She looked at the clock on the wall and found the time to be two-thirty. Her gaze shifted to the office window overlooking the front porch and driveway.

"*Les amis,*" said Heather, and Le Roi's tail made a side-to-side sweep. It was then she noticed the Uber decal on the windshield.

Heather made for the front door, twisted the knob on the deadbolt and threw the door open. Le Roi wasted no time in welcoming Steve and Candy home. Sugar skipped down the stairs, shot past Heather, and wrapped her sister in a hug. "I thought they wouldn't release you until tomorrow." Princess sniffed the oxygen concentrator that hung from a black strap around Candy's neck.

"She's a quick healer," said Steve. "The doctor liked her blood/ox levels and her ability to whisper."

Rasheed went to the back of the vehicle and took out the first of several loads of flowers. In the meantime, Sugar helped Candy up the steps and into the home. Princess seemed at a loss in deciding which sister needed her the most.

Steve, Le Roi, and Heather followed. She noticed Candy point to the living room instead of the stairway. The sisters settled onto a leather sofa facing the fireplace while Heather directed Steve to the recliner close to Candy. Heather had a loveseat all to herself that gave her a good view of the sister's faces. Rasheed busied himself with scattering arrangements of flowers throughout the home.

Heather asked if anyone wanted something to drink. Candy raised a hand. A scratchy voice said, "Hot tea with honey."

Steve said, "Make it two."

Rasheed's voice came from the direction of the kitchen. "I'll make enough for everyone."

Heather tilted her head as she made a general comment. "Candy, welcome home. This is such a pleasant surprise, but not totally unexpected. Steve is the reigning champion at keeping important information to himself."

"Hey," said Steve. "That remark hits too close to home."

Candy's smile seemed to brighten the room. The machine at her side hummed, and Steve took over with an explanation of Candy's release from the hospital. "It's been a busy day for Candy. The doc ordered new X-rays first thing this morning. Respiratory therapists made multiple visits, and even a speech therapist made an appearance. What sealed the deal for her release was no sign of infection and the improved oxygen levels. She'll stay on the oxygen concentrator and out of the cold for as long as it takes to heal. They also recommended we not have the fireplace burning."

Heather looked at it and said, "I was so busy, I didn't think about keeping it going today."

Steve's next words came as a slight surprise. "Lieutenant Douglas came early this morning. He and Candy had no trouble communicating with him now that she can write again. It was police business, so I used the occasion to grab a cup of coffee."

Heather knew that Steve could have stayed but left to avoid antagonizing Lieutenant Douglas. It was a small but important step in repairing their relationship.

The tea arrived, which gave Heather a chance to point the conversation in a different direction. While Rasheed played the part of tea server, she spoke of her dad moving to the reunion home with Heather's freshly arrived team members from Texas.

Heather noticed Candy trying to stifle a yawn. Sugar noticed it, too, and placed a hand on Candy's arm. "It's naptime for you. Princess and I will take you to your bedroom. I'll help you get ready for bed then come back down and take care of your guests. Princess can stay with you. She's the best bed partner I've ever had."

The sisters drank their tea then excused themselves. Steve waited until they were upstairs before he directed his words to Heather. "This will be a good time for us to talk to Sugar alone. I've been putting off this conversation."

Rasheed said, "I feel this might be delicate, and I don't have a strong relationship with Ms. Sugar. I'll go to my room and read unless you wish me to stay."

Heather said, "Thank you, Rasheed. That's very astute of you. A good detective knows when not to participate in conversations."

Rasheed left, leaving her, Steve, and Le Roi to wait for Sugar to return. Steve said, "It feels cool in here."

"Do you want a fleece throw? There are several in a basket."

Steve gave his head a little wobble. "It's not the lack of a fire that's making it feel cold, it's what I have to tell Sugar."

"Did you hear from Leo again?"

"Yeah. I told Candy. She can speak better than she's letting on. Sugar will need her after she hears what I have to say."

Heather considered Steve's cryptic words along with his pensive demeanor. The worry lines in his brow were as deep as she'd ever seen them, so she picked a safe question to ask. "Is that how you got the doctor to release Candy early?"

"I did some fast talking but hit a brick wall until Candy told the doc she'd check herself out if he didn't sign her out. He didn't like it, but he's a very busy man and now she's upstairs. Rasheed will need to take her for respiratory treatments for a few days starting tomorrow."

They sat in silence until Sugar came down the stairs and joined them in the living room where she grabbed a throw and took a seat on the couch. She then slipped off her house shoes and tucked her feet under her.

Steve began the conversation. "Sugar, I need to ask you some questions related to our investigation into the threatening letters."

Heather watched as Sugar stiffened, then cast her gaze toward Steve. "You know, don't you?"

"I suspected it the day you and Randy came to Heather's office, but I wasn't positive until today. I hoped it wasn't true."

Sugar spoke her next words as if pleading for mercy. "I told him it wouldn't work. We'd already begged and borrowed all we could from Candy. She said I should leave him and come live with her." Sugar looked into the fireplace at nothing but cold ashes. "Candy even offered me a job as a costume seamstress and usher. Randy promised me he needed only a little money, and he'd be able to pay back everything. He said that if the first threatening letter didn't work, he'd find another way. I should have left him then."

Heather asked, "How did he mail the letters with postmarks from Branson?"

"We've been sponging off Candy for a long time. When things got terrible, I'd call, and she'd invite us to stay with her. He'd stay sober for a while and work at Candy's theater while we lived with her. That lasted until Randy said he was well enough to go home. Then we'd return to Texas, and he'd go back to his old ways."

Sugar issued a crooked smile. "I did everything but answer your question, didn't I?"

Her question didn't deserve an answer, so all Sugar got was silence. This prompted her to say, "Randy knows some people in town. He paid them to mail the letters for him. He never told me their names."

Steve chimed in. "Some people can only stand so much success before they fall back into their old patterns."

"That describes Randy," said Sugar.

Steve turned his head in Sugar's direction. "Was it Randy who gave you the bruise that Heather saw?"

Sugar's head dipped, then raised slowly as she looked up through cloudy eyes. "He never laid a hand on me, no matter how much I complained or how drunk he got."

Steve nodded. "That's good to hear. It shows he wasn't all bad." He raised the pitch of his voice. "Did you know the man who attacked you?"

"The men. There were three of them. No, I didn't know them. They kicked in the door of our apartment and worked me over while one of them stood behind Randy with a meaty arm wrapped around his throat and a gun to his back. They told Randy he'd better come through with what he owed. He had a week to find the money, or he'd come home to a dead wife. You can't believe how relieved I was when you called and told me to get on Mr. McBlythe's jet."

Heather asked, "Did you ever consider divorcing Randy?"

"Every day for the last ten years. You may not believe me, but I committed to leaving him after those men beat me. Call me a coward if you want to, but I believe they would have killed me if I hadn't come here."

Steve rubbed his hands together as if warming them. "Yes, they would have, but they killed Randy instead."

Heather's gaze shot to Steve. No wonder he'd dreaded this conversation.

Sugar gasped and wailed, "No," as she covered her face with her hands.

Heather retrieved a box of tissues and sat beside her on the couch. Three tissues and a shuddering breath later, Sugar said, "I knew deep down it would end this way. It had to."

Steve reached for Sugar's hand. "Candy knows; she's waiting for you to join her. She said this is the chance for it to be like when you were girls growing up. No secrets and big dreams for the future."

# 31

Two days had passed since Candy returned home and Sugar received the news that she was a widow. Now that there was no threat from Krampus, peace once again reigned in the home on the hilltop overlooking Branson.

Heather had called Pam, her personal assistant, and told her to take care of all funeral arrangements so the sisters could get on with the rest of their lives. Sugar agreed that nursing her sister back to health was better than traveling back to Texas to watch a casket being lowered into the cold earth. They'd travel together in the spring, when flowers bloomed, and pay their respects to Randy, a man who had succumbed to the temptations of the world. They gladly accepted Steve's invitation to stay with him.

Heather sipped a cup of tea in Candy's home office and looked out the window. Steve and Rasheed would return soon from their morning walk along the lake at Branson Landing. They'd arrive fully caffeinated, with traces of sugar from donuts on their jackets. Steve claimed the first half mile they walked was to work up an appetite and the mile and a half stroll that followed was to work off their indulgence.

She then recounted her activities over the last two days.

Most of that time had gone to her father and the aquisitions team. Steve was left to sit quietly, listening to an audiobook and waiting for one or both of the sisters to sit with him in front of the cold fireplace.

Steve's return on this gray morning brought a surge of energy into the home. "How are Candy and Sugar this morning?" he asked.

"They had their breakfast and are upstairs getting ready for the day."

"Run up and tell them you and I are leaving. Rasheed and the dogs will stay here with them."

Wondering what her partner was up to now, Heather did as instructed, slipped on her coat, and made her way to the car. Steve was already there waiting for her. Two seatbelts clicked and they were off, heading down the steep driveway. "Are we in a hurry?" she asked.

"Not in a hurry, just excited. Chief Fry wants to see us as soon as possible."

Upon arriving at police headquarters, Heather saw nothing out of the ordinary, other than several unmarked black SUVs. She related her observation to Steve.

"That's good," said Steve. "I was worried my plan hadn't worked."

Heather led Steve into the building. An officer held the door open for them and said, "Chief Fry is expecting you. He's in his office."

They walked quickly, but Branson's top cop wasn't in his office when they arrived. This didn't seem to surprise the officer who said, "I'll tell the chief you're here. Have a seat."

Heather settled Steve in a standard office chair in front of the chief's desk and sat in the chair beside him. Steve said it reminded him of being sent to the principal's office when he was in the sixth grade. "I hope he didn't drill holes in his paddle like Principal Moore did. It left interesting white circles on my rosy-red cheeks."

Heather's snort came as heavy footfalls preceded the chief's arrival. He breezed in and took a seat behind his desk before speaking. "I don't have much time, but there are a couple of things we need to discuss."

The chief leaned forward. "Thanks to you and your buddies in high places, the drug ring here in Branson is on its way to being dismantled as I speak. The deliveries to the apartments come three days a week, but the days alternate every other week. This is the week for Monday, Wednesday, and Friday. Today is Friday, and the delivery of drugs has already taken place."

He took a quick breath and continued, "The DEA is using drones that can stay up higher and longer than anything the Bird brothers use. We'll be watching them as their delivery and dispersal vehicles come and go from the apartments. The drones will follow all the vehicles leaving the apartments. When the last one arrives at their destination, federal agents and local police will make their arrests."

Steve said, "You don't have to give us all the details. We've both had enough experience with the feds to know they'll use a big net to catch as many people as possible and close other drug houses. What I want to know is, did you secure warrants to raid the two homes where the Bird brothers and Nate live?"

Chief Fry leaned forward. "Thanks to Lieutenant Douglas, his confidential informants, and a scared kid with a funny name, we have warrants for the arrest and search of two homes in Kimberling City and their vehicles. We'll wait until we're notified by the feds that their arrests and raids are taking place."

Steve said, "And to think that all this is happening because Nate wasn't satisfied with the money from distributing drugs. Yet, I understand his bitterness when life deals you a losing hand."

Chief Fry's head dipped and returned. His lingering gaze at Steve held a look of deep respect.

Heather put in her closing comment. "It also helped that an

alert cop pulled over Jay Bird for having a muddy license plate, and an inquisitive lieutenant was in the area."

The chief said, "It's almost as if someone told them where to look and what to do."

Something still didn't add up, so Heather asked, "We appreciate being kept in the loop, but why did you really call us down here?"

"That was Lieutenant Douglas' idea. He wanted to let you know how much he appreciated what you've done for him, and for Claire. The idea of using leverage on Jay Bird worked. He's busy today, and will be long after the feds spring the trap on the drug traffickers."

Steve said, "He'll be up to his ears in paperwork for several days. I expect the raids will take place in multiple states over the next ten hours."

"Once again," said the chief, "you're on target."

Steve said, "Starting this afternoon, Heather and I, and a group of friends from Texas will be staying a week in a reunion house. We'd love for you, your wife, Lieutenant Douglas and Claire to come visit us and give a final update on the case."

"I'll pass that on to Douglas, but I can tell you now not to expect me and my much better half. We're going on a cruise."

Heather's voice sparked with excitement. "What kind of cruise?"

"A Christmas market river cruise in Europe. I'm looking forward to seeing Munich and, despite all the trouble Candy had, I'm looking forward to seeing the Krampus."

Heather couldn't help but shudder. "The cruise sounds absolutely magical, but tell your wife to stay away from Krampus."

They wished Chief Fry good luck on the raids and safe travels in Europe. Once in the car, Steve chuckled.

"What's so funny?" asked Heather.

"You are. That's your fourth exuberant reaction since you arrived in Branson and it adds confirmation to me knowing what your project is. I think I'll wait and tell everyone at the same time."

Heather released a puff of exasperation. "Tell me what you think it is, so you can start gloating and drag it out all the way to Christmas."

Steve wiggled his head from side to side. "No thanks, I'll wait."

Heather mumbled, "My next-door neighbor and business partner is Krampus."

Steve held up his hands in surrender. "All right, I'll tell you. I don't want you pouting your way through the holidays and ruining everyone else's vacation."

Heather twisted in her seat and looked at him. "I'm listening."

"The clues were obvious. The first was the water show at Branson Landing. That spoke of entertainment. The second was the hotel on the hill overlooking the lake. You reacted strongly to luxury and lodging. That hotel told you there's a market for something exclusive in this area, something people are willing to pay top dollar for."

Steve waited for a reaction. He didn't have to wait long. "Dad taught me not to race others to the bottom. A surprising number of people will save their money to enjoy the best products and services. Quality wins in the end."

Steve kept talking. "The third and fourth things that brought about extreme reactions were boats. The Showboat dinner cruise on Table Rock Lake and the European river cruise the chief and his wife are going on." He paused dramatically before asking. "How am I doing so far?"

Heather didn't want to swallow her pride, but she had to admit, at least to herself, that Steve was closing in on the prize. She took a deep breath and said, "Put me out of my misery. What are my dad and I working on?"

Steve rubbed his chin. "In my mind, I'm seeing a long, narrow cruise ship on Table Rock Lake. It would be like a

European river cruise, but on the lake. The staterooms, food, and service will be first class. Entertainers could get on in Branson, and the ship could go upstream for miles. You could even drop anchor near Silver Dollar City and tender passengers to shore."

Heather retained some of her pride when she said. "You made the same mistake I did in thinking too small. Dad loves the idea of lake cruises on luxury boats all over the world. Branson may or may not be the best place to test the waters."

It was Steve's turn to groan. "Test the waters. Nice try, but that's almost as bad as some of Rasheed's parables."

# 32

It was ten minutes after one in the afternoon as Heather watched her airplane sink below thick, gray clouds and touch down at Branson's hilltop airport. She informed Steve, Rasheed, and Sugar that it wouldn't be long before they would be on their way to the reunion home with a full complement of guests. Bella was the first to come through the door. She looked like she'd stepped off the page of a high-end winter clothing catalogue. It came as no surprise when she went straight to Steve and enveloped him in a hug.

Steve responded by saying, "You're still the best hugger in the world. How was your flight?"

"Smooth until we came down from altitude. The landing gave new meaning to rock-and-roll."

Heather caught Bella's attention by looking directly at her and raising her eyebrows in a way that asked a question without words. Bella shook her head and mouthed, "Later," without saying the word.

What followed was a scrum of hugs, greetings, and questions. Heather focused on Briann, or perhaps it was Briann who singled her out to give details on the flight. Either way, Jack's daughter had much to say. "The flight was super awesome. The pilots closed their door and let me take Roxann and Juliet out of their cages. Juliet is the Golden Lab and Roxann is the Doberman. They're both perfect angels once they get to know you. Do you like the Christmas scarves I put on them? Bella says they coordinate well with their service dog's vests."

"They're stunning, and Bella should know," said Heather.

Jack arrived with both dogs on leashes. He handed his daughter the leather leads. "Go introduce yourself to Miss Sugar and then introduce her to Roxann and Juliet. Heather and I will stay here."

Heather watched the confident girl approach the woman she'd never met when powerful hands gripped her shoulders and Jack's lips covered hers. She didn't know how long the kiss lasted, but it wasn't long enough. His smile was the first thing she saw when he drew back. She placed her hands around his neck and pulled him toward her for a repeat performance.

They separated again and he said, "Merry Christmas."

"It is now that you're here."

Bella and Steve joined them, as did Adam, Bella's husband. "Hello, Heather. What's the plan?"

Heather felt heat rise in her cheeks when she saw that everyone had gathered around her and Jack. Calling on the poise that had been ingrained in her, she raised her voice to give instructions. "We have three SUV's to transport everyone. Rasheed, Sugar, and I are the drivers. We'll pull up to the entrance. Everyone needs to take their suitcases to the curb. Adam, Jack, and Rasheed will be responsible for loading the dogs and luggage. Then, we're all going to the reunion home. The chef has all sorts of goodies waiting for us."

Sugar and the two dogs walked with Heather to the parking lot. "I'm going to stop at Candy's and pick her up. She's promised to bundle up, stay inside, and not move from a warm chair. She insists on meeting everyone, but we'll go home when she gets tired. I'll take Steve and the two new dogs with me, if that's all right with you."

"It's more than all right. I know Candy is excited to meet Roxann and you should walk the yard with Juliet. Take your time coming to the reunion home. You and Candy need to bond with your dogs. Steve will answer any questions you might have." A series of thoughts came to Heather that made her smile. It was going to be a Christmas to remember.

The three SUVs pulled to the curb in front of the airport's main door. Their appearance made Heather think of a presidential motorcade. Jack, Adam, and Rasheed made quick work of loading luggage, dogs and people.

They arrived at their communal home fifteen minutes later. Jack took in the scenery. "Great view of the lake. Are you sure there's enough room for this crowd?"

"Plenty. Your mom wanted to share a bedroom with Briann. I guess you could say I'm sharing a bedroom with Princess and Steve is sharing his with Le Roi. Everyone else has their own bedroom with private bathrooms." Heather pointed, "My dad is staying with the acquisitions team in the home next door along with Junani, who had to promise her mother she wouldn't stay nights in the same home as Rasheed."

People grabbed luggage and followed Heather in through the front door. She paused, stepping to the side, and announced, "I put sticky notes with your names on them to help you find your bedroom."

Carrying and rolling their burdens, everyone made their way to the stairway. Heather and Jack stood out of the way and examined the great room. Whoever did the decorating had spared no time or expense. It looked like the set of a Hallmark Christmas movie, complete with a ten-foot-tall tree in the corner by the fireplace. The smell of freshly baked gingerbread hit her. She looked into the dining room and saw the table covered with bowls and platters of all manner of sweet and savory treats. The chef had outdone himself.

Lunch was a come and go affair with the mob grazing like cattle instead of sitting down to a formal meal. Their numbers swelled when Allister and the acquisitions team joined them. Steve, Candy, Sugar, Roxann, and Juliet were the last to arrive. Candy unwrapped a thick scarf from her head and took a seat in a wingback chair with the Doberman on her left side. Steve sat next to her with Le Roi on his right. Heather thought how much they looked like proud grandparents at a family gathering and took a photo of them.

Heather turned to Jack and asked him to whistle. A two-note shriek pierced the air and all conversation ceased. Heather nodded a thank you and projected her voice. "I want to thank everyone for rearranging your schedules. I hope you're as thankful as I am to share this time with you. We have several activities planned, the first of which is going to Candy's theater tomorrow night. She regrets she won't be performing any more this season, but she's improving, which is what's important."

Steve spoke as the applause following Heather's statement died down. "I'm pleased to tell you that I spoke with Branson's lead investigator this afternoon and everyone responsible for her injuries is now in custody." He held out a hand for Candy to take. "I also learned from Lieutenant Douglas that he found the time to slip an engagement ring on the finger of the woman who is taking Candy's place."

Candy pulled Steve's hand, and he leaned over to hear her whisper.

"Candy says it's about time he found the time and courage to ask Claire. You'll get to meet her tomorrow night after the performance."

Steve kept talking. "And speaking of gifts, Heather has one she'd like to give to a very special person."

"I can't take credit for it because it's a regift. My father rushed to Branson when he heard I was in the hospital, along with Candy. My condition wasn't serious, but he came all the same, which is another thing I'm grateful for. In true McBlythe fashion, he purchased a car so he would have transportation while he was here."

Her father spoke up. "I thought it would come in handy, and it did."

Heather nodded. "To make a long story short, he gave it to me. I don't need it, but I know someone who does." She turned to Sugar. "Do you have the keys to a gently used car?"

"They're in my purse."

"Good. Keep them and enjoy your car. You'll need it to drive to work tomorrow night."

The sisters looked at each other. Candy nodded and Sugar burst into tears.

Bella stepped forward. "While we're giving gifts, I also have a gift to give." She approached Steve and handed him a small package.

"What's this?"

"Open it and see."

All eyes were on Steve as he tore off the Christmas wrapping from the small box. He lifted the lid and pushed aside the tissue paper. He ran his fingers over the contents as a puzzled look etched his face. Then he smiled as he lifted the tiny shoes for all to see.

Comments of "Oh, how sweet" and "Congratulations" were heard around the room as applause broke out.

Adam joined his wife. "I told her you'd probably already know."

Steve smiled. "I've been practicing looking surprised. When did you two find out?"

Adam put his arm around Bella and said, "The day you and Rasheed left for Branson. She wanted to tell you in person, but I was sure you'd know before we arrived. None of us can fool your sixth sense."

Bella spoke up. "One thing you don't know is the names we've picked out. If it's a boy, he'll be Stephen. If it's a girl, we'll call her Maggie."

Heather smiled as Steve reached out his hand to the young woman who was like a daughter to him. The man who once despaired of life being good again, especially at Christmas, now sat with tears rolling down his cheeks, a smile of contentment on his face. All it had taken was the announcement of a very special child at Christmas.

---

## FROM THE AUTHOR

Thank you for reading *Tinsel, Trees, And Treachery*. I hope you enjoyed your mystery escape to Branson, Missouri as you turned the pages to find out whodunit! If you loved it, please consider leaving a review at your favorite retailer, Bookbub or Goodreads. Your reviews help other readers discover their next favorite mystery!

You never know what will happen next in the world of Smiley and McBlythe, so be sure to join my Mystery Insiders reader community. It's a great community of mystery lovers that are the first to hear about new releases, discounts and other mysteries I've enjoyed. After you sign up I'll send you a *reader exclusive* Smiley and McBlythe mystery novella!

Happy Reading!

Bruce

Scan the image to sign up or go to brucehammack.com/the-smiley-and-mcblythe-mysteries-reader-gift/

## MURDER ON THE BRAZOS

**A floating corpse. A county on the verge of chaos.
One man's race against corruption.**

When Fen Maguire handed over his badge nine months ago,
Newman County was clean and safe—a legacy he thought would
endure. But the drug dealer's corpse drifting down the Brazos
tells a different story.

With the victim's house torched and evidence implicating the
new sheriff's father, Fen's artistic retirement is cut short. His
discovery of a hidden drug cache and coded notebook reveals a
web of corruption that runs deeper than anyone suspected.

As the new sheriff stonewalls the investigation, Fen must dust
off his detective skills. Armed with his artist's eye for detail and
his investigator's instinct for deception, he races to unmask a
killer before Newman County becomes unrecognizable.

Scan below to get your copy of
*Murder On The Brazos* today!

## ABOUT THE AUTHOR

Bruce Hammack, a native Texan, began his professional writing career in the tenth grade when the local Lions Club sponsored a writing contest for students in civics class. To the amazement of students and teachers alike, he won the prize of a twenty-five-dollar savings bond.

After retiring from a career in criminal justice, Bruce picked up the proverbial pen again. He now draws on his extensive background with law enforcement (and criminals) to write contemporary, clean read detective and crime mysteries.

Bruce has lived in a total of eighteen cities around the country and the world, but now calls the Texas hill country home with his wife of thirty-plus years. When not writing, he enjoys reading a classic mystery, watching whodunits, and travel.

---

Follow Bruce on Amazon, Facebook, Instagram, Bookbub or Goodreads for the latest new release info and recommendations. Learn more at brucehammack.com.

Made in the USA
Coppell, TX
27 December 2025

67254500R00152